To Cathy,

Thank you so
much for sharing
this evening today
in Bristol!

12/10/23

GEMMA RUIZ PALÀ (Sabadell, 1975) is a Catalan journalist and writer. Her first novel, *Argelagues* (2016), was a great success in Spain. *Wenling's* is her second novel, for which she spent years visiting nail salons incognito to capture their conversations, atmosphere and vibes. Her third novel, *Our Mothers* (2023), won the Sant Jordi Prize in 2022. This was the first time in nineteen years that a woman had received the prize.

PETER BUSH has translated a number of Catalan modern classics, including *Black Bread* by Emili Teixidor, Mercè Rodoreda's *In Diamond Square*, Joan Sales' *Uncertain Glory* and *Winds of the Night*, and Josep Pla's *Life Embitters* and *The Gray Notebook*, which won the 2014 Ramon Llull Prize for Literary Translation. In 2015 he was awarded the Creu de Sant Jordi by the Catalan government for his translation and promotion of Catalan literature.

Gemma Ruiz Palà

Wenling's

TRANSLATED FROM THE CATALAN
BY PETER BUSH

HÉ/OÏSE

PRESS

First published in English in Great Britain in 2023 by
Héloïse Press Ltd
4 Pretoria Road
Canterbury CT1 1QL

www.heloisepress.com

Ca la Wenling, © 2020 by Gemma Ruiz Palà.

The English edition is published by arrangement with
Gemma Ruiz Palà c/o MB Agencia Literaria S.L.

This translation © Peter Bush 2023

Cover design by Laura Kloos
Edited by Laura McGloughlin and Robina Pelham Burn

A special mention to Robina Pelham Burn for her expertise on the acquisition of English as
a foreign language by native Chinese speakers.

Text design and typesetting by Tetragon, London
Printed and bound in Great Britain by CPI Group (UK) Ltd, Croydon, CR0 4YY

The translation of this work has been supported by the Institut Ramon Llull.

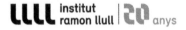

ISBN 978-1-7397515-5-5

TRANSLATOR'S NOTE

Barcelona is a multilingual city where many people speak Catalan and Spanish and other languages with different degrees of fluency depending on age, origin and social situation. Bilingual exchange and the meshing of different cultures are at the heart of this novel, and I have italicised speech when characters use Spanish in the original to help readers in the English-speaking world experience that. It is a city where you are often and quite naturally engaged in conversations in which three or more languages are being used as a matter of course. There is no reason to erase that reality in translation.

谨以此书献给我的朋友刘玲玲，
感谢你让我学到的一切.

Why do I do it? You know, I wonder why too. I'd have to go back to the heady days when I was all into novels and movies at sixteen, when my nails started to crack and I asked for an appointment at the dermatologist. Go to the pharmacy and ask to see the Roche-Posay range, came his immediate advice. The shades are very subtle, he followed up, his specs halfway down his nose. He wedged the frame, coughed four times, charged my mother a straight 5K (the old pessetes!) and handed me the prescription: a manicure.

I couldn't say whether it did me any good. I've rarely worn my nails as I brought them into the world. After that conversation I kept repainting them. I stuck with the varnish from the pharmacy for what seemed like forever, they even stocked it for me: *Vernis fortifiant protecteur, 3, beige*. Until I caught vintage fever and the Fifties look. Not to the point of coveting a second-hand Chevrolet; I mean I was crazy about that cool swinging style. I was mesmerised by those American women shut up in their spotless Formica kitchens kneading blueberry pie, stirring punch, knocking it back on their tod and obsessing

7

about grabbing their suitcases and heading down Revolutionary Road. I was mesmerised by the lives the Von Trier in my year had captured to perfection in a short that was truly gory. They mesmerised me, and I couldn't resist an aesthetic that gave my fingernails quite a different buzz.

The drawback was first going to film school with a blood-red manicure, then asking if anyone wanted me as an assistant of an assistant of an assistant: it made me far too visible. More so then, at the end of the millennium, when friends couldn't care less about nails. As for those into documentaries, my forte, better not even go there. They gripped their ciggies tight and looked at me in disgust out of the corner of their eyes. Real-deal docu-makers roll their sleeves up, get their hands dirty and hate poseurs, they hinted without saying a word. And so as not to seem a naive, lonesome ninny, I had no choice but to extend my adolescent phase and return to that ever-so-subtle number 3. I had to shelve my red delirium for when I could retreat into my shell in the holidays, which was also when I could have a ball with the books that movies had forced me to set aside. All alone, in plastic flip-flops, under the olive tree at my grandparents', indulging in books, with – you bet – bright, gleaming nails.

I remember the September I made up my mind. The queasy stomach when I started my first – paid – job at a production company, and the zero censuring of my nail polish: not a word was said. That would happen. Later. And the oil slick spread and spread… And we come to today, when tobacco and nails have swapped places. Now almost nobody in our line of work smokes, and almost everybody is flash, fash-conscious and paints their nails. Most of all, the real deal, the ones who roll their sleeves up and get their hands dirty. And lots in my shade of red, too.

I reckon I should shout this from the rooftops: I was the Trojan horse in that world of cameras, tripods and microphones. 'The oppressor wouldn't be so strong if he hadn't had accomplices among the oppressed themselves' was what Simone de Beauvoir said, right?

And I examine my hands. Not a single cuticle or hangnail. My architecturally trimmed and blood-red nails. I look at them and admire them, they're stunning. But I swear blind that the dermatologist wouldn't have prescribed that 'subtle' nail varnish as my treatment if the you must-be-kidding keratin had been a boy's and not a girl's. The medical prescription was the original sin. I can see that now... The doctor with the sliding specs wasn't the first, or the only one, but his contribution should be up there with all those who shaped me for the outside world: presenting me as a woman.

I quite agree that styling your hands is small beer compared to other practices in the beauty industry, like removing floating ribs. If you scrutinise your skeleton and imagine the scene, you soon realise that painting your nails remains a fairly benign woman-as-object indicator. One you could perfectly well do without, if you examine the whole set-up with a cool head.

Once you start examining markers of femininity, you've really hit rock bottom. Because you look at your hands again and clench them in a fist. You unhook your summer dress, see those waspish waists and swirling skirts, and curse your bones. You press your heels deep into your shoes. You gather up all your trinkets and weigh them in the palm of one hand. You

9

open all your lipsticks and want to smash them to smithereens. You squeeze out the last mascara and swear you'll never again go near a make-up counter and start hollering. To be or not to be? To be like this? Or that? To try being this? Or that? Before you finish the self-interrogation and contradictions pour down on you, you hit the floor and almost black out, but drag yourself up as best you can, half on a chair, grip the shelves and seek help from your other gods, from an understanding deity. The female variety, naturally.

The luck that comes with so much substance is that it's easily spotted. I got down from the chair with the thousand pages of *The Second Sex* on my shoulder, and, butt on the floor tiles, I started all over again. It had been fifteen years since I'd savoured a monument like that. Well into my twenties I still hadn't left the nest, I was fooled by fashion; they lifted up my shirt and I didn't even ask why. Now I'd tipped into my forties and the analysis, the context, the power of the arguments I read in Simone de Beauvoir stuck to my fingers like fresh polish. She'd written it fifty years earlier and penned a portrait of me! My very own malady! Spot on! I had to rein in my euphoria so I could relish what I was reading, and spent well over a week rooted to the middle of that passageway. Never a thought those days for the post-production studio that awaited.

I finished the last page, uncrossed my legs and went straight to my computer. I now knew my problem was everywoman's and that the 'feminine condition' was a male thing, now I knew we'd never been able 'to be', full stop, that they'd always invented us. Now I knew that knowledge is half the battle and you had no choice but to negotiate with yourself the marks of femininity you wanted to retain, then sally into the world and gleefully defend them morning after morning, and I wanted to hear that spelled out. And be struck by the voice that had hit bull's eye with *On ne naît pas femme, on le devient*.

And I find it in a 1975 *Questionnaire*. A standard television set, leather sofa, multi-camera take, mostly guest–interviewer exchanges. The interview lasts fifty minutes and Simone de Beauvoir doesn't waste a second, she's a machine gun rat-a-tatting lucid thoughts ready for the page. She responds without hesitation or pause, doesn't get flustered. She keeps her hands folded on her knees and when the cameras focus on a specific detail, what do I see? A manicure with short, square nails, blood-red like mine.

Why do I do it? Well, it's all down to Simone de Beauvoir.

1

You'll never catch her twiddling her thumbs. When she's doing your hands, she does only them. Even so, she never wastes a moment. Her eyes never rest, she's always on the go, and the first to greet anyone coming in. She gets there before anybody else has time to clear their throat. No surprise the strap on the front of her tabard is always slipping. If I knew how to sew, I'd tell her to take it in a bit. But I don't, I'd have to fetch my auntie. They all wear the same dark-brown outfit, double-breasted, black-edged. I like it, it smacks of Jedi gear. Not the standard boring fuchsia uniform you find in most nail salons, as if we women weren't allowed any other colour from the spectrum.

Her kids arrive. From school, a religious one I think, from what I glimpse on their tops. They rocket through. Only arrived from China six months ago, but hell do they home in on me. They've brought me the jam jar with the bean they're germinating as if it were a carnivorous plant and that makes me laugh. I don't know if their mother told them to, I reckon she must have, because she always sends them to say hello. Whenever they parade in front of me, I'm flummoxed: I want to get it right.

She wears a Mireille Mathieu fringe, as my mother would call it. She'd say that regardless of the age or musical taste of the

13

person she was talking to. If you're not of her era, or in tune with her *chansons*, Google them.

The hairdressers are all male, and one is her hubby. He strikes me as more in the pop-rock groove. He'd easily pass as the soloist in the group that's often on the radio, and wears outrageous quiffs. They have two or three part-time women, depending on the day. Temps for small jobs, sorting nail polishes, cleaning and tidying equipment. One full-timer does feet and massages.

Then there's the queen-pin. The heart and soul of Yang's Hair Salon. Wenling is her name.

2

'*H*i, love! Manos!?' 'Yes, *mans!* How are you, Wenling?' '*Good, thank you. You no want magazine, you always book... Wait a bit, OK?*'

And after wondering a while whether to read *The Blazing World* by Siri Hustvedt or surrender to the hum in the salon, I hear '*Come on, lovely!*' It's my turn.

'Which region did you say you're from?' '*The south, the city of...*' No way, the name escapes me again, eludes me just when it was on the tip of my tongue. 'You said your people worked on the land?' '*Yes, all mountains in my city and rice not good, in my city greens and a lot... a lot...*' I recite a variety of greens but don't discover what veggie most filled their bellies. 'What did you do before coming to Barcelona?' She was a sales assistant in a chemist's, I gather, because she says *shop* and points to the hand cream, nail polish, shampoos and lacquer. Then she really fires off. Tells me: '*In shop... I free! Head not thinking, head flying! I young!*' A thirty-five-year-old woman saying that, thinking of herself as old. Now toiling every minute, with children, just imagine... 'Of course, with two,' I say. '*With three!*' she corrects me as she stares at the pop singer. I have to stifle a laugh with the hand she's not painting.

Now it's her turn. '*You no children?*' And I spin her a tale of the twists and turns that subject has brought into my life. I'm totally upfront. I give it a bit of a gloss, but it's stark. Wenling doesn't miss a trick and when I stop, she hits the button: '*You not have any, good for you. Boyfriend?*' 'Yes, I do.' '*He nice?*' 'Wonderful!' I say, vociferously, like a loudmouth bragging about his car's performance. '*So you no kids, you rest! I never able, never alone, always work.*' 'Don't you ever go to the beach on Sundays, when you've shut up shop?' She looks at me as if to say, you won't catch me in the sea, never, but I do go for walks. '*I go beach and mountain for kids.*'

But now Wenling's nose is full of those sweet, synthetic smells that bring back her youth. She doesn't want to leave her chemist's. And drifts back: '*I in my city, so young... Work many hours, no sit all day, but when shop shut...*' And now she pretends to bolt the door and disappear. '*When shop shut... I so happy! I with Xiaolu, my friend-sister, and go out, walk, laugh!*' She looks up. And her eyes seek out those castles in the sky.

Did any survive? Who demolished them?

3

When she replies *so-so* it means something isn't right. She'd just come from Sant Pau Hospital and couldn't understand why her girl's blood test had to be at midday. '*Very late... Haijun small to have empty tummy so long.*' She'd begged them twenty times, earlier, please, but they'd rudely sent her packing: 'Next!'

'Give me the note, Wenling.' I dialled the number. 'Hello, as you didn't take any notice of her, I'll put it another way...'

'Eight twenty-five that same morning alright, madam?' All sorted in ten seconds, and I didn't even turn nasty.

'Is that it? Is your word enough? She doesn't have to come and get a new form?'

'No, madam, change noted, good day, madam, sorry for the bother, madam.'

Smooth as silk. I aped her 'madams' a few times, and we began the manicure on a high.

*

Defects bring us together. The day of the cold sore, Wenling had been waiting on me. I'd also had a real beauty for weeks. I'd got a godawful one and she must have seen me applying the latest quack ointment in the mirror. Such faith. She'd been waiting on me to find out what it was and where you could buy

17

it, but I'd not been back. Until one evening when I was on my way to the metro, she bumped into me. She was lounging by the ticket window looking into the street, shaking her head. She jumped up and hit the window. '*Stop, tell me what put here.*' Her grimace said it all, together with her gesticulating finger. 'Boil up thyme leaves,' I told her. No sense her wasting her cash too. 'And make sure you cool it down, don't splash the hot herbal brew on yourself,' I told her, puffing out my cheeks as if blowing on a bowl of soup. They call them beauty salons but we ought to say patchwork hubs.

4

A whitlow is to blame for the invention of the modern manicure. It was on the finger of Louis Philippe I, the last French king. Instead of being alarmed by the bad end met by his predecessors, the guillotined Louis XVI and exiled Napoleon, he could only think about Louis XIV and his death from gangrene. The populace was up in arms again, but Louis Philippe I of France didn't want to be troubled by talk of revolution, he had enough on his plate living with stinging pus night and day. He had everyone summoned to the Palais-Royal, for we know how testy kings get when their sores can't be wished away. And everyone means everyone. Doctors are the first hapless souls forced to lance the purulent bubble eating away at the nail of his second finger, but as penicillin is yet to be invented, they fail. Dentists are then recruited, just in case the implements they use to treat tooth rot and abscesses can do the job. Pure butchery. They even try blacksmiths, who are used to dealing with iron hoofs. Another failure. Parfumiers and their best essences, cooks and their best butters, cat's morning piss… All to no avail. The blister swells and the royal head despairs. Louis Philippe I of France orders them to get rid of the whitlow whatever the price: cut off my finger!

A drastic step, clearly. But it's what often happens if we delve into the past of other peoples. Europeans were feeling their way in the dark when it came to curing infected nails. It was a long time since ancient Egyptian kings and queens had used something else as well as gold, turquoise, lapis lazuli and red agate to ensure their entry to the next world. Their mummies opened the doors to eternity in dignified style thanks to the red hue that henna brought to their impeccably manicured hands. The Arab peninsula's elites discovered aeons ago that looking after your nails and painting the keratin was a splendid status symbol: a good manicure always invited deep reverence. And no one could beat the sophistication of the imperial dynasties of China. At the height of the Yuan dynasty, the nobility let their nails grow several inches and eased them into exquisitely decorated, precious-metal sheaths. Here we are, people chosen to live a life of luxury, proclaimed those pointy hooks that never scratched – servants did it all.

Nineteenth-century Paris puts on airs but is ignorant of such refinement. And the knife-sharpeners are polishing their blades when they spot a skinny young lad racing towards the palace. Royal advisers bring a glass of cool water to help him recover his breath and listen to what he has to offer. He is quite taciturn, because he doesn't say that he's learned what he will do to the king of France from his mother, who learned it from her mother, who learned it from her grandmother, who learned it from her great-grandmother and thus it linked into a chain of women that went back to the birth of the first spark of human intelligence. The skinny lad will speak only through a shammy leather and a twig of orangewood. He gently rubs the nail and slowly begins to remove the cuticle with the twig. And it works: wherever you are and whatever your status, when you treat skin with the necessary care, you will be rewarded. The tears Louis Philippe I sheds when he sees his finger restored and that sausage banished are double what they were when, as an exile in Switzerland, he learned that they had beheaded his father.

5

She never removes her face mask, but that day she does. That day she has to pause the world. That day she has to be sure I have understood. And that nobody else has heard. Wenling looks around, pulls down the elastic and whispers: '*No, lovely, I no mother.*'

She's telling me she was intending to leave her children in China with her grandmother and I assume she means her mother. But she isn't. I reckon both must be really young, and I phrase it delicately when I ask how you survive when your kids are so far away for so long. Sometimes making yourself understood is harder than climbing a mountain with a chest of drawers on your back. But we work at it, take deep breaths, and climb to the top. '*I no mother and I never all my life see mother.*' That's quite something else. Losing her one day versus never having one. '*I no photo, I not know!*' And with her hand she drew the world's saddest oval. Can you imagine, not knowing what your mother's face looks like? No, Wenling, I can't... She's no longer staring at me; her eyes are on the far ocean. I don't dare pry any further.

'*Father, yes, he alive,*' she says, coming back to earth. '*Sixty-seven.*' Such staccato brevity doesn't augur well, so I keep quiet. Putting me in the picture about him means telling me about her grandmother. One fine day her father offloaded her with a 'you'll land on your feet'. It was hard bringing up a granddaughter. But her grandmother toiled away and acted as mother, father and Holy Ghost. '*I cry a lot when she die.*' She swells her belly and says, '*Haitao.*' It happened when she was eight months pregnant with the boy. '*Grandmother always put me first, and teach me everything, I cry a lot, a lot…*' I hear those same tears from China to Honduras, to Argentina, to Ukraine, to Morocco, to Pakistan…

Grandmothers are the cement that fills the cracks across our world. Theirs is massive, humble, unseen labour, always hidden away. Cement is also what they have to swallow as punishment for so much ingratitude.

'*You look like mother? You have photo?*' I blow one up on my mobile and she gazes at it with reverence.

6

'Hello, young man!' says a lady with eyes only for him, rasping like a hold-up merchant. '*I've escaped for a jiffy, can you do me now?*' He laughs. '*You always running, no catch train here!*' I've noticed Wenling's husband always has ready banter, is always cheerful and on the ball. And that's a real gift. He grows on me by the day, I must stop calling him pop singer.

'*Take a seat, no problem.*' He holds a gown for her and gives her a Lindt chocolate. His customer's body warms to the sweetness of it and she flops down. She owns the hairdresser's three doors down. Her son always grumbled when she told him to do her hair, or did it too roughly, so she lost patience with him. She says, '*In your country you are closer, children here have no respect.*' And a moment later, whispering, she adds: '*Or next to none.*' As if to soften the mortal blow that had silenced us all. '*First you not sure, now you always with me,*' he says, riding the joke. Because at the start she'd only come for a manicure, but on the quiet she couldn't keep her eyes off him. Half-stunned, half-jealous. And she couldn't hide it. One day he squared up to her and let rip: '*Hey, I am hairdresser twenty years!*' She rose to the bait: 'Hey, I forty!' And they became friends. 'Stop writing so much and let him cut yours one day, dearie, he's ace!' The hold-up merchant now has me in her sights. I reflect that recording

24

everything I see on my mobile isn't as in your face as holding a notebook. Even so. She's right enough, WhatsApp all day long! I say WhatsApp to kybosh the word 'write', so it doesn't figure in the minutes. 'You bet one day I'll tell him to cut mine, if he comes on your recommendation!' I play along. 'Yes, dearie, you won't want any other hands near you.'

I should take more care, as I soak up this traffic as it comes and goes, varnishes, cuts, washes, rinses, souls bared, mud thrown. Or they'll catch me in the act, doing my fieldwork.

★

'I'm from the piano school; I've come to see the boss,' she told the husband. '*OK, go in.*' I peer and see her kiss Wenling twice and produce papers for her to sign. They've not been here a year and she's got them into piano lessons already. She's really into life here. Not like the young hairdressers. I look at them and it's like they're always hovering inches above the tiles, they never touch down. Maybe tomorrow they'll find better work in Valencia, Paris or Milan. Or if there's a downturn, they'll return home, tails between legs. Having children also means putting down roots. So you can hold on, wherever you fetch up.

What about Wenling's husband? What does he think? Where has he got to while she thins out and layers the young man who came in singing 'Devórame otra vez'? He recognises the customer who's just left the massage parlour: '*You here…*' She responds: 'Hi! Ah, you're…' And tries to place him but can't immediately. She closes her eyes and… 'Got it! You're the youngster from the tapas bar on Plaça del Sol! The one that serves the pork stew they found so tasty!'

A lady walks in saying she can't come until her soap has finished, and starts making excuses. 'Hey, dearie, I'm hooked, and I suppose you think I'm silly.' She's seventy-five plus, short hair, brownish-red, and backcombed. A neighbourhood icon. She chatters nineteen to the dozen. 'May I ask you where you find the classy clothes you always wear?' What am I supposed to say, it's not the first time she's asked. She's not expecting my reply. I say second-hand shops and she struggles to hide her distaste. 'Just as well they give them a good wash nowadays before selling them on... Just as well.'

Wenling finishes a girl's nails and before starting on mine she greets the soap lady, Eulàlia, by name and asks after her husband. 'You know, dear, he's at home,' and she opens her fan. 'He's managing...' '*How much older?*' Wenling enquires. 'Seven, my dear.' My eyes go straight to her magazine, to glean info so vital to life. *Brad Pitt and Angelina Jolie, the keys to the divorce of the century.* Bucketloads of hyperbole, a photo just of her, mascara tears, in the dumps, weeping... yet another Pietà. They spare us a photo of him; everyone can imagine the grinning, handsome, preening male, the usual. We're still stuck with the same old macho press. 'Hey, take it, if you want it, dear!' 'No thanks, I was only looking... I only wanted... Besides, those magazines make me furious...' 'Furious? How funny!' Senyora Eulàlia laughs in my face. And she's right, up to a point, I didn't explain myself at all well and I look as if I've got a screw loose. Wenling understands even less and says, '*You speak Catalan, I no speak.*' 'Well, you better get a move on, or your kids will wipe the floor with you!' And she does understand that, but in case she hasn't, Senyora Eulàlia reinforces the message by tapping her on the forehead with her fan. '*But I too old!*' 'You? At your age? Too old? My God, you must be having an off day.' And I have to laugh, because she is right too.

'*Señora Eulàlia*,' asks Wenling, '*my kid's teeth like that at night*,' and she grinds them. '*What you think is?*' 'Perhaps she's constipated… her tummy needs a clear-out. Have you been to the doctor?' '*No, too little thing for a doctor.*' 'Well, go to the pharmacist and ask for some remedy or other.' I don't have a clue about kids' illnesses, but her face is so worried… One second, I say, gesturing to Wenling to let go of my right hand, and I call the pharmacist below my apartment. She prescribes an essential oil with no side effects, one that basically gives you a good clean-out. '*You can try this, Wenling.*' I jot it down. '*They're holding it for you at this chemist's, in my name.*' She grabs the scrap of paper and I hear her pronounce it. For the first time.

7

Today isn't Wenling's day. The string of comments zipping from one end of the shop to the other suggests she's fallen out with her pop singer. I'll keep a low profile while I wait.

I focus on the old grandma the youngest hairdresser is just finishing. He's affixing a loose, white, windproof hairnet to her head. She's had what they called 'a good comb' in my grand-mothers' day. It's almost what they now dub the 'final touch' but without the high price tags English always carries. Maria dels Àngels had to perform wonders, quickly, no wash, using only the end of a comb: lengthening the life of those hair-ends that only see the hairdresser's mirror once a month, if they are lucky. The grand weekly wash-and-set is only for the well heeled.

The youngest hairdresser sprays on the right amount of lac-quer to keep it in place and holds a mirror to the rampart at the back. 'Real lovely!' says grandma, and now he begins her ration of neck massage. Her eyes close in pleasure. '*I really come for the rub, you know,*' she tells him with relish. The hem of her dress is coming unsewn, the cuffs of her blouse are frayed, and her spectacles belong to a bygone era. In the manner of customers my fishmonger calls 'priorities'. A curse knots in my throat. It's aimed at all those who vote, approve and sign off shameful

28

pensions from which many can't even save the ten euros a wash-and-comb costs here.

Rub over, old grandma comes back down to earth. 'It does me more good coming here than going to the doctor's,' and she touches her gammy leg. The youngest hairdresser hands over her walking stick and accompanies her to the door. He doesn't let go of her until her good leg gets into its stride and she can limp along by herself. I watch them holding hands. '*Goodbye, Señora Mundeta*.' And he gives her such a look as she disappears up the road. Such tenderness etched on his face when he walks back in. Maybe we can salvage a small portion of a human race that's so gone to the dogs.

'*You come to me, lovely!*' Wenling summons me. I'm on my way! 'Shortish, straight and colour number…' '*I know, clever!*' I say no more, and she chatters on. '*I too angry, yesterday husband no want go walk, and all Sunday at home because he very tired, better say nothing*,' and she seals her lips. Today I fancy a silent manicure: I have had it up to here with all the Mundetas of this world.

8

Rachel Doyle was seventeen and so self-assured. Always the best marks, the best answers, the best presentations. And always outlandish… Her class looked at her as if she were green with a horn growing from each side of her forehead. But they had to listen to her and never open their mouths. They knew standing up to her only made it worse. Her latest fad: old people. Posters around the whole school, a stall, badges, information sessions… When Rachel Doyle had a bee in her bonnet, there was no stopping her. 'My friends, why on earth do they frighten you so much? Why do you avoid them? You'll be like them one day!' And as what began as a reproach always morphed into a harangue, someone or other would sign up. True, only two were recruited to this cause. Persuading all those masses of throbbing hormones that the best idea for a Friday was swallowing ibuprofen with a bunch of old ladies was a battle lost before it began. What on earth! A candid-camera jape, most concluded. And, sure, there was a camera, a quite visible hand-held one carried by Rachel Doyle that afternoon when she, Vanessa and Gabrielle turned up at the old people's home in her home town of Commack, New York. She recorded the first session from start to finish. Because it wasn't a doctor's visit and they hadn't come empty-handed. They stood here with the camera, three nail files, two nail varnishes, moisturising cream and one name: Glamour Gals.

It was thanks to her grandmother that Rachel Doyle had founded this scheme to provide companionship. She had been put in a home in Nevada and Rachel could only go in the holidays, and always wanted it to be a special occasion. One day she had the bright idea of taking her for a beauty treatment and had to argue the toss with the residence manager. He saw he was up against a brick wall and decided to give her the necessary permission. The fortune she had to pay took all her savings, but seeing her granny go back to the home looking so fresh and radiant after a few caresses was worth its weight in gold.

Initially, the ladies in the Commack residence stared at them as if they too thought the three young gals must be green with horns either side of their foreheads. A manicure session? For free? For us? Old has-beens nobody cares about? What a crazy idea! That first day, the Glamour Gals showed that converting disbelief into wonder was a quick-fire art.

Twenty years later, now an official, grand, non-profit organisation, led by founder Rachel Doyle, with over two thousand volunteers, training schools, student grants and premises in sixteen states, they still find amazement on faces as sessions kick off. The Polaroids they have taken as goodbye presents ever since that first afternoon in Commack haven't changed: they bear witness to the pink, smiling, sparkling faces that follow that first miracle.

*

William Koehler Senior Center, Mahopac, New York. The Glamour Gals on this mission are from the town's high school, and sixteen to seventeen years old. 'Values, communication and the history of our lady neighbours, three in one!' explains Jenna, the group leader, at the presentation they will make on Monday in class.

Paper tablecloths weld the card tables together. On one side, the junior squad: all laughs and determination, their arsenal at the ready. On the other, the senior squad: high hopes giving them butterflies, guarded conversation, hands held out. They file for a while, wrap a refreshing napkin around hands, dry them, and ask what their favourite colour is. As each nail varnish is opened, a life flows out.

'Frances, but call me Frankie,' eighty and British. 'From which British city?' 'Tee-hee, that's a good one,' she answers, well amused. 'There's none that compares to London, my dear. World War Two, you did hear about that, didn't you? And now you know, I'll tell you I was evacuated as a kid.' Her childhood was frozen at zero in 1948, the year she arrived in the States. That's why she always gives the two names, because she was born twice. She wants her nails white, lilac and silver, to cheat the routine. Because it's great here; the only drawback being days that are all the same colour.

Felicia, eighty-five. 'What a treat for us!' She can't get over it, it's fantastic! She wasn't rich, she could never have afforded a manicure, children and so much work, never ever! Felicia tells her glamour girl: 'I was born in Cuba, *m'hija*...' 'That's great!' she replies. '*Yo aprende un poco de español*.' The last time her nails were painted was when her granddaughter got married, and that was twenty-five years ago! She laughs a wonderfully toothless laugh and chooses her polish: 'I want a deep red, like frijoles!'

32

Graziela, ninety-two. 'Fifty as an executive secretary,' she emphasises with the pride of the perfect. Graziela March, because exterminating the fleas of new arrivals wasn't the staff in Ellis Island's only job, she says as if she were back there. They battered luggage, respect and surname! 'Italian family, my real surname is Marchese, that's much more distinguished,' and she points to mother-of-pearl pink.

Cynthia, seventy-nine. 'I love your hands,' the glamour girl tells her. 'Please say that again into my other ear. Oh, thank you! I heard that properly.' Her hair is her mother's; her hands her father's. The best of both! And that's how she carries them with her all the time. She caresses the nape of her neck and gazes at those long film-actress fingers that she only wants painted with a clear varnish. 'What about you? Do you know what you have from yours? It's vital to know.'

And after the first to and fro of the brush, roles are soon reversed. Now it's the elder ladies who are asking the glamour girls what they want out of life. And they suggest doing a round of possible lines of work. 'Not a manicurist, I bet?' Graziela opens fire, mischievously. 'No way!' says Jenny, the leader, getting off her chair. And one by one they strut their futures: engineer! Music producer! Lawyer! Archaeologist! Digital artist! Governor of New York! 'Wow, good for you!' says Graziela, and orchestrates a fine burst of applause.

Now the nails are trimmed and varnished, it's time for a group Polaroid. It's no longer the only souvenir, now that each glamour girl has a smartphone in her pocket, and the flashes are fit for a première: 'Frankie, show me your nails! Felicia, please do that again! Graziela, smile! Cynthia, look at me now!' And they upload that entire repertoire of twisted fingers, freckled hands and arthritic joints to the stellar cloud of these young folk, to where they keep all their deities: Instagram.

9

Today the youngest hairdresser is giving a retired school-teacher the works. He's concentrating so hard you'd think he was handling atoms. The perm is now al dente and he's unravelling the rods that look like wire rather than plastic. He rolls and twists them in, one at a time. It seems incredible that a bunch of waves flowing halfway down her neck will be the end result. She tells him she's not been for four months because she broke her humerus. '*I remember, your hair very pretty.*' She said 'humerus' quite deliberately, and after thanking him for his compliment, she repeats the reason why and touches the bone in question. Now the hairdresser understands. '*Yeah, hospital no good…*' The retired schoolteacher continues her medical report. She's lost eight kilos, and you know, that was a positive, but as for her hair… she was really fed up about her hair. How drastic, she'd not been for so long! That made as much sense to him as humerus, but he guesses right and titters. 'You've done me proud! It looks a treat!' The retired schoolteacher has had her say and grips the seat to get up. '*Wait!*' He makes her sit down again. '*Wait a bit, it last longer.*' He's a perfectionist, the genuine article from this hairdressing school. He's spotted a wave that's subsided and battles with the ends of three different combs until he gets the figure of eight right. That's it: '*Now you can.*' I feel like putting out a flyer: 'Important message to all retired ladies in Gràcia, this is the place you'll find your real artist!' Because if the flyer said you'll find your glamour boy right here, nobody would understand.

And now Senyora Eulàlia comes in and greets the retired schoolteacher: 'A sight for sore eyes, Senyora Catalina! So pleased to see you again!' 'Hello, love,' she greets me. 'You and I are on the same wavelength, aren't we?' and she walks the length of the salon in order to deposit her shopping trolley in the little backroom. Without saying a word, as if she were at home. I can smell the herbs for a broth from here. 'I'm having my hands and feet done today, so I'll be here for a while,' she tells me with a wink, and comes to wait next to me. 'You know, it's so relaxing! That's why I come, love, and for the company... for the company, I'd be lying if I said otherwise.' Wenling signals for me to go to the manicure table and Senyora Eulàlia follows.

She sits us down, swish, swish, swish, with her fan, and brings us up to date: her hubby is getting over his poorliness but she doesn't know if he's really better, because he's the doddery kind. My mind finds her phrase 'doddery kind' invigorating, and her blast of fresh air has an immediate effect on the conversation: 'Hey, Wenling, how's your kid? Tell me, love, *did she get over that gritting-her-teeth malarkey?*'

She gave her a natural cure for a week: it didn't do her any harm, but it didn't do her any good either. Because it wasn't as if she was constipated. At night Wenling kept an eye on her and she ground her teeth as usual, and she had to ask the doctor for an appointment. '*He say lot of kids' teeth like that because too much*

36

to do after school, sport, English...' 'We're in a fine pickle, love, so young and a bag of nerves already!' *'Tomorrow dentist put...'* She looks for the image on her mobile and shows us one of those transparent plastic mouthguards.

I've not said a word so far, I can imagine what it's about. If I was ten like Haijun and had been transplanted from my home, school, city and planet only the day before yesterday... from my whole world. I try to put myself in her shoes and reckon that teeth grinding at night is not the half of it. Her world was her grandparents; mother and father were only labels, voices on the phone, summer visitors. *'Your girl not here long... find hard to fit in, all new, it's difficult.'* I hear myself imitating her Spanish. I want her to grasp that at the very least I have the right to hold an opinion on the subject. And Wenling gets me, that I'm hinting there's grief that comes from nostalgia, and she shrugs her shoulders. *'I know... but in China say: If tree change land, die; if person change land, live. My kids get used to here bit by bit...'* That 'here' is her wager. And it also has to be theirs.

'Today I worried about school,' she suddenly tells us. The fact is Wenling has a problem this afternoon. Last time it was a real sacrifice to leave a packed salon to go to a parents' meeting, and nigh on torture to do it and not understand one word of what the teacher was explaining for more than an hour and a half. And she can't think what to do. *'Well, ask for a time just for you, love!'* Senyora Eulàlia is always on the ball. 'Come on, I'll write a note for you!' *'Yes, that better!'*

> *Dear teacher: Wenling, Haijun's mother, prefers not to come to the parent–teacher talk today because she found it very difficult to*

follow last time. She asks if you can please give her a time to meet you, so you can tell her what you tell the other parents. Many thanks for your patience and understanding.

10

She was wearing her motorbike helmet the first time I saw her. Stressed out, texting, her expensive leather backpack half-open, a La Central tote bag bringing up the rear. Chaotic. Sophisticated and with an air of distinction, as people used to say. She didn't look local. Kristin Scott Thomas lost in Barcelona. And with a bun in the oven. A good six or seven months.

'*Hello, lovely, why you no take this off?*' Wenling asked, helping her with all her baggage. She also called her by her name, but I won't be the one to take her helmet off. In here she'll be Kristin.

She was dazzling, as if she'd just been for a swim on another planet. I couldn't take my eyes off her. Naturally, if I'd have established eye contact, it would have spoiled everything. I had to make do with verging on neck strain and cervical disaster and listen in behind Ágota Kristóf's *Claus and Lucas* trilogy.

First she said, 'If you only knew, Wenling… If you only knew!' and laughed. A bit like a madwoman who knows what she's about and dances her way through life. But the moment she becomes oblivious to the danger, she lets go and it all floods out.

★

39

Summing it up as 'the story of an expectant woman in love' may not seem a big deal. Or at least not worthy of note. It's technically correct but short on detail. And a game changer. Certainly Kristin fell in love when she was expecting. Just at that second when men stop licking their wives and kiss only their foreheads. Precisely that second when the parents-in-law call daily to ask if the girl has kicked once or twice; when parents gift clothes fit for Norwegian royalty, neighbours feel up her belly on the slightest pretext without her say-so, and hospitals apply their protocols for the deactivation of human bombshells. There, feeling the first move of a mutation that would change her from an individual into a piece of furniture, Kristin spontaneously overthrew every taboo. And fell in love.

She didn't just say hello; their eyes devoured each other when Kristin entered the Pilates studio where he worked. And without ever exchanging a word, one day they happened to exit together. Side by side, close, not daring to brush against each other, fearful of freezing there and then.

She heard his voice for the first time when he told the receptionist his name. She'd made no mistake. It was sweet, gentle; a voice that treated people well. She hadn't yet opened her mouth, still hadn't removed her helmet. It protected her; Barcelona is a small world. And it was in that first bright-white bedroom that smelled so clean that Kristin began to feel her power. It was stellar, infinite, no doubt about it. And irresistible. And Kristin didn't give it another thought, accepted it, and it was completely natural for her clothes to feel a few millimetres tighter by the day.

She did all she had to do and felt the power to boot. Of course, she muttered to herself on the street, left an office folder in a taxi and burned the pan for a fourth time, but it was all going marvellously. Her husband couldn't get over it, we should have more than one, if you're going to be like this all the time. And everyone she bumped into found her happier and prouder. That's what pregnancy does for you, love! You bet!

First they agreed to keep to neutral apartments, it was more prudent. And, heavens, they weren't short of friends who enjoyed love without the paperwork. But it was a hassle having to keep to their timetables. Because the power didn't like to be kept waiting. When they wanted to see each other, it had to be instantly. And they had to risk leaving their safe dens. And it turned out that Kristin's bump was as good or better protection as entering everywhere in her helmet. It was her safe passage.

It wasn't that they got many shifty looks or raised eyebrows when they asked for an en-suite double room, or a corner table in a bar. Were they so up for it? So horny? Soon-to-be parents so keen to copulate? But what else could they be if not a proper couple, properly blessed? Pregnancy, that female state of sexuality everyone dares desecrate, had an unsuspected bonus: it immunised against suspicion. Raised eyebrows were always followed by slaps on the back, and congratulations!

They burned up petrol from one end of Catalonia to the other. They enjoyed siestas in the prettiest hotels in the Empordà, dined under the stars in the Delta and made love on a Costa Daurada beach. Darkness was falling, the only people left in the beach bar were the bartenders, who took a look to see where the muffled laughter was coming from. Not even a unicorn could have made that impact: Kristin unbound, her big bump out there, round and silvery like the moon. They closed in a flash and beetled out. They didn't hear or see them. They kept humping, living the power.

★

'*And when child come, what you do?*' Wenling is down to earth too. '*I don't know, I don't know…*' And Kristin's eyes lost their sparkle, darkened like a beach whose moon has been stolen, and the future dangled there, among the microparticles of lacquer the arty hairdresser was sprinkling over Senyora Eulàlia's combed mahogany perm.

Kristin gave birth to Lila. One day I was waiting for a manicure when she came in to show her to Wenling. They'd come straight from the paediatrician, a young Argentine who'd been totally bowled over. '*Your child is so full of life! She's been laughing since the first check-up! Tell me, what were the circumstances of the pregnancy?*' Kristin was petrified. '*The circumstances?* I'm not sure… the usual, I suppose,' and she winked at Lila: Hey, shall we tell him?

11

Today I really will. I'll follow the hairdresser customer's advice and do so wholeheartedly. Today I will. '*Hello, lovely, hands.*' I'll say hands and hair! 'Just hands,' I say. Half-heartedly. I wanted him to do my hair and today I've pulled back yet again. The thought of my friend Sesi puts the brake on, she's the friend who rules over my head. And that's been the case for ten years, will she think I've lost it when I finally tell her? Sesi will understand, she will, the next time I ask Wenling's husband to cut it and find a way to tell her. But my legs tremble at the very thought.

'How are you, Wenling? And the kids?' '*They fine, thanks.*' 'Do they like going to school? Are they getting to grips with the language?' '*Yes, they do well.*' 'And did you see the teacher?' '*No worry. Tell you later.*' And her eyes twinkle because she can see I'm the peacemaker already snapping her fingers if someone has to make a fuss.

I find the twins a real joy. They don't like going to cafés. They always want to spend the afternoon here. The first walks in, the one who calls her Wendy, and she's so upfront. She comes from the Barceloneta on purpose. '*It's seven stops! Half a dozen hairdressers in my street and I come here.*' 'Nice hairdresser's,' says Wenling's husband, summing up why she makes the effort.

'*Hello, Gripi!*' Wenling welcomes her. She doesn't reply, she's stuck to her mobile and about to clear up my doubts: '*Lourdes, it's your twin Agripina, you've still not made it to the hairdresser's!*' No, Wenling didn't get her name wrong, but he did: '*Wash hair, no mobile now, Gripe.*'

'It's not "*Gripe*", you idiot! "*Gripe*" is the flu! Agripina or Gripi!'

It was inevitable. Roman emperors always get their comeuppance.

While he washes her hair, she tells him what two-thirds of the customers say: she's been in hospital. Three weeks for Senyora Gripi. Two on account of water on the lungs and one because the porters dropped her. '*They forgot the safety catch and… clatter-clatter-bang! You know, it even gave them a big fright.*' She shows him where she still has the bump. '*You see? Here! Make sure you don't fry it with your dryer!*' This Gripi has a great turn of phrase. I adore her.

I gather from Wenling's *so-so* that the meeting with the teacher didn't go well. She's soaking up subject matter, especially maths. But there is a problem: Haijun is very quiet, she reprimanded her for it, and when she speaks, her voice is so soft she can hardly hear her. That dismayed Wenling as much as if she'd been stealing rolls at breaktime. I say, 'Well it's what I was saying the other day, I find that so understandable, given that she's had a second birth here only a short time ago. And even so she's still doing well. *This is quite normal, don't you worry*, the more time goes by, the louder she'll get.' I'm so sure of this that I think I shouted, when it's better not to sound so categorical.

Wenling isn't so sure, and she asks me if I can go and have a word. '*Maybe she tell you why…*' 'Right away,' I say enthusiastically. I hope nobody notices I'm not the answer to everything, an issue like this isn't like writing a note, or squaring up to a hospital secretary, my comfort zones, as they say nowadays, when most women will walk away and leave you to fend for yourself.

And while my nails are drying… 'Haijun, can you come here for a moment?' I ask her about school, the subjects she likes most, if she has lots of homework or plays any games. All very basic, I admit, but quite enough to coax her into being… a bit chatty! Hadn't we agreed she was ever so quiet? She goes to the playground with a little gang, she doesn't stand in a corner all by herself: it's not wilful isolation. She likes to be with her girlfriends, a lot: proof of her sociability. But in effect, for now, Haijun only listens. 'Why?' 'Well, I still don't get every word and they speak very quickly.' 'Is it the same with the teachers?' 'It is with some, not with others.' 'Does it depend on whether they speak too quickly?' She nods and that's a real eureka and hallelujah combined, and she smiles, relieved of a burden that I'd say can be easily sorted. Two simple questions and it turns out that the Great Riddle of the Silence of the Newly Arrived Child has been solved. Smashed to smithereens, because Haijun doesn't want to kill off conversation, she wants to talk even more.

I indicate my nails aren't dry yet, that I have all the time in the world, go on, go on… And she asks what the difference is between western and eastern Catalan. I'm flabbergasted. 'Are they asking you to learn that when you're only just beginning to learn how to speak?' Oh my god, three cheers for our canny curriculum! 'Well, the way I speak, the way they speak in Barcelona and roundabout, is called eastern Catalan. And what they speak here…' I look for a map on my mobile and point out Ponent, the Franja between Catalonia and Aragon, the Ebro Delta, Valencia, 'is where they speak western Catalan.' 'OK,' she responds in a *neutral* Catalan, 'but what's the difference?' That's the slap in the face I deserved… 'I haven't been a great help, have I?' She lets out a giggle I find priceless. 'That's fine, you explain.' 'Well…' I take a deep breath, 'one difference might be the way the letter "e" is pronounced…'

I hope no philologist is in the room. Or that he ignores me. Because I reckon that the most practical thing is to give her a mini-recital of atonic and neutral and long and short vowels by singing a line from a lovely children's song, 'Les nenes maques al dematí': '*L[ə]s nen[ə]s maqu[ə]s* is eastern Catalan and *l[e]s nen[e]s maqu[e]s* is western.' 'OK!' she exclaims, all enthused. 'And is it eastern or western Catalan in Madrid?' 'No Catalan in Madrid! They speak Spanish in Madrid, like Senyora Gripi, right?' '*Així, així,*' she says, using Wenling's favourite Catalan remark. And before she returns to the backroom, I come out with what I'd wanted to ask from the day I saw the letters on her tracksuit.

'Hey, Haijun, which school do you go to?'

'To the Sisters,' she shouts proudly.

'*The Sisters?*' hollers Senyora Gripi. '*The Sisters are bastards!*'

As if the doors to a fake ceiling had sprung open, the flood is biblical, Taoist, Talmudic, Buddhist, Koranic… Wenling and Haijun stay deadly still. Me too, but I'll have to do my best to come to the surface; they don't move. I spit, cough, breathe in the little air around and, finally, recover my voice.

'What are you saying, dear?' And more quietly, '*I'm sure she doesn't mean now, Wenling, I'm sure she's referring to the past.*'

46

But Senyora Gripi's was no knee-jerk reaction, and she's not stopping.

'*The Sisters played a nasty trick on me!*'

And I almost collapse to the ground. Should I kill the subject so Wenling and Haijun aren't even more upset and embarrassed? But then I'll never know what horrible injustice Senyora Gripi suffered.

'What period are you talking about, Senyora Gripi?'

'*You know, several years ago, in 1966…*'

'You see! A long time ago, Wenling!' Just look how those two have frozen!

'*I see that… It wasn't my intention… But nobody can erase that nightmare!*'

And before she lets fly, I slip in a bit of context for mother and daughter.

'I mean, there was a war here…'

I realise I must switch to Spanish, so Wenling gets every word. '*After the war, the period Señora Gripi is talking about, those who won the war were a dictatorship, Franco, a dictator, a military man, a criminal, a…*'

'*A pig, a sadist and a murderer!*' Senyora Gripi rounds off my list.

'*And lots of people were very afraid here, Wenling, and convent schools…*' and I emphasise '**in those days** *didn't treat you properly if you didn't think or do what the church and the military both ordered you to, and they hurt people like Señora Gripi.*'

Granted, I could have phrased it better, but Wenling and Haijun calm down.

'*That's right!*' Senyora Gripi backs up what I said. '*They wouldn't let me register my children because I was a single mother. Can you believe that, Wendy? My husband left me and I had a seven-year-old boy and a five-year-old girl to bring up, that's the truth, and he disappeared overnight and those bastards,'* back on her hobby horse, when we thought we'd got back on track again, *'those bastard Sisters tell me they don't want a mother without a father, Wendy, that I'm a bad example for the school, and they put my children out in the street! I went home sobbing like Mary Magdalen, and will never forget that day! Never!'*

Wenling gets up, goes over to her and holds her hands. A tear rolls down Senyora Gripi's cheek. Haijun looks at me, my eyes tell her I don't know what to say and she understands that it's not the moment to break our silence.

Now the three of us are with her. We walk up the Carrer Gran on a damp, dark autumnal day in a Barcelona that is occupied territory. First she shoots out of the Sisters like a bullet, driven by her rage. But now Senyora Gripi is in a quandary and doesn't know where to go. Whether to try her luck in another school, or leave it all to the nanny and go into the grocer's. Senyora Gripi is one of the defeated too, and she hesitates. But she doesn't wither away; she is like gorse. The blazing, resilient kind. Really something. She'll forget the bleach, wipe away the darkness and support her children, and that's the story so far. The other history. The one without exclamations or monuments. The one we have never honoured. The one we owe to so many Senyores Gripis.

12

I've hardly mentioned Wenling's little boy. He's playing the rock, paper, scissors game with a fair-haired boy twice his size. His father is giving him a trim and needs the patience of a saint. Because those two act as if they are in their own world, as if hair-trimmer and barber don't exist. 'Rock!' He peers out from behind Haitao. 'Haha, paper!' The fair-haired boy shows him an open hand and spins his chair around. Another! There's no stopping them. Luckily an eight-year-old's head doesn't take long. They go inside, but there's no let-up. The din carries on as if they were still playing next to us. There's so much boisterous glee, I even have to stop taking notes on my mobile.

'Pol! Pol!' The fair-haired boy's mother walks into the salon. 'Come on, Pol, time to go home!' '*He fine with us*,' says Wenling. 'You bet, if it was down to him, they'd be together all day! Let Haitao come to our place for a while, Wenling.' 'Yes, please!!' The two boys peer out. 'No,' says Wenling. '*Haitao a nuisance.*' '*Only for a snack, come on, Wenling,*' Pol's mother insists. '*No, Haitao eat very slow, a nuisance.*' And they implore, act up, indicate it will be impossible to disentangle them. 'Look at us!' they shout as they entwine arms and legs. Wenling smiles but doesn't back down, and Pol's mother isn't keen to pressurise but she tries again. '*They're having a great time, right? Not just for a teeny while?*

49

You sure, Wenling?' '*When their holiday, yes.*' The kids hold their breath, Wenling is weakening. And says, '*OK, at the weekend.*' '*I'm sorry, we're away this one. The one after we'll be here, what do you reckon, Wenling?*' '*Yes, fine, the weekend after.*'

The boys go crazy. They celebrate like they've won the League, the Cup and the Champions League: Whoopee! Whoopee! Whoopee! I note the whoopees haven't moved far from where they were when I was a little girl: in the corner, far from the party. Haitao and Pol string out the whoopees a couple of times as they return to the backroom. The weekend after next is a long way away, they have to make the most of the pact signed by their mothers. They don't let up, and start chasing each other, jumping and pissing themselves with laughter. I tell you, a good number of us would like a slice of that joie de vivre. We'd get one just by watching them. 'That's enough, Pol, come out of there!' Now the mother who'd been so reasonable starts to lose it. It's half an hour since she looked at her watch and told him it was time to go.

Haijun sticks out a big sister's tongue at them and brings her school bag over to me. 'You help?' 'Of course! *You can paint them later, Wenling, I not in hurry.*' '*You sure? My girl not a nuisance?*' 'Not at all! Shush now and let us be!' And she isn't upset by my brusque tone.

We start with Spanish, finding the subject in the sentence. I use the old questioning technique and Haitjun gets it immediately. Thirty years on, I listen to myself talking verbs, asking whether the wretched plural *eran* goes with *perros caniches* or *Julia*.

I tell myself it will be a different kettle of fish with Catalan when she says it's time to practise accents. I'm amazed again.

Soon even more so: Haijun doesn't get one wrong. She immediately tells me when I ask her where the accents go on the
words I shoot at her – if, that is, they have one. *Cardiòleg*? On the
'o'! *Ressò*? On the 'o'! *Atmosfera*? No accent! *Càmfora*? First 'a'!
Terraplè? On the last 'e'! *Paràbola*? On the middle 'a'!

I run through thirty and she doesn't get a single one wrong.
I can't get over it. The girl must have a fantastic memory; she
hears them in class, and, bang, never forgets one, because she can
only have heard those fancy words in her Catalan class. *Càmfora*,
paràbola, *terraplè*… Not even I use those nouns. And am I the
only one thinking you could change them for *adaptació*, *enyoradís*
or *nostàlgia*, and give students the same practice in allocating
accents? To make sure the kids weren't so 'quiet'?

I'm still mulling that over when I hear her ask: 'Something
else, something else!' It's great when kids can never get enough
and I'm thrilled. 'What is your favourite instrument?' 'The
piano' – really just a knee-jerk answer. Oh, she's so happy.
'I play piano! Difficult to find the right notes but I like it!
Something else! Something else! What instrument you play in
school?' And she bursts out laughing when I make fun of the
dreadful guy who tried teaching us the recorder.

Because he wasn't a teacher or a musician, simply a supporter
of Franco. Ex-military, into the bargain. I avoided going to the
Sisters, but I came from the sticks, where the progressive schools
you find in Barcelona were a pipe dream. Musical pedagogy was
so much science fiction. Every recorder lesson was torture. The
ex-military fellow made us call him *Don* and threw the board
duster at our heads if we giggled when we blew bubbles instead
of notes. He didn't even know how to teach us the most basic

thing like how to blow. That hoodlum had never got beyond the 'soldier-on-your-feet-off-with-your-sheet' stage and that's why he'd managed to wing it as a music teacher in a Catalan state school till the end of the Seventies, when he retired with every honour and bonus. Thanks to our ever-so-exemplary democratic transition. Such a unique whitewashing of the dictatorship and its butchers.

13

I was intent on combing Barcelona district by district. To find out who did manicures and pedicures, who was on the receiving end, whether there was any feedback or interaction, and what sort. All the fault of the standards of femininity we'd been landed with, the idea you might strike oil if you rethought everything from every perspective. One fine day I saw that the manicure had everything to offer. Once it was established as a basic badge of my femininity, I needed to keep it up and make sure I got the best. And just as not having the patience of a twenty-year-old means you dig deep into your pocket and pay for one, it can also mean you make something of your time rather than waste it. I've always been fascinated to find out what people say and how they behave when they think nobody is watching.

I'd started by scrutinising nail salons abroad, when they were still few and far between here. I had a well-oiled routine, grabbing free time between shoots, clearing off without the troupe. I yawned, I pretended I couldn't keep my eyes open, I couldn't hear them – 'Sorry? How? What?' – and the team had to wind up. They'd tell me to go and get some rest, go on. They'd do their thing, I'd do mine.

Manicure salons had lots of potential; it wasn't like propping up a bar and pretending to knock back shots. Because apart from the idiot barmen, I was fed up with innuendo from the leering guys next to me. What's this dame doing here all alone, how many has she put away, what if she's on the game, what if… None of which you'd have to put up with if you were a guy. There's no comparison, however much writers and film directors have vamped up the romantic allure of bars, pubs and cocktail joints: truth doesn't exist in the bottom of a glass, and the rattle of a cocktail-maker has no more mystique than the swish of a nail polish brush. No more persuading guys to guzzle.

Quite the contrary, a manicure salon is a sure-fire guarantee I won't stumble home and will be well supplied with notes for my private fieldwork. Every little service in a salon brings a quite remarkable variation in humanity. Customers who aren't the icing on the cake. Customers indifferent to the person so carefully cutting, filing, hydrating and seeing to the well-being of their extremities. Zero marks.

The number of zeros I registered became scary. You wouldn't believe that in next to no time I'd reach five per cent of half the human race. But the more *nuls points* I collected, the more motivated I was to listen, note, portray and extrapolate. I established common patterns, identified common features… It was a job and a half deciding why we have become so animal-like.

That contrast in humanity comes courtesy of a disappointment. From the moment the 'And the Oscar goes to…' wasn't announced for our short and we left the Kodak Theatre empty-handed.

Aimee's Nail
Los Feliz, Los Angeles, California
Manipedi: $30

Customer 1. Sunk into her chair, eyes on her cell phone, feet soaking in water. She doesn't look at the manicurist even when she lifts them out of the bowl, or when she dries them as if she were a newborn babe, or when she shows her the sample range so she can select a colour. A load of bags scattered around her – from boutiques on Rodeo Drive. She looks like the real LA deal. The real post-European colonisation deal. She doesn't pipe up once. The usual zero.

Customer 2. Real post-European colonisation deal too. Absolutely the deal, chatters away non-stop. Into her phone. Budgets, bank transfers and revenues. Can't wait. She frees up her hands when the manicurist requests her hands the third time and resumes business. She utters a sole word: yeah. In duplicate. File or clippers, yeah-yeah. Squared or round, yeah-yeah. Shorter or longer, yeah-yeah. It will be a miracle if she guesses her taste right. She looked her in the face as if she hadn't seen her. Barely a 2.

Customer 3. LA local since the age of eighteen. Since she married so they didn't deport her to Mexico. She and the manicurist hit it off straight after the introductions. He was twenty-five years older, she was a *chavita*: what you must do to get papers. 'Nightmare-nightmare-nightmare-nightmare,' she repeats with her eyes closed. Now her kids have grown up, she'd like to separate, but the guy has had an attack of angina. She crosses herself at the very thought. She asks the manicurist to paint her nails black, just in case. They both burst out laughing. The customer then asks her what she's doing, whether she's studying. And when the manicurist tells her, she says: 'That's amazing, well done, never rely on a man!' A ten like a Rolls-Royce: the first I award.

Manicurist 1. Sad-faced, open-toed sandals, a grey bun. Grandmother.

Manicurist 2. Careful, cloth slippers, hair pulled back in a ponytail. Daughter.

Manicurist 3. Super cool, supersonic Nike trainers, long hair flecked with blond highlights. Granddaughter.

I get no. 2, the daughter, Nhung, from Vietnam. From South Vietnam, she specifies, and points to the plasma overlooking the salon: Little Saigon TV. Coming to America at the age of ten doesn't mean she is American. Though her daughter is, one hundred per cent. She's the Aimee on the sign but she only helps in summer; she's finished her first year at university, languages. English, Spanish, German, Chinese… She's lost count, and her mother never got beyond the basics. She laughs though she's not amused. *She left her heart and her voice there.* We look at her at the cash register, then I take a longer look. Smallish, skinny, still lively. Keeps going, but never able to forget all she's given up.

And what they say must be true: Vietnam stories come with lots of tears. In those days they cried enough to fill the world's oceans. The days when Nhung's mother fled. The days when a war died and a way out was born.

14

It's Tuesday, 29 April 1975, and a voice on the American Forces Radio declares: 'The temperature in Saigon is 106 degrees... and rising!' A hand presses a button and a record sings out:

> I'm dreaming of a white Christmas
> Just like the ones I used to know
> Where the treetops glisten
> And children listen
> To hear the sleigh bells in the snow...

The ditty that had the cheek to dream of a white Christmas in the muggy heat of South East Asia is the precise electromagnetic flake required to set off Operation Frequent Wind. A highly ironic, scumbag evacuation code and name for a blustering military operation to activate a line of history that in plain terms meant retreat and defeat.

The US of A flees from the Vietnam War to the background music of the bestselling Christmas song of all time, a tail of shame between its legs, a record haul of deaths, countless numbers of raped Vietnamese women, Agent Orange sprayed around so barren land will continue to be toxic, and baggage it is as much a bother to carry as to mistreat: they prefer to say 'American dependants' rather than 'collaborationist South Vietnamese personnel', and have promised to lift out all sorts in that manoeuvre.

There are high-ups, military and pilots. There are bureaucrats, spies and torturers. There are doctors, office workers and interpreters. And their wives, naturally, especially the hostesses who organised all those receptions. And there are children, and bundles, and suitcases and typewriters. And there are hangers-on, those fleeing because they too are scared of communist revenge, but they are forlorn, no uniforms, no patrons, no cash, no papers. And they all pile in, push and shove in the eye of the storm.

The US of A has told them it is grateful for all their years of loyalty, that it won't leave them in the lurch and will protect them from reprisals and certain death. And will do so in evacuations by helicopter from a bombed-out airport, and it will be fantastic. By helicopter? Everybody? Everybody... they can. Everybody... they can fit in. Everybody... that comes after the first-comers: Americans and Western journalists. They don't use the word 'white' but it makes their job easier amid the chaos. It's also a big help to promise 'to help those who helped America' with your fingers crossed behind your back: in the moment of truth, the South Vietnamese will be the most abandoned. And not from any lack of will on the part of hapless American pilots who sweated to the last. But what had been chronicled as 'the world's largest helicopter airlift in history' can shrink and look quite pathetic, depending on how you see it. When a whole country is under the thumb of a single master, try to find the brave guy who will stay on and welcome his successor, rolling a cigarette on the terrace of the Majestic. There are never enough helicopters.

*

Whenever people talk about the last days of the war or the fall of Saigon, it always comes up. The historic photo of the helicopter, the terrace, the guy holding out a hand and the ladder packed with South Vietnamese desperate to climb on. They are near the American embassy, which at this point in time doesn't have enough iron fences or guards as so many people push to get in, with time running out. The terrace in that historic photo is more like a little open space with a deck in the middle where a helicopter could never land, even if only for a dare. It's like wanting a falcon to land on the palm of one hand. Yes, it does touch the deck, does land, and people do scramble. The people with the sharpest elbows and most ear-splitting shrieks surge forward, trample on and flatten as many bodies as possible to reach it.

But helicopter entrails are soon stuffed. And a helicopter's glory is short-lived, is like its little insect siblings: life is short, make way for the next. The video that unfreezes the photo and shows what happens next makes that clear. You see the whirling iron devil lift off, leaving in the lurch the ladder horridly laden with people. The guys our optimistic perception had already helped pack into the helicopter along with the fellow holding out a hand. The guys our redemptive passion had already crammed in – hold on tight, deep breaths, legs crossed, heads spinning – as the 'copter shudders and whirls towards two concepts that begin with 'ex', which everyone wants to keep at bay until the time comes when you love them more than your own father: exodus and exile.

And on the horizon, another word those lucky enough not to be left clinging to that ladder find sprouting on their foreheads the moment they are inside the vessel. A label they all read when they are disgorged in Southern California: Saigon is now Ho Chi Minh City, they are now dubbed 'refugees'. And it makes no odds if they are from the south, the good guys who fought on their side, the ones civilised by the French, converted by missionaries, the meek and obedient who swallowed two spoons of the Truman Doctrine before going to sleep in case they'd caught a whiff of communist air. It makes no odds. 'Your country doesn't exist,' you have the same faces as the Vietcong who killed our boys, so young and full of life, the same faces as those who left us war-wounded, and as far as I or we are concerned you can rot in these tents for centuries to come, and be thankful we believe in God and aren't heartless and didn't leave you in the sea to be fish fodder and that we've piled you into Camp Pendleton.

15

Combing Barcelona district by district was the idea, right? Well, there's no way I can jettison Wenling. My hands are now hers, it is what it is. And my feet... I thought I could take my feet anywhere and get a pedicure on the sly in order to collect supplementary data to record contrasts in human behaviour. Well, they're sabotaging my efforts, they're fed up with serving as a pretext. They won't let me cross any other thresholds. And I wasted days in that tug of war. My nails flaked and grew, just like my lies. '*No feet no, thanks, yesterday cut and painted nails.*' And I'm more shocked by how deceitful I've become than by the pruned-down grammar I've espoused that would cause a furore in the Spanish Royal Academy. Down with pronouns and articles! If they're more bother than they're worth, off to the dungheap!

Come to think of it, my yoga teachers do it too. They say: *Left arm go in front right leg. Left leg up, right hand takes left knee.* And so on and so forth with the whole sequence of postures. And everyone gets it, right? You know, I'm a dab hand at imitating the Spanish Wenling has only been able to learn like a thief, in snatches from customer to customer. And I realise this now as I write: I do it so she feels I'm closer to her.

Let's forget that then. I'll not be going elsewhere to get a pedicure. My fieldwork will have a single field: this one.

'*Sit down, lovely, you feet first, afterwards hair, my husband eating.*'
'You're not eating?' '*I later, when children out at school.*' I hear '*chil-dren*' and break out in a sweat, poor kids. Fact is my brain's too worn out for another language class, even though it's a doddle the way I go about it.

Since there's no sign of them, I jump in and say that she's never shown me her friend-sister. 'Do you have any photos?' Her face lights up. '*Yes, she always sending, she very just so, when finish feet, I show.*' 'Hello!' Haijun comes out from the back and I don't get to see Xiaolu's face. 'I recognised your voice!' She's so bright! '*En sèrio?*' I should lash myself whenever my gob comes out with an error like that! What kind of Catalan is she going to learn if I keep coming out with *bueno*, *vale* and *en sèrio* every other word?! I correct myself: '*De debò?*' 'Yes, and I hear you speak Spanish to Mother.' 'Just now I did, I speak half and half, really. With you, as you go to school, you can learn it, we will practise Catalan, right?' 'Great!' And she turns to look at her father, who tidies her ponytail as he walks out, simply to irritate her.

They talk in Mandarin and I don't need to know any to translate the good-natured tone. However, Wenling deciphers for me. '*Father say she bigger by the day and he shorter, say she not seem family, find Haijun in the rubbish.*' The look on my face makes them laugh more than the in-joke they decided to share with me. 'Come off it! *What are you saying!?*' 'They're joking, Haijun, don't you believe them!' She hugs her father from behind as if she's trying to strangle him, but any doubt has been killed off: father and daughter exchange absurd grimaces that couldn't be more alike.

She goes off to school dragging her brother behind her. My feet are perfect, and Wenling runs inside to have lunch. I'll remind her some other day of the photos of her friend-sister, now the moment of truth is nigh. '*You hair with me? You sure?*' I don't have time to get a word out before he replies, '*No worry, no worry, I know, your hair easy.*' Maybe my hair, but the rest of me is bone-hard, kid. Wait a sec! I use my hand to put the brake on him and with the other show him the photo on my mobile of a cut Sesi did one day. 'See, like this.' 'I know, I know,' he doesn't even take a look. '*Like here, like it is here, but longer,*' he points to my head and pulls the chair towards the mirror, just in case my sight is weakening. I swallow my pride with a mouthful of saliva and say nothing.

It would be wasted effort: he's moved on, concentrating on his tools. He clips deftly, oblivious to my grief, although it all looks fine. But when we reach the critical areas, oh mother of mine! I can't breathe, I'm on edge. Careful! My sideburns! My fringe! They mustn't be too short or too long, too wispy or too thick. And there I am, scrutinising each decision, staring at his every gesture, my jaws in lockstep with every clip. You get that my love for Sesi is unconditional, right? Nobody wants crazy people in their life.

I gradually relax, we've survived the Bermuda Triangle and I'd say there are no victims to mourn, my fringe and sideburns look fine, thank you very much. Now I'm more relaxed, I can see him as a hairdresser and not a threat. And, quite simply, he is fantastic. What a twist of the wrist, what aplomb with the thinning scissors, what skill with the comb. Sesi: if you saw him cutting, you'd befriend him too, I bet you would.

But we're not done yet. Now it's the turn of the nape of my neck, which requires another set of skills. Because that little ponytail must be a bit lower and a bit round, but without his dexterity being too obvious... I don't know if I'm making myself clear. '*No worry, I know, I know...*' And he resumes his clipping. It's a miracle when he gives me the small hand mirror so I can have a look: he's shaped it perfectly! It's amazing. I drop the towel, the bib slips off and now I can't remember if the washbasins are to the left or right. '*Wash hair here!*'

Letting someone else rub your skull... Don't we realise this small act brings the greatest of pleasures? When did we stop doing this to each other? Why did we let them take this from us? So foolish...

He gives it a thorough rinse and '*Now that's done, dry hair.*' But that's one step too far. '*I dry, I dry, no worry, I always dry myself, I'm manic about that.*' The other two hairdressers don't know what to do when they see me grab the dryer so force-fully. One wonders whether to stop me, but admits defeat. That could be dangerous, I'm armed, after all, and he lets me get on with it. 'You've done a really good job, *thank you, a great cut.*' 'Listen,' I tell him as the dryer buzzes its last buzz, 'I don't even know your name... What is it?' Wenling has just finished her lunch and is walking towards him. '*You call him Loco. Loco!*' She peers over one shoulder, '*Loco!*', then peers over the other. And laughs herself silly. And he does too, though he pretends to look fed up.

They didn't touch each other, but I'd swear I saw a sparkle in their eyes.

16

It's a holiday, they're not showing the soap and I only spot Senyora Eulàlia. 'Hello, love! *Manos?*' 'Yes, *mans*, how are you, Wenling?' '*Good, thanks. Your turn now, no people come today.*' The artist is sculpting Senyora Eulàlia's curls, and he – let's stick with 'he', because I don't know if I prefer to revert to 'pop singer' than call him Loco – is having his neck muscles kneaded by the masseuse. 'Hey, lad, it's your lucky day,' I tell him. '*Hair alright?*' he immediately asks. 'Yes, it's lasting really well, thank you!' And he shuts his eyes, loving his massage.

I want one as well. Night would fall, I'd yield to the pitch-black and melt away. Just the thought of it brings me to the brink. My head's about to drop on the manicure table. '*You very tired today, you say nothing!*' 'You're right, Wenling, today I'm…' The exact word for my state of mind exists and it is 'slothful'. But I have to leave it at simply dead, *muerta*. '*You relax…*' Wenling mindreads my longing and gives me an extended hand massage. She acts as if she were wringing my fingers. She stops the circulation, lets it go again, stops it, lets it go again, stops it, lets it go again. And I don't know if this is a textbook reaction by my blood or if it's me, but I spring back to life. And now I realise her face also looks very washed out, and that worries me. '*You look pale, you don't feel well, right?*' '*I tired today…*'

Yesterday night film on my mobile.' And she flickers her eyelashes. '*But I happy too!*'

Her girl brought home wonderful marks for the last semester, really good, in maths, Catalan and everything. 'She's quick on the uptake, Wenling, I'm always telling you, she's like you! Did you know that we inherit intelligence from our mothers?' She shakes her head rapidly as a grin spreads over her face. 'Yes, yes! Really!' I repeat. 'Good marks *in school*, I'm sure, I'm right, aren't I?' '*Well…*' She starts off very shamefaced, but has to confess, '*Is true, good marks always. But very poor, and I no can continue study.*' She says it with heartfelt sadness. '*Until what age?*' She lifts her facemask slightly and counts in her language until she reaches… '*Sixteen.*' 'And what would you have liked to study?' I'm afraid I've over-complicated the tense of the verb, but she doesn't need to think twice. '*Mandarin. To write.*'

That infinitive cuts me to the quick. I gave up on writing. Wenling didn't; she was struck down by the usual bolt of lightning. The same one that struck my grandmothers eighty years ago. The same one that electrocutes so many other women everywhere. You can't pay to learn? Well, you're fucked. A dry storm, books abandoned on the shelf and another beast of burden for the herd.

'*My grandmother already old and I help.*' And Wenling first went to look for work… at a tattoo shop? She draws on her wrist, but I don't reckon that can be right. And no, she didn't do tattoos. When she draws the third circle, the penny drops. That's it, watches. 'A watch factory!' And I stand up as if I am shouting 'Bingo'. You should zoom in on us, when we manage to read thoughts. '*But very difficult, very small, not do right.*' I think about

67

the phrase '*feina de xinos*' – 'work for chinks' – that we use all the time, not giving it a second thought. As if the gift for the most fiddly work is innate. As if what comes with birth isn't the land where we toil and the labour conditions that are legal there, as if that isn't what ties us to this or that job and gives us a decent or disastrous life.

'*And after the watches?*' '*After, iron.*' I understand that but can't credit that a sixteen-year-old girl can be hauling around lumps of iron in the shape of tubes, beams or whatever now comes to mind. 'You? Iron? But that weighs a lot!' '*Not that much, boxes,*' and she acts as if she's wrapping up... boxes... of iron? Wenling looks for her mobile to find the translation but it doesn't pop up. We won't get to the bottom of that, so what, let's forget the iron. And we both think alike: '*No bother, iron not last long, then more, I work lot of thing, I very poor,*' she repeats again. And now her face wrinkles and she looks like death warmed up.

After the factories came two clothes shops and, finally, the make-up counter where Wenling was young, happy and free with her friend-sister Xiaolu. '*But that all in past... I no longer think.*' And suddenly, solemnly: '*Lovely, I only think one day.*' And she comes straight out with it, with all the numbers, the 15th of May 2006. The day she set foot in Barcelona. '*When I die, I remember this day.*'

17

The poster says: Welcome to Hope Village. And painted underneath: Operation V.I.P. And in brackets: Vietnamese Integration Program.

Shy of telling it as it is: a selection of people made from the usual Very Important People. A poster that gave a welcome to the South Vietnamese who didn't deserve to be piled in tents on the Camp Pendleton naval base with hordes of their compatriots would hardly have been the style of an international Christian organisation dedicated to aid, development and advocacy like Food for the Hungry. They were the people who'd bought this former TB sanatorium in Weimar, Sacramento, California, refurbished it and would now do good by converting it into a resettlement centre for Vietnam War refugees. The fact that important refugees such as South Vietnamese civil servants, generals and that jewel Nguyen Cao Ky, the former prime minister, were hidden among the hordes they salvaged from Camp Pendleton was a minor faux pas.

VIPs for sure, but it's not all a bed of roses in Hope Village. There are hostesses who set up all those soirées that have become rubber plants parked unnoticed in a corner. And there they rot. That former sanatorium is the opposite of Camp Pendleton, and they have no complaints. Here they treat you like humans.

Children are well fed, beds have heads and feet, there are proper brick-built bathrooms, a mass of trees and deer who vie and leap outside the window... But if you're not emblazoned with medals, it also means you don't get calls from US diplomats or meetings or references or future opportunities. And being at zero in a foreign land makes nostalgia flourish. It springs from the refugee label they bear on their foreheads, and the past is everything: it's all Saigon, it's all my house, my mother, my father, our food, Notre-Dame, the river, the mists, the sunsets...

And in that state, painfully trailing flowers, stems and roots, those twenty-or-so women take themselves early one morning to the Hope Village reception as requested. Today it is they who, for the first time, have a special guest. Those who have a smattering of English, who are well educated and well mannered, who don't yet know they will be the chosen few, are the ones directed into the study room. You can wait for your visitor here, you can take your seats now. Fortunately, otherwise they'd have collapsed to the floor.

Off-screen she is even more luminous. Sparks of brilliance that should have blinded the man who only wanted to parade her body. Her last films have barely caused a ripple, or have been straight flops: surely none of the twenty chosen knows there were any after *The Birds* and *Marnie*. So what. She would change nothing, she never hesitated when it came to giving up her career. It's plain from her face that nothing can beat being rid of those claws scoring her flesh. The crows' claws eager to gouge out an eye and eat her alive were a walkover in comparison.

Tippi Hedren preferred to stop Alfred Hitchcock plaguing her life, she wants to be free to do whatever she wants, as well as take the odd role that comes her way. Not ones like those, of course, he made sure she was blacklisted, to make her pay for not letting him rape her. But everything has its pros. And the bonus of a career truncated by the all-powerful Hitch's revenge against the actor who stood up to him and rejected him with one almighty shove is time: time at her disposal. That's why Tippi Hedren is about to open a refuge for exotic cats that the wealthy buy on the black market and cast aside when they're no longer fun kittens. That's also why Tippi Hedren has volunteered to work for Food for the Hungry and has taken under her wing South Vietnamese women who were once drifting on the China Sea in nutshells. Boat people who fled on the first thing they could grab hold of after being left dangling from so many ladders.

However, this Hollywood star hasn't come to Hope Village today to complain or gripe about her lot. Everything she suffered is a secret she carries within herself, you still can't say a bad word about that pig Hitchcock. The hue and cry won't kick off until he's dead, and that's a good five years away. And Hedren doesn't want to harp on about the plight of her fellow American women; these women have enough sorrows of their own. No, Hedren is a woman who clings to ideas and for nights on end she's ruminated on what will happen to those refugee women she's been told are living in Hope Village like souls in limbo. What will happen to those 'wives of' who have neither a trade nor aid in the USA?

Hedren has come to put some suggestions to them, and she launches into it. She'll summon typists and dressmakers to see who has the nous to learn those skills, and teachers of English for when they have to fend for themselves in the outside world, and as soon as they can read well enough, they'll receive driving manuals, for if they go to Los Angeles, that will be key, then the courses she's already timetabled with someone or other, and she also wondered… Suddenly, Tippi Hedren stops and looks at them.

They're all hanging on her every word, mouths open and breathless. 'Is everything OK? Are you following me?' Aside from her words, whether in full flood or few, what has really made its mark, what those forty eyes have been glued to from the very start, is what crowns her dancing fingers: an oval, coral, gleaming, majestic manicure. The most daring takes hold of her fingers, two others are spellbound and all twenty are soon chorusing their admiration. Hedren doesn't need a second for it to click, she says, 'Got it!' before rushing out in search of a telephone.

*

Tippi Hedren sweeps away all their doubts. Doubts which have come from their husbands, rather than the chosen twenty, and are spokes in their wheels that don't stop them. It's not a problem if your husbands can't see the potential, darlings, I'll set up appointments with volunteer opticians! Eighteen chuckled, the most daring out loud, and one who had run her own nail salon in Saigon said it was time they rolled up their sleeves. Hedren got the message: good! She showed them what basketball teams do before going out on court, and after those twenty-one high-fives the decision was taken: she would train them to be manicurists. Go for it!

She said yes on the phone right away. She could count on her every Saturday, she was a single mother, she knew that you need a tribe to survive in this world. 'Women help women, that's our slogan!' whooped Dusty Coots, one of Hollywood's most prized manicurists and sculptress of Tippi Hedren's wondrous hands. It took eight weeks. Eight Saturdays in a row Coots grabbed her box of tricks, flew dead-tired from Los Angeles to Sacramento, turned up in Hope Village, asked for a strong coffee and started the session.

She reviewed the hands the chosen twenty had done as a sample, they reviewed procedures again, cleaned off the varnish, washed, trimmed, filed and repainted. Come on, make those cuticles more precise, smooth that nail a bit more, polish the sides, make the varnish perfect! Very good, now do it again, and even better! Until there was nothing that could be improved on, then they had a party.

Rooted to the spot and holding a cocktail, Tippi Hedren seemed miles away when the most daring of them blurted out: 'Tippi, what are you plotting now? You know you look as if you're planning a typhoon?' A typhoon by the name of a Professional Licence Certificate. All that good work needed accreditation. The chosen twenty had to be able to go out into the world with every guarantee; the fact they'd been students of Dusty Coots couldn't be framed and hung on any wall.

The excuse they made was that registration was closed. We're very sorry, our groups are full. But their insistence on finding out which side, ah, which *side*, in Vietnam those twenty women were from said it all. Directors of beauty schools who'd have struggled to point to Honduras on the map and showed scant interest in world geography. The letters Tippi Hedren sent to demand places could be as fierce as you liked; she could underline her name and the Food for the Hungry logo at the centre of the letter heading. Nothing doing. Rejections came thick and fast.

Until the couple who ran the Citrus Heights Beauty College saw there was money to be made, and answered positively, 'Let's do it.' All they must do was dress in white from head to toe. And pay the twenty enrolments up front in cash, naturally. Then they could start.

With blouses, housecoats, sanitary pyjamas and all the whites they'd collected from that second-hand shop in Sacramento, the chosen twenty clambered into the coach. Spruced up and beaming, their minds set on absorbing everything imparted in the coming four hundred hours of class in that academy.

They weren't so cock-a-hoop that evening when they came back. They were exhausted and those white outfits always bore stains that needed soap and water. But they would change, have a bite to eat in the dining room and before going to bed would go back to the study ward to ask each other questions about the anatomy of hands, the composition of varnishes, the fixing of fake nails, and the right rhythm for a massage. Their husbands would look on from the bedroom ward. Shell-shocked.

Roles had changed and would change even more. When ex-prime minister Nguyen Cao Ky vanished from the VIPs in Hope Village very early on, only they were left. Now the men said goodbye at the bus stop, put up with the children, killed their boredom as best they could and said hello in the dining room when their wives returned very late from the beauty college. References and important calls had flown off with the ex-prime minister, and those civil servants and generals had to learn that breadwinners in America weren't exclusively male.

After four hundred hours in class all twenty brandished their Professional Licence Certificates. It's a tremendous achievement, wrote Tippi Hedren from Africa.

They are still owed the certificate for the challenges that were to come. It ought to recognise 'The entrepreneurs who invented a new business', but the pen-pushers who should have expedited and signed them were unaware of what was in the offing. Even though the nail salons the South Vietnamese manicurists conjured out of their sleeves now move billions of dollars a year. No joke. Until quite recently they were ignored by the United States Bureau of Labor Statistics and there was no trace of them in the North American Industry Classification System. Collective non-existence, no sign of their activity or growth. Now they've been included in the census and statistics, inevitably as they're making so much cash, but still not all premises are considered worthy of being registered: the small freelance establishments surviving as best they can don't make it, they're still on the slipway.

Nor does Tippi Hedren earn any royalties from the Treasury Department for her copyright. Nor does anyone say of her that giving a life to those twenty refugees was more than an act of charity. It ended up being an exercise in role reversal that created a new branch of the economy. Without her special visit, her dancing hands and the majestic manicuring dexterity Dusty Coots gave them, without her intuition and stubborn will to rescue the chosen twenty from that pit in Hope Village, there wouldn't be a nail salon on every street in the United States and practically the whole world by now.

And how come it spread like a trail of gunpowder? The chosen twenty pack their cases and settle across California. They soon see that only top hairdressing salons have manicurists, who cost a fortune, and they take the gamble of renting small premises to open the service up to all pockets. Customers respond, spread the word, the fame of their manicures attracts twenty more daring women, and new waves of refugees arrive, and you don't need lots of capital or wonderful English to set up a nail parlour, and it's a success, and success runs riot, and another twenty come and repeat the experience, and yet another twenty talk, write, teach each other, get loans to open their small establishments, and their men come on board, and don their coats and start removing varnish, and the most ambitious open beauty colleges like the one where the first chosen twenty were trained, and set up cosmetic material warehouses to supply the sector. The network spreads and spreads until today the 'Viet-salon' is synonymous with small manicure and pedicure premises open 12/7. No appointment needed, and you leave with movie-star nails for next to nothing.

*

I will never know if Nhung's mother, who gave me that manicure in Aimee's Nail in Los Feliz, Los Angeles, ever ended up in Camp Pendleton with her ten-year-old daughter. Or if she was lucky enough to be selected for a transfer to Hope Village and even saw with her own eyes the chosen twenty being trained.

Or if she was one of those who had to row, row and row with her hands and all her might so the skiff that was already barely afloat didn't fill with water when she saw the belly of the vessel that was coming to rescue them. I will never know what her path to exile or exodus looked like, or what elbows she had to shove on those final days in Saigon. The shouting, the biting, the bodies she had to push out of the way to make her exit. But the word 'refugee' must sting on her forehead and inside her brain, that I can imagine.

And if I shut my eyes and see her again at the cash register in her nail salon, or steal another glance at a body worn down by so much hardship, I'd do it differently, I'd change the ending. Now I'd not pay thirty dollars for my mani-pedi, say goodbye to Nhung and walk away. Now I'd wait until it was time to shut up shop, I'd sit on the floor and listen to her telling her story as stories of Vietnam must be told: in tears.

18

The temperature in Barcelona is eleven degrees… and rising. It won't be a White Christmas here either, however much the piped music dreams. Early morning and it's jam-packed. '*Today wait an hour,*' he says with some regret. He also tries to convince me: '*No worries, not so long, you sit, right.*' 'That's fine, we won't be shooting again until after the holidays, I don't have to work today.' Or so I say. Because I quickly put away the book by Lucia Berlin and take out my mobile: I'll be tapping away all day.

Wenling could only manage a rapid hello and a half-glance; she's grating Parmesan at piecework rates. Packaged in the three colours of Italy, the flakes of epithelium leaving the grater would fool the most demanding gourmet.

A customer informs her neighbour: 'I once made a meatball for our Christmas stew!' I never hear whether it was a disaster or prizewinner, the dryers are on full blast.

And now there's the start of what might be one hell of a hiccup. They summon to the basin the woman who spoke of her meatball and Senyora Mundeta waves her stick to say no way, that it was her turn. Wenling takes her head out of the pile of cheese and waves the white flag: '*Yes, Señora Mundeta, she coming before and now back again, you wait a bit, alright?*' She's not at all convinced, snarls but says nothing. No blood spilled, it's Christmas.

That was the daily bread in my grandmothers' hairdresser's. There they did almost come to blows. Your bastard turn. Keeping it, losing it or violating it were matters of state. And if the turn was hallowed, there were distinctions in that establishment that were even more so. A grand lady clad in a long overcoat always made it plain she wasn't going to be kept waiting. Long coat, tall, from a well-known family, she was always going to win out. She was also adept at ensuring she stayed in everyone's good books, with gracious greetings to all and sundry. And they all turned a blind eye to her queue-jumping. But the one with bad habits was a woman whose husband was in the secret police during the dictatorship, and more Papist than the Pope, always harping on about both sides being equally bad. This poor lady lacked an overcoat, breeding and personal charm, and made up for it with a barefaced cheek. She couldn't have cared less if there were customers who'd been waiting since lunchtime. When she walked in, the rest of humanity had to move aside. One afternoon my grandmother, who was pacifism personified, stood up and pointed out that it was unfair. And the problem was the fascist situation; the word took her so by surprise she couldn't tolerate it. She made it clear she was having a fit, causing havoc all round, the salon owner in tears, brushes rolling across the floor, doors slamming, bans issued. Interfere with turns in Maria dels Àngels' place and all hell was let loose.

The jingle bells from 'All I Want for Christmas Is You' start ringing and Kristin walks in. '*Hello, love! Manicure?*' 'Yes, and pedicure as well.' '*Wait a bit there, right?*' This is non-stop, is it the end of the world? What if we come to the Christmas table with unvarnished nails? Won't we get a meatball? I'll try that next year. If I dare, of course.

Haitao, like a ghost: high spirits in a Father Christmas hat, whooshing through the hairdresser's on his skateboard. He leaves the backroom when he sniffs his sister is back with Suchard *turró*. Their faces are a picture. 'Great to be on your hols, isn't it, kids!' They laugh, cheeks smeared with chocolate, so happy. Their mother sees it differently. '*They a nuisance, better at school, you keep an eye?*' 'Yes, I'll make sure they don't give anyone a chocolate manicure!' They're a receptive audience and both laugh at my quip.

'*He first, only need a haircut, alright, dear?*' 'Whatever the boss says!' And I let Wenling take my arm and slip in Senyora Eulàlia's husband. 'Only,' she says, 'those toenails look like horns! I've never seen any so thick and crooked, a frightful sight, it hurts just to look at them. And the way the poor man howls when the pedicurist pulls his socks off, I don't know how he had the guts to walk all the way here… 'Don't give him any sympathy!' Senyora Eulàlia taps me on my nut with her fan. 'I've been telling him to come for the last two months, he's a stubborn tyke, not even when I begged him! You know, love, you need the patience of Job…' and she straightens the two strings of pearls she's put on for today.

Haijun has been told to ferry in clean towels and put them on the shelf. She washes her hands and gets to work. Half-heartedly, it must be said. '*A vint-i-cinc de desembre, fum, fum, fum…*' she hums to lighten her load. Senyora Eulàlia gets up and takes two envelopes from her pocket. 'Here you are, darling, one for you and one for your brother, my log has pooed before time...' and she pinches her cheek.* I feel the two books in my bag that I've chosen for them, the ones I wrapped in the brightest colours. The ones I didn't dare take out.

'Let it snow! Let it snow! Let it snow!', an annoyed chorus about the snow we won't get, and there's quite a din now. Haitao parks the barrow full of dye they'd made him fetch and he walks off and sits on the sofa at the back as if he's just returned from a stretch of forced labour. 'Have you got *Fortnite*?' he asks the customer reluctantly fingering her tablet. 'Hey, no room on the sofa, duck!' a girl covered in piercings tells Wenling when she sends her there. The boy and the customer with the tablet squeeze up and the girl with the piercings now finds room, and as they've not got their own games, the three of them leap on the spaceship Haitao is driving, and he's now full of vim and beans. He screams, 'Wowee! Wowee!' when they dodge an asteroid.

Wenling never stops, my head spins just to watch her. 'You'll be clapped out tonight,' Kristin tells her. '*They more*,' and she quickly gestures to us to stand up and waves the hairdryer. 'But you're thinking about everything, your children, customers and house.' '*That's true...*' 'Ask your husband to give you a massage!' And like the people who heard Nicholas Copernicus dare place the sun at the centre, Wenling responds from deep down: '*Ooooh, what you say! No massage ever!*' 'No! Well, that's not on,' I chime in theatrically. '*Yes, I better change. You know any good husbands?*' Kristin is stunned by her joke and I have to intervene.

---

* At Christmas in Catalonia some homes have a log or branch, *un caga-tió*, that's covered in a blanket and fed leftovers from the beginning of Advent until it's rapped with a stick on Christmas Eve and defecates presents.

'Mine is pretty good, Wenling, he really is. I know I'm always telling you, but…' '*Hahaha, but he taken, you lucky!*' I ask her how long they've been together. '*Twelve, daughter now ten…*' 'Seven for me.' '*I more!*' and it sounds as if this contest's winner will be the loser. Kristin must have read my thoughts. She keeps quiet about her six years and a day, but nods vigorously.

My early prezzie is to have befriended the retired schoolmistress, Senyora Catalina. I've always admired in silence her constant OMGs, and today I told her so and the floodgates opened. She's from a Majorcan family, has been living in Gràcia for three years and might have been an actress if she weren't… The 'if she weren't' that comes with being a woman. In the Sixties and now. Because rehearsals were in the centre, in the evening, after finishing studies, 'The best time of the day,' she says, fluttering her eyebrows. And with her love of the theatre, great voice, expressive tone and wavy hair, the best roles were always, always reserved for her. She played them all: Medea: 'Oh, hands and mouths, that I love more than anything!'; Antigone: 'What divine justice have I transgressed?'; Juliet: 'What's in a name? A rose by any other name…'; Marta: 'I was not born from the land and after the rains, like a pitiful animal'; Doña Inés at All Saints: 'Be silent, for God's sake, Don Juan!' 'But no friend lived so far north, nobody came up as far as Travessera de Dalt. A young girl couldn't come back at night by herself, and they made me give up.' She trained to be a schoolmistress and down came the curtain. Yet one more thwarted career. Unfathomable, the number of curtains that have descended prematurely.

Senyora Catalina wants to go back to her roots, to Palma. 'In the meantime, we'll keep meeting here. I've been coming for two years now, a regular, they do it nicely, are pleasant and, OMG, the wonderful people you meet!'

I get Haijun and Haitao to come to the till while he takes my money, and I dare: I give them my Christmas books. '*And what do you say?*' their father asks. Because they immediately glue their eyes to the titles, read the blurb, compare the two… 'Thank you! Thank you!' They react quickly. Wenling watches from the other end of the salon and I gesture that there's no need, don't get up! '*Wenling very happy with present… and I too,*' he says, very embarrassed. I'd like to say something apt and realise I can't, not yet. 'Wenling calls you Loco, but you must have a real name, right?' And all his face muscles go crazy. He stiffens, trying to stop the laughter, but his muscles are out of control. '*Me? Easy, Yang, like this place!*' What a fool, I'd not seen that, but of course! 'I'm not sure I agree…' He looks at me aghast: '*Why?*' 'Because, I mean, who's in charge here?' 'Wenling!' he replies straight out. 'Then it ought to be: Wenling's Hair Salon!' '*You right,*' and he splits his sides. '*I pretend boss!*'

I'd unilaterally changed its name some time ago. I left their street and Max rang. 'Where are you?' Now I don't say 'coming from the *xinos*', which is what I, too, used to say at the start, nor 'from my Chinese friend's', which is what I would soon say instead; the word 'manicure' never features. 'Hi, you've caught me just leaving Wenling's.' I stopped in my tracks. 'Hey, you still there? Wenling's,' I kept repeating to myself. 'Hey, Wenling's… I now say Wenling's…'

Now I have to attend to Senyora Gripi, who enters in a state. '*I've brought three boxes! They're for Wendy, but this is for you.*' She stuffs a *polvorón* in each of my coat pockets. '*And don't say you don't like them, if you've never tried these, you don't know what you're talking about. They're from Tordesillas, the best! And not just because that's my neck of the woods, naturally.*' I kiss her twice, pledge my unconditional liking for them, and say I must run. Max is waiting for me to go and buy our *turrons*. Wenling's Christmas special will be a pizza, today she won't have to cook dinner and the kids go crazy: '*When shut, I ring, today we a different night too.*'

The piped music sings 'Baby, It's Cold Outside' and it's true. It's not freezing, but there's a chill in the air. Blessed deliverers who work on Christmas Night: glory to you as well!

19

I'd prefer Top Christmas Songs. Today the screaming drives you crazy. It's coming from that boy. His poor mother, I know her, she's from Cal Pep, the fruit store, incredible mangoes, always just right, and her husband slices them so nicely... It's my guilty pleasure when I come back from work. The next time I see a takeaway from Boqueria, I'll look the other way. It's in such bad taste to say every ten jars of fruit kill off a lifelong fruit stall when you're still scraping the fork you used on your exotic mango.

The fruiterer ended up leaving. Not because of me, because I kept my tinned fruit thoughts to myself. She had to accept defeat and stand up with her hair still sopping wet. Truth is her boy's screams put everyone's nerves on edge. The girl who does the pedicures sang him a little ditty, Wenling's husband tried to amuse him with his brushes, but he bellowed away. Water off a duck's back: '*Kid's head very hard*,' said Yang, after they had left.

The festivities are petering out, manicures too. If every-body was keen to make a good impression for Christmas, it's all so casual for Twelfth Night. Not many of us today. I take out the script I've got to correct but don't look at it. I glance at the *Lecturas* the boy next to me is reading, I wonder what world-shattering news I'll glean from its pages. It's the birthday of: Serrat, 73. Ricky Martin, 45, OMG. Ana Torroja, 57. Edurne, 31, who the hell might she be?

A hardened know-all tries to wind Wenling's husband up over shampoos. 'It must be the real thing, there are people who refill them with cheap liquid soap when your back's turned…' He feels slighted, but Yang responds with only four words: '*Take a look, please.*' He's stuck the L'Oréal dispenser in her face so she can read '*fabriqué en France*' and he's brought her the paperwork from the last consignment. 'I see, I see,' she says, wrinkling her nose. And the audit continues; now she wants to know whether they have the Three Kings where they come from. '*No, not in China,*' Wenling replies. I see the grief on her face, as if putting on that show isn't enough of a burden. 'That's incredible, no Kings at all?' Course it has helped a lot that our know-all blew it up, almost turning it into a drama.

Wenling puts her hands in to soak one last time and takes her mobile from her pocket and puts it on loudspeaker.

I recognise Haijun's voice and Wenling's military staccato. The usual: whether you're up yet, whether you've washed your face and made your bed since you've been on holiday and your mother took care you weren't dossing around until it was time for lunch. I'd bet anything the conversation went something like that.

Know-All must have deduced something else, as she's now looking at me offended as if to say that Wenling and her daughter are chatting in Mandarin *to spite her*. Come off it, lady, we're Catalans! All our lives we've been told we speak Catalan only to put people's backs up! Surely you don't want to act like that?

I said that with a meaningful look, and I put her in her place: she had to back off.

★

The fact is Wenling always makes her children toe the line. Say hello, be grateful, don't make a fuss, do your homework with no crossings out. It may not be fashionable but it's quite natural to me: my sister and I spent our whole lives saying no to biscuits. And the boxes were left unopened. Artiachs, Cuétaras, Trias and Birbas, the ones I most hated turning down. The ones along the sides, wrapped in shiny paper, bet they were the chocolatey ones. I was so desperate to eat one! But if asked if you wanted a snack, there was only one answer, as far as my mother was concerned. No, got that, girls? No and thank you, thank you on your lips the whole time. And biscuits were but one example of our strict upbringing.

★

'I'd never ever use the colour you always do, my girl. It's... it's Gilda all over.' A little stab. Miss Know-All has got it in for me.

'Well, I'm not too sure about that. I know the film by heart and after the slap from the idiot Glenn Ford, you know, when she hides her face behind her hands, you can see them and they're clear, Rita Hayworth's. Like yours now.'

'Not at all! What do you mean, my girl?'

'Nothing, dear, nothing at all, except I get your drift. You say "Gilda" but really mean "common". But, you know, I don't feel insulted, quite the opposite. I think my red is so pretty. It's

GEMMA RUIZ PALÀ

the colour of our monthly blood, our strength, our power, the colour of life itself!'

Oil on the flame, a touch of feminist medicine. Miss Know-All says, 'Holy Mary Mother of God, all that studying, and what a terrible young generation,' and rocks back in her chair. She blows on her nails, turns the page and rip! A furious tear zips through *Hola!*

I think I'm adapting. Today alarm bells didn't go off when he touched my mop. Today I didn't do my usual parallel cut. Maybe they do add concoctions unauthorised by the EU to their products in this hairdresser's: we end up delightfully high. If Miss Know-All were right, I'd expect her to celebrate rather than denounce it.

But I'm not totally out of it, I hang in there, and catch them. One customer elbows the one alongside and they both snigger when the masseuse comes out to summon her next client, a young lad. Relax, don't make too much of an effort, the collective imaginary works more quickly and more subtly. Right now that snigger is downloading a whole armoury of clichés. It comes from way back and has a father, the automatic response that makes us associate 'oriental woman' with 'pulsing sexuality'. The same father as Madame Bovary's.

*

All three of us were looking down the well when the men arrived. I don't know if my brothers managed to escape, how long they lived, or in what state. I could only hear their cries from inside the sack. The pitch-black dark on that night, in that well, took them from me forever. Father had gambled half his flock, he'd lost the other half he didn't have, and he threw himself into the well of shame. He pushed mother in too, so he didn't have to walk alone. They could only collect his children. It was already light when the men unloaded me in front of another man. They stood me up, told me to strip, show my teeth, and began hitting my calves with a branch. The more I dodged, the faster and higher they hit. The more I hopped and jumped, the happier they looked. The man said it's a deal, she'll do. I'll take her. He handed them a small bag and called to a woman. 'Take her,' he ordered, 'wash her, instruct her. Soon she'll give her first performance.' I was thirteen when they told me to dance for foreigners, thirteen when they turned me into the Kuchuk Hanem you have read about in your languages and that today you will hear about in my own words for the first time. You should know that Kuchuk Hanem isn't a name. It just means young maiden. And on the first day I cried as long as the Dance of the Bumblebee music lasted. Tears that they took such pleasure in making a young girl dance as if she was fighting off a wild animal while she shed all her clothes. Choked by the dead weight of the first foreigner on top of me, the tears, blood, sweat and bitter slime they made me swallow. They said all the foreigners came to see our ancient temples. Perhaps they believed we – the people of my land – were so much dead stone too. We were not, but were forced to act as if we were. My body was already granite when the man with the inky fingers appeared. The one who paid for two nights with me and found that enough to dare write about who I was. The man with the inky fingers stole my voice, pulled my skin off and inflated it with air made of lies. He wrote that I was a dancer and I tell you I was a slave who had to perform for them before lying with them. He wrote that I was a machine that didn't distinguish between one man and the next and I tell you I was a girl who'd been chopped to pieces. He wrote that I revelled in lasciviousness and I ask you what kind of desire can be fired by the flesh of someone who denies your will. He also wrote that I wasn't a woman but a world, and you believed that nonsense too. The man with the inky hands was evidently one of your best spinners of yarns. That must be true, because even today you look at the women from my land and the land where the sun rises with the lustful eyes of his fantasy. Now you know Gustave Flaubert knew nothing about my life. Or my death. I can't swear I caught the disease from him. But I can vouch that the infection came from foreigners like him. They called it the French sickness and at twenty I was covered in its sores. I didn't want to wait for my flesh to rot. One moonless night I slipped out and went in search of my parents. I went to find a well. And now I live in the enchanted waters left by the last rains wherever they fall. Only when you disturb their calm with a stone will the waters break that spell. Only when they are a mirror once more will you stop there and the waters open up. And you will see who I really am, and learn my name, and hear how my words sound and everything that is yet to be said. Do not be afraid to rewrite the jaded histories of the women from my land and the lands where the sun rises. It is much more frightening to leave her like that, head underwater, swollen and blue, without soul or heart.

★

But these words weren't written anywhere. They departed with the last rains. The scriptwriters of colonialism belonged to one side only, were but a few: a handful of hot-blooded Europeans repressed to the marrow and so hungry for that last crumb they dreamed up so much bread. Madame Bovary's father was the most influential. Gustave Flaubert would be the first to emblazon his correspondence with the detail of his passionate desire to bed that young Egyptian girl, which he'd then feed into the attitudes and bodies of his protagonists: Salomé, Salammbô and the Queen of Sheba... And such a prized pen must inevitably create a school: a constellation of writers who are still read today, enjoyed, revered and granted credibility. From then on, all oriental women, from Egypt or China, princesses or shepherdesses, would be shaped according to their biased template. From Kuchuk Hanem on, all oriental women would be described in that same fantasised, sexualised fashion. Forever and ever thereafter, as if it was the word of God.

Because the decolonising of territories didn't lead to the decolonising of minds. Our heads are still full of those delights. The film sexual tourist Gustave Flaubert narrated with such gusto is still shown, tomorrow, the day after too. And that's why it's still so very normal for Asian women to have to tolerate us censuring their movements, suspects in the equation: Orient equals sex, Orient equals licentiousness, Orient equals submission, Orient equals silent and passive. And why we still undermine their dignity with the insidious jape about 'a happy ending'.

*

One of Miss Know-All's barbs did sting. And it's silly, another question from me won't make up for her 'No Kings?', but I ask it all the same. I ask Wenling when they'll celebrate New Year, and immediately regret doing so. All I can add when she tells me the date is what the animal will be this year, because we've fabricated so much folklore and merchandise around it, and are thus well informed. But I don't know why they celebrate it when they do, or what delicious dishes they cook and munch, or what it means. Or how upsetting they find it to be so far from home and their families on such an important date. Too late. *'Love, it's the year of... Do you say "chicken"?'* she asks, wrinkling her forehead. 'Chicken is the child, don't you mean the father, the rooster?' 'Yes!' she replies, guffawing. I look at her and know she's unsure. *'How say "gallo" in Catalan?'* '"*Gall*", like the Christmas "*gall dindi*", the turkey we ate a few days back.' *'Of course, lots of customers say "gall dindi"! I've got it!'*

You won't see it written because it would seem longer than a day-long fast, but from now on I'm going to speak to Wenling in '*Digui, digui*' style, that teach-yourself-Catalan series. In everything she says, word for word: *gallo-gall*, *pollo-pollastre*. Won't that make it very heavy? Don't worry, I'll add plenty of spice.

She finishes an amazing manicure and says, *'Thank you, lovely, now I eat.'* And she walks inside. I glance at the clock on the wall. Is it that late? Well past a quarter to four. She waited until she'd finished me.

'I also see how the ladies laugh, don't you take any notice...' The masseuse comes over, and wants to speak to me. *'Here everybody normal people, massage and that's all. And I very happy because have*

many doctor, nurse, computer women clients. You not worry, I good, I name Fen.' She squeezes my shoulders and that's worth an hour's massage.

I pay feeling all wobbly and when I open the door Pol squeezes by. 'I've come to see Haitao!' Hearing his voice, Haitao rushes out. After big hugs, they shake hands, hop and jump and smile. Trapped, I stand there for a few seconds, half in, half out. We carry so much dead weight from the past in our pockets that seeing that pair is always a relief. It makes me feel energised about the future.

20

I'd like to go in. Just a quick visit to say goodbye. I'm in a tizz. I slow down. Forwards. Backwards. Forwards. But now I'm there, and tongue-tied. That boring habit of starting off every sentence with a no. 'No, you know, I just happened to be walking by... No, no hands or feet, I've not got time... No, well, just for a few minutes... No, I just wanted to know how it was all going...'

Strange to say, I find them with their feet up. It must be television soap time. Initially, they both look surprised. But Wenling gets it. '*Come in, lovely, sit down, I so pleased you pop in!*' And we start chatting as... as friends do.

They're a bit worried because they'd like to have more customers; paying their workers' wages and the rent every month on the dot is a struggle. And then there's the mortgage on their apartment, the children's school... '*You know, like all families.*'

The premises belong to a Catalan gentleman who also owns Pep's fruitery, her customer's salon and half the street, Yang tells me. Not cheap, but they're managing, for the moment. And if they are, it's thanks to their long opening hours. It's the only way not to lose money, although it's so hard, and '*very, very tiring! His back always hurting,*' says Wenling. A mood of gloom hovers over us and silences us.

'*You travel China?*' Yang suddenly blurts out, breaking the lethargy. '*Yes, she tell how one day, she travel to China when a young woman*,' Wenling now reminds him. And I too understand how if I lived at the other end of the planet, I'd like to hear someone utter names from my country. Bringing the subject up, out of the blue, just for the sake of it, so they'd say: yes, I was in Barcelona, Montserrat, Castellterçol, in Menorca. And for them to repeat themselves. Barcelona, Montserrat, Castellterçol, Menorca. I'm delighted to rehearse my itinerary again. 'Yes, Yang, we have a cousin who lives in China, and he acted as our guide in Beijing, Xian, Pingyao and Shanghai.' '*Of course, the famous*,' says Wenling, laughing, and rounds off this day that has turned out to be surprisingly rewarding. '*You and I one day to my city together!*' And today she doesn't wriggle out of it: today I learn that Wenling comes from Qingtian City, in Zhejiang province.

On her mobile she shows me the highlight of her city: *the stone sculptures*. Don't give any to me, I want none in my dining room. Although, naturally, the result from the effort of toiling on the skin of those hard mineral rocks deserves a round of congrats! She scrolls through the images. Trees entangled with seaweed and shells. A temple overhanging a precipice, two chubby children pushing a cart, a majestic tiger frozen in full flight, a basket of fruit that says 'eat me'... Even Mao was turned to stone by the artisan hands of Wenling's neighbours. And it's no laughing matter, because the first brave souls who dared travel a bit further, and a bit more, did so to seek new markets for these carvings. And ever since then, people from Qingtian have been very clear that you earn nothing by sitting under the tree waiting for a hare to run past: you have to shift yourself to find one, wherever that might be.

*

Qingtian county: 'nine parts mountain, half-plain, half-water'. Territories that from days of yore had to flag that calling card are in a bad way. A sign they weren't suckled by gentle souls. A sign that rice didn't come easy in Qingtian. When its hills weren't being swept away by torrents before the harvest, it was being withered by drought. Because if clouds didn't do it, who was there to soar on high to irrigate?

And after weighing up the pitiful options they'd been handed, Qingtian people decided to plant the skirts of the mountains with what became their second talking point: sweet potatoes. Because those tubers thrived wherever: their skins weren't so picky, they managed on too much water or too little, enough would thrive to feed them. But those tubers weren't that meaty or saleable, as was clear from the little cash they had to buy rice in the market, and they got called all sorts because of those sweet potatoes. Never marry a skinny cat from Qingtian! Only a spoonful of rice per pot of sweet potato! So went many sayings. They live on dried sweet potato until the day they die! They're a bunch of starving sweet-potato eaters!

Qingtian folk were shamed to the core and stopped looking at their mountains so forgivingly. If you can't give us grub, give us something else to live off, gents! And the mountains agreed to being scraped and gave their response: a shiny stone that peeled away, each layer glowing with a different colour. Stone soft enough to chisel and make sculptures out of. A stone so unctuous to touch that the cognoscenti would label it 'pyrophyllite' and it would finally give Qingtian a good name.

Palaces and monasteries across the empire rushed to commission seals made from stone from the Qingtian mountains. Few spread ink so neatly or imprinted seals so precisely. Buddhas and mythological figures sculpted by Qingtian artisans were also much in demand, and well-off individuals across the empire purchased them blind. But being so exclusive could mean scant buyers, sparse profits and hunger pangs once more. And that fine day arrived at the end of the nineteenth century and the beginning of the twentieth.

The people of Qingtian had heard that in the lands of the barbarians to the west they held fairs and exhibitions of handiwork like theirs. They could advertise their wares, extend their repertoire and find customers everywhere. The nature of those lands had always forced them to look lively, to go roaming, even cast themselves into the sea, if needs be. They rapidly created a collection of miniature sculptures, loaded them on their backs, and went off. From Qingtian to Shanghai, from Shanghai to Marseilles, as they landed in Europe.

From the start it was a great success. They were given prizes and much else at fairs. The prizes encouraged them to travel from port to port, from city to city. First, with only the miniature figures and pyrophyllite seals, then with whatever they could pack into a suitcase; trinkets, porcelain, tea, ties, tablets of soap…

However, prizes weren't enough for souls who had to stand eighteen hours a day and sleep jammed like sardines against half a dozen other guys, after wolfing down a small helping of tasteless noodles and sipping a glass of tepid water. Because their spirits soon dropped at the sly looks from those who stopped to be nosey. The sly looks that never went away and spat out 'Chinky Chong'! But those Qingtian folk, jammed against half a dozen other guys like sardines, counted the day's takings and turned them into yuan. They thought of those back home, of all the rice they could buy and wiped away their tears. And next morning, back we go, they washed their faces and sold in the street again, hoping to do good business.

From Russia to Portugal, clickety-clack, clickety-clack across the whole of Europe. And once they'd sized up the entire continent, most preferred to stay in France, a number in Italy and a few more in the Netherlands. But the odd one said, I'm off further down, close to Africa, daring to explore a country called Xibanya, where nobody from Qingtian had yet to set foot.

In the Thirties a bunch chose Barcelona, Valencia or Madrid as their final port of call. In the letters they sent home, they explained that they weren't much valued in Xibanya, but at least they weren't singled out, and that was a boon. And it wasn't a bad place, it really wasn't. The climate was benign. As were the people, once you got to know them.

To this day, as happens when people leave their land, as has happened ever since the world began, they go to where they will find acquaintances. Of those who opt to leave China and live in Xibanya, most are still from Qingtian. And now there are many women from Qingtian. They no longer go up and down with suitcases. They observe, wonder where they can make the most impact and roll their sleeves up to learn. And in everything they do, they try to ensure that their labour shines a greater light, or at least as much as those first little pyrophyllite figures did at fairs and exhibitions. Because they too have not travelled miles and miles and made sacrifices to no avail.

*

'*But no eat stones!*' Wenling's husband is quite a spoilsport, he knows what's what, and both shake their heads at me. It's impossible to live over there. As a kid Wenling had to eat sweet potato rather than rice. Apparently everybody eats what they fancy nowadays, but one thing's for sure: every day a few get richer and most get poorer. More luxury skyscrapers, and more bald mountains, he laments, because twenty years ago everyone respected the land and there was scarcely a single traffic light; now they call Qingtian 'little Hong Kong', because of the multicoloured lights illuminating the place when darkness falls. And people so into consumerism they're sick in the head, so crazy about spending, and if you don't wear a change of clothes every day, they look at you like you're a loser, not like here. 'Hey, you need to get to know us a bit better, we can be a bit loopy too.' My finger signals there are screws loose and we joke, but not for long, because they want to finish portraying their China and who'd have thought it: their point of comparison is our welfare state that's quietly teetering on the edge, because they're chopping it down. But it's all that Wenling and her husband have known, and that truth lights up their eyes with all their new discoveries, a roll call of all they've made up, a jingle I know by heart: '*Here hospital and medicine for children, here old folks paid every month and children can study. Here, if people work hard, they can live. Here they live.*'

A single verb. Alone, unqualified, unlimited, un-attenuated. To live... And the mountains of cloth many of us accumulate to undermine it, rather than paring it down to its purest conjugation.

Now I have to tell them that I dropped by because we won't see each other for some time, because I've been invited to talk about documentaries in India. It doesn't mean I'm on a par with that Catalan gentleman who owns half of Gràcia, but I too have a decent income. Enough in the bank to allow myself a week's holiday in the middle of January, spend some money and fly through the skies to Kolkata. '*Have good time, lovely!*' they chime as one.

21

TS Northeastern. What kind of badge is that? Or what kind of name? Because it must be a name. It's clear enough on the hairdresser washing the customer next to me: Taruni.

Floor 1 in Kolkata's Taj Bengal Hotel. I won't attempt to describe the 'intensity' of its streets. You shouldn't necessarily read that as a sign that yours truly is made of ice, because I felt the shakes and bumps as much as any of you who have been there. But I stayed only a few days, and as a lot of dross has been written and filmed on the subject and I've lots else to chew on, I preferred to press the 'Spa' button in the lift. And act as if I was betraying Wenling. Because I've given up writing files on other establishments, but no way did I want to miss out on this manicure.

For sure, the manicurist treating me doesn't seem to be from Kolkata. It can't be that they've stolen her identity because she's not bred locally, now can it? But who knows? The atmosphere is quite rarefied. I register the same slippery looks from the two male customers and the three females. The same dry, elusive cough that can't bear so much tension, the same nose that feels uneasy, the same embalmed faces. From nought to zero in terms of humanity, the whole lot. When they emerge all spick and span, I hope they inject a bit more oomph into it, these sad creatures. They don't open their mouths all that time, so it's hard to pinpoint their origins, but it wouldn't be rash to guess from somewhere between the petro-monarchies and the Commonwealth and they alone are colonising the whole of the beauty salon in this Kolkata five-star hotel. I must be the only representative of a country that doesn't pass muster on economic grounds or geo-strategic values, to mention two indicators.

It is so silent I dare not break the ice. I intuit that our Mediterranean mentality wouldn't go down well. The manicurist managed a curt hello and got stuck in. But now she looks up from my hands. She says sorry, she forgot to consult me on the colour. I ask her if they have any red.

It's not easy. Most of the varnishes on her chart are variants of fuchsia, each one drearier than the last. And most quite iridescent or glittery. I make the point. 'Oh yes, guests here like extravagant nails, but I don't…' She rummages for a few seconds in the last drawer on the little counter and comes up with a small bottle. It's orangey, and the dried gunge suggests it's from the predynastic Egyptian period. 'That's the one!' I yelp enthusiastically. It will fit the bill, however past its use-by date… 'Are you sure? Do you want me to ask for more polish?' 'No, no thanks, I was looking for this colour.' I don't want to give her grief over paint that in five days will be all flaky. And I make the most of that little burst of conversation. 'I'm visiting Kolkata for just one week. I'm from Barcelona, nice to meet you.' 'Nice to meet you too!' And her spontaneous elation only points to this being not the custom: two petro-subjects and a Commonwealther are so shocked by our exchanges that their cheeks turn tomato-red. Blood's beginning to bubble and give life. For their sakes I'm pleased.

'My name is…' I'm KO'd by a string of five or six syllables. She has to repeat it before I can pronounce it half properly. No chance I can write it down. When I leave my manicure session, I confirm my zero ability to reproduce it. You now see why she asks for them to etch only TS, right? Customers who asked after her name, however few, made her suffer, and were tongue-tied like me. But it wasn't her idea to be given a coordinate as a surname: Northeastern. From the north-east.

TS comes from the Himalayas, her culture is Lepcha, and her country, Sikkim, an ancient kingdom hemmed in by Nepal, Tibet, Bhutan and India, which annexed it in 1975 and involved it in its fight against China over Tibet. Hence the coordinate. They hung it on her on an off day.

The historic recognition of mutual frontiers still festered – OK, if we accept that the Autonomous Region of Tibet is China, we'll also accept that Sikkim is India. It still festered, like a road that's recently been tarmacked, and the Chinese president was visiting India, a visit at such a giddy height nobody should come out spattered in tar. No splashes in the soup, no Tibetan-looking face in sight. You pull the stops out to avoid uncomfortable situations when you hold power: anybody not blessed with an Indian-looking face was forbidden to go to work during that crucial visit. And the best way to control them was to label them like carriers of the plague, so that someone like TS wouldn't escape and turn up at her place of work in the basement of the Taj Bengal Hotel. She, who wasn't even from Tibet, that most dangerous agent of counter-diplomacy. Her face might remind some Chinese statesman who treads the floor of that hotel that indeed there are still Tibetans in this world, they've not been swallowed up by the earth, the Dalai Lama lives on and, alas, is exiled in India.

We find that out because they've not changed her uniform label from that day on. Sloppiness and baseness makes a rhyme of sorts: if ever a Chinese government fat cat comes back, the job's done. And the slight has been perpetuated.

I reckon you must be in a real state to commit an offence like that. Although perhaps not as deranged as when that bastard Franco came to Catalonia and they put my republican great-grandfather behind bars on Via Laietana. TS had assumed I was Italian or French, naturally she knows nothing about us but listens sympathetically to my account of post-war repression.

And what about those mummified customers? They'd completely gone out of my head. When I look for them after my conversation with TS, they've scarpered except for one petro-subject. He's right up against the mirror using eyebrow tweezers to twiddle with a tooth. I can't say whether he's been listening to us or chose that as a good move to camouflage himself. It may very well be that he wasn't at all interested in the story of someone from so far away and so beneath him, and that he's a lecherous pig.

Now I must leave too. The ten minutes have flown by and my nails are dry. 'Take care,' I say, and give her two pecks on the cheek because I don't dare give her a hug. 'Next time the manicure will be in the place where you belong, but I wish it could be here with me!' And now I do put my arms around her neck.

22

'*The boss is on holiday.*' As I don't react, the very young woman I don't know has to repeat herself. '*The boss, on holiday.*' 'You serious?' And she laughs. '*Seriously, seriously... I'm Jin, pleased to meet you!*' She seats me at the manicure table and we start chatting. That '*on holiday*' was still spinning around my head, but hearing her and seeing her bustle distracts me. Of course it does. She's a live wire.

She left China at the age of twelve and ended up in Riudellots. '*It stank of pigs! The first thing I thought when I arrived here, whenever you opened the window,*' and she squeezes her nose, '*yuk!*' We laugh ourselves silly. Particularly when I tell her it's how I always feel when we go to Vic. My friends from the Plana don't buy that, *they* say I'm making it up, but the pong from the collateral damage inflicted by drying sausages always does my head in.

After La Selva came Barcelona, Madrid, Seville, Valencia, Malaga and, finally, the Canaries. Her mother lives there and owns a bazaar, but she prefers Barcelona. She's twenty and is saving up to buy the lease on a bar with her boyfriend. '*Manicuring for life, you must be joking.*' She's made her mind up, she's got a strategy. I detect a familiar attitude in Jin. I reckon it's the right to choose. She recognises that and stands up for it.

And wants to explain how leases work: '*You think it's weird and it's because you don't understand that it's our custom for the family to give you money*.' And when she says the whole family, she means all and sundry, friends too, everyone chips in, everyone helps get the ball rolling, trust and family credit is their oxygen. Above all, your parents, naturally. And that's why her mother never shuts on Sundays and spends only the minimum on their three meals. His parents too, they stash everything away so their son can get on track. And while they've not got the dough for the lease, she is studying Spanish and English, '*for the future*,' she tells me, '*because I don't want to be stuck in a bar forever either*.' Well, I see that, but I'm annoyed Catalan isn't one of her priorities. It's as if she's read my thoughts. She only studied it for a year, she goes on, till she was thirteen, because she had to start working, and so many moves made it a blur. But she used to speak it, and if she were to stay in Barcelona, she'd like to learn it properly.

'If she were to stay… she would like…' The subjunctive and conditional are obviously not on our side. I start turning over the weak points in our language and a voice disperses them. '*Wenling isn't here!*' he tells me as he walks in laden with bags of fruit from Cal Pep and looking worried. '*Father headache, yesterday tickets and this morning goes*.' Hell, just what I was saying… On holiday? Wenling? It had to be force majeure. And now that Jin can see I'm not a fly-by-night customer, she tells me the truth.

Wenling's father has been diagnosed with a brain tumour. He won't last more than a month. We both look devastated. She has more reason. She tells me her grandfather has got lymphoma and tears well up. '*Sure he is eighty, but I was always with my grandparents, they are the most important people in my life...*' She says that so firmly... A grandfather who was also cement-solid... '*In my country a lot of cancer, specially in the region we come from, Zhejiang.*' There is no research to prove it because there can't be, because the government hides it, she tells me as if we were in a horror film, but the land, air and rivers in her province have been polluted, as a result of that silly nonsense of building more and more factories. That's why they count their sick and their dead as if they were counting flies on a muggy evening at summer's end. '*Little kids with lung cancer in my village! Kids! A lot of them! Do you think that's normal?*' She takes one of my fingers and touches the end of a nail. '*You can go, take care, right?*' She gets up and gives me two kisses. 'See you!'

*

Tomorrow it will be a week. It's a bit soon for my nails. But long enough to ask whether Wenling is back and how her father is. Yang greets me. Today he's let his quiff droop, badly.

'*No-oo! No-oo! Wenling next week manicure no-oo!*' I don't know if elongating his vowels makes his plight more explicit, because that's the effect. Like someone who's repeated the same thing three hundred times and makes it three hundred and one with you. Sounding desperate, if not a tad more than that. '*Don't worry*,' I respond at once, 'let Jin take me, she did a fantastic job last time!' And now he jumps to his feet. Claps his hands and looks as if he surely needs the window ledge. To throw himself out. '*No-oo! No-oo! Jin China! Grandfather!*'

'What!? Has her grandfather died? Jin's in China as well?' And every loose end I tie up is one fewer knot for him to unravel. '*Yes! Yes!*' He shouts triumphantly. 'Really? *Jin grand-father dead?*' I say it staccato to be one hundred per cent sure, because I think it can't possibly be true. '*Yes! Grandfather Jin dead!*' He opens his arms, relieved.

Now we've reached this stage, I throw caution to the wind, and I dare: 'Wenling's father? He dead too?' '*Almost!*' And he starts laughing, he infects the arty hairdresser with the old ladies and I join the party. Nerves must surface sooner or later, and best they do so with plenty of foam.

The laughter soon peters out and we calm down with a few final 'Ays'. 'That's really bad luck... I'm very sorry for Jin's sake, the poor girl.' And when I am about to leave, I'll come back next week: '*Hair get long, sit down, wait a minute.*' Well, better obey. Oh, Sesi knows only too well. She told me I was a lost cause and gave him the professional green light. A glance at the front, a look at each side, and one word: perfect.

A quick look around before I get my book out. I reckon I won't take a bunch of notes today either. There's only one girl and she's bored out of her mind while Wenling's husband finishes flattening her ends. Nothing there. A guy, with a few wisps, who'll be clipped in a flash. But, hey, he wants scissors to cut his four wisps. He asks, please... but rudely... He snarls 'electric razor' as if they'd threatened him with death via the carotid. The carotid... It must be one hell of a mess when they cut such a key artery. Wispy would be a goner, if the hairdresser artist's scissors slid down his neck, slash. I'd be better off reading a book.

I open *La filla estrangera* and on cue the children start making a racket. They arrive from school as we all did: frantic, sweating

and hungry. And lots of us went straight to a shop: to Juanita's clothes store, Malet the grocer and Canal the tailor. My sister and I had a cutlery store as our headquarters. Look, that's where they make scissors and where we sold and sharpened them…
'A good book?' asks Haijun. 'Very good! It's by a writer who knows lots of words and talks about important topics. Her name is Najat El Hachmi, can I read you a bit?' And I make her hold her breath for three pages. Both of them in fact, because Haitao comes nosing around and is rooted to the spot too. I look up to see whether they're still there: hooked. I wonder how I can make the most of their fascination and immediately think of *InfoK*. 'Do you know what that is? If you take a look, you could learn more great words, and better understand Catalan, and you'll want to read the books I always bring and you won't be able to stop yourselves!' But first *Info K*: play.

It's my turn now. I leave the mobile with the kids, but in no time they're huddled around me. I was in such a hurry I didn't click the whole programme, only a clip, and they want more. 'There you are!' It was a report on a school in Viladecavalls that recycles food and turns it into compost for the garden they've made in their playground. They find it such fun to see young kids like themselves that they ask me if one day the Sisters will get a look in. My guard is low, because although I know he is a good hairdresser, I'm still keeping a wary eye on what he's doing with his scissors, and I don't give it a second thought and say: 'I'll ask them if they're intending to film at the Sisters…' 'Oh, you know…' Blast! I've put my foot in it. 'Yes, I work in documentaries and they're in news, in the building next door.' 'And you on the telly?' 'Sometimes…' 'You look, you look!'

says Haijun. Haitao repeats it even louder. 'Yes, look, look!' his teeth full of sweets he spatters over us. A little bear drills into my neck, bits of liquorice on the mirror, his father's arm and the floor. And he scolds him: '*You dirty! You wash!*' The fact is it's dripping from his nose and everywhere.

While we wait for him to get back from the bathroom, Yang washes my hair. Eyes shut, I realise I won't know if he's given me a crooked fringe or shorn off my sideburns; the children meant my mind was elsewhere. I dry myself on the towel and they pull at it. 'Come on, put it on, put it on!' I reckon the last documentary must have downloaded. I mouth the name of the most famous militia woman who never was and she writes perfectly on search: Marina Ginestà, and clicks. The poor things can't understand a word. 'It's more for adults,' I tell them, 'the *Info K* we were watching is better for you.' But they see me and go haywire. They freeze the image. 'Look, look!' they chorus and show their father. 'Who is it? Who is it? Who is it?' He puts the shampoo down and comes out from behind the basin, taking care not to stumble. He comes over and looks at the mobile, he says *her* and points at me as if it was nothing out of the ordinary. This guy is incredible.

23

'What?' and he gets me.

'*Father not dead.*'

'Hello!' his son greets me, and I ask Yang if they are behaving themselves.

'*Yes, better without their mother,*' he replies ingenuously.

Haitao immediately contradicts his father by grabbing his arms and legs time and again: he's after his mobile. He grins as he pushes the boy away and finally relents.

'*All day on phone to mother! If father the same, Wenling back Friday.*'

'I don't think I can make it on Friday, we'll be filming… give her a kiss from me, Yang.'

'*Kiss? Hahaha, kiss is for boyfriend and girlfriend!*'

I would be so sad if one day they were gone. No, not sad. No, I think I would feel ill.

24

That looks like her. She's finishing a hand massage on a girl who is so close to falling asleep. I sit down nearby, I don't want to get in her way. I say nothing when she looks at me, but she never misses a trick. She sees me and we shake hands.

I'm shocked to see Wenling looking so pale and wiped out. Because of the journey, the father she left dying there, the call that will tell her he's gone and the journey that will bring. He's in hospital, with his wife, she tells me. And with all her fingers on her neck she gestures as if strangling someone. The tumour shut down his brain, now it's attacking his breathing. I say, 'No need to talk.' But clearly I don't really think that and as always when I feel stressed, I gabble on, and now ask her about Jin's grandfather.

'It's very bad luck, for her too, poor dear...' '*Yes, but Jin grandfather very old.*' Not quite '*his time was up*', but almost. A faux pas. Wenling's father isn't seventy yet and, besides, I've just broken a sacred law: never console someone by mentioning someone else's grief. I wind up that exchange as best I can, by chattering on. I ask her if she wants me to bring melatonin so she can get some rest. '*Pill?*' she asks. 'Yes, for before you go to bed.' '*No, thank you, no pill!*' she says, pouring cold water on the idea. '*No worry, in the morning drink more coffee, thanks, lovely.*'

How different the world would be if harsh words didn't always come first. If the first thing they taught us about other people's languages was love and compassion, who then wouldn't dare to be a good person?

25

I always face the same dilemma now. Whether to ask about her father or not. On the brink as he was, he ought to be dead by now. But if he were, she wouldn't be here, she'd have departed to do her duty as a daughter with a proper funeral. No matter whether he behaved well or poorly when he was alive, tradition demands that Wenling says her goodbyes by pulling out all the stops. And, poor fellow, he's never going to improve, however much I express my concern. I add another weight to the scales, thinking how all of us are depriving her of her right to put him out of her mind. If every customer that comes in reminds her of her father, her father, her father, our good intentions will only add to her suffering. She thinks about him enough without our encouragement: I now see she carries her mobile in a small cloth bag around her neck. So she doesn't miss the call, I guess. She must be expecting it all day. Don't mention it again, I don't ask.

'*Hello, lovely, manos?*' 'Yes, *mans*! How are you, Wenling?' '*So-so, thank you, you wait a bit, right?*' I flop down on the sofa and spot David Beckham. His face is stuck to the glass door. It's the first time I've glanced his way and I don't know what he's doing there on a poster for hair cream. His quiff doesn't stand out one-tenth the way his gleaming teeth do. What alien-like whiteness. It looks like he's covered them in chalk and wants to persuade us to have a taste. Yuck! I look away. The lady next to me is reading a page in *Lecturas* that's advertising, I kid you not, 'the latest in dental whitening'. They must get it every Thursday at the Beckham household and it must be an education.

Before starting on my manicure, Wenling gives the kids a few instructions. 'Chinese homework!' Haijun translates for my benefit with a look of shock-horror. 'Difficult?' 'Very!' They go every Saturday but during the week they have to practise calligraphy; whenever they're forced to, they moan. Chinese has fifty thousand characters. 'Hey, it must be very difficult.' She immediately goes to get her writing pad. And listen to this because now I'll ask the goofiest question: I ask Haijun if she writes Chinese with a pen or... a paintbrush. Yes, you read correctly, 'a paintbrush'. 'Hahaha! No-oo, with a pen.' 'You must think I'm really daft?' 'Just a bit, hahaha!' And now we've started to have fun, Wenling takes the reins. '*You, lovely, manicure, take your seat.*' And says something to the children as they walk into the back, come on. '*They study, not just play,*' she tells me, ditching the frown she adopted a few seconds ago. 'My fault, sorry.' '*No worries, lovely,*' she smiles, taking the cotton wool and starting to remove the old varnish.

While she cleans, I free-associate. And my thoughts, which always wander freely and never dodge thorny topics, fly straight to adoptions. Of Chinese girls, to be precise. My first boss was doing a Chinese calligraphy course when I met him. I could swear they did it with a brush... While they were waiting to be told to go and fetch them, he studied the culture and country of birth of the girls who were to be his own twin daughters. I was lucky enough to see them arrive from China that July. How they clung to the mother they had so missed, how they learned to digest the new food, how their heads grew thick hair, how they discovered the pleasure of having a bath, how they grew taller, developed little personalities, laughed. I was very young, I'd never been in the front row watching such an ebb and flow of emotions, so it became etched on my brain.

But the echoes from a cherished memory can soon turn you into a blabbermouth if you don't keep your wits about you. Because I shared that with Wenling, as if she was going to feel exactly what I felt. I was so naive. As if she wouldn't translate the words 'Adoption of Chinese Girls' into the 'One-Child Policy'. And as if that neutral bureaucratic language didn't come with thirty years of human-rights abuse.

And being the wise Solomon I think I am, it wasn't that hard. But imagining the way this policy damaged so many millions of Chinese women should have forced me to think things through. And you never stop to do that. If you do, you might realise that good fortune for the few implies misfortune for many.

That Wenling refused to respond and didn't look me in the eye when I told her of my experience of meeting adopted Chinese twin girls wasn't because she didn't understand what I was saying. She was indicating that the reverse side of such a loaded subject would require her to use loaded words too – political control of reproduction and maternity, state interference with women's bodies, mass sterilisations, selective abortions, female infanticides, the abandonment of girl babies – and she didn't have mine and I didn't have hers. Hence her silence. So we'd drop the subject, so I would drop it. After an embarrassed pause, she said: '*For me this very difficult, very sad…*' And I immediately sealed my lips.

Where the hell is 'Learn to keep quiet' in the Ten Commandments? They're useless, even on that front.

26

Today I've a metallic voice for background music. *No tengo ningún gato. La sopa aún está fría. Mi amiga tampoco viene mañana.* Wenling's Spanish teacher is a mobile app and displays a marked allergy to humour. Wenling doesn't miss a step while one customer's nails are drying and another's hair is setting. She keeps repeating sentences generated by the app until she gets the pronunciation right. *No tengo ningún gato. La sopa aún está fría. Mi amiga tampoco viene mañana.* Not surprising it's so mournful, such a wet blanket with no cats, cold soup and no friends. Just as well it's virtual and not a sourpuss in person. I downplay my hello and sit down silently and act as if I'm reading. And try to hide. I can't help it. I watch how she sets things out, organises, arranges. If her realm weren't a neighbourhood hair salon... She'd be flying so high. Wenling only has four walls and a telephone, but she knows what's going on beyond her nose. That must be why we all go there in search of refuge.

*

'*I'm not a ghost, girl, it's me!*' Wenling switches off her miserable teacher and walks towards the young woman who's just come in. '*You a long time!*' They hug each other and the story doesn't end there. I'm included. Or rather they keep me around.

Because Wenling intervened, told me to sit down and started to prepare my hands while listening to what she was saying. 'I'm Mireia, that red is so cool, hello, so pleased to meet you.'

She's nineteen and has been a customer since she was fifteen. She splashed out everything she earned from babysitting on being waxed at Wenling's. It was the only thing that didn't pluck her soul from behind that thick carpet of hair. I should say Mireia belongs to the first generation that's throwing off the yoke of depilation, good for them, to treat their hair as if it doesn't deserve extinction, as if it's just one more feature of their organism with an essential purpose and function. But, hell, my colleagues who let their hair flow didn't have hair as dense as she had! She didn't have the heart to let it be, sought an ally among local beauticians and submitted to her treatment. And she found no one with hands like Wenling's. Or with her attitude. In posher places you find snobs who turn up their noses. Because Mireia has the standard two piercings in her ears, like most sweeties still do, simply because they came into the world with a vulva. However, when the holes are a bit risqué, oh dear. It's quite striking that earrings in offbeat places most annoy those not geared to wear them. Mireia has three in each eyebrow and two in her nose. And they have sharp corners, those that don't beg forgiveness for existing. 'They don't label you in this place, you love it too, don't you?' She looks at me with such pretty blue eyes... I am relieved to see the enamel on her teeth is tarnished. Yes, I believe that one thing compensates for the other, I admit. What's appalling is that beauty is still portrayed as dangerous for women.

Mireia has also got tattoos. I can see the tail end of one

escaping when her denim blouse's sleeves are rolled up. And two luridly coloured flowers explode on her ankles, between her leggings and open, half-laced trainers. Comfortable wear, reasonable enough when you've just given birth.

'*You?! You have baby?!*' Wenling pulls her face mask off. 'That's right, darling, *I'm so young*, that knocked you for six, right?' So long without seeing her. That was why. She lost track of her and her belly.

When she was two and a half months gone, she went to live with her grandparents in the village where they spent the summer on the Costa Daurada. Mireia's mother is one of the neighbours the real estate rabble turfed out of the area. At the end of the day, it was better to take out a mortgage on a small family apartment than fork out on a rent that had been tripled and have to live on air. Now, they can break bread on the Costa and enjoy the sea breeze.

But today Mireia was fed up with the village. She couldn't stand any more aches, tendinitis and back pains, and asked her mother to go to the pharmacist. She's dispensed with breast-feeding and isn't ridden with guilt like so many mothers. When you have a salary, time and books, dialogues with your con-science can protract everything. She only needed three months of maternal experience, then a bottle and formula. No sooner said than done. She warmed up water, emptied the powder in, checked the temperature and gave it to her baby. 'Thanks, Mum, love you!' And with the change from the pharmacist's she bought a ticket to Barcelona.

'Gràcia gets scummier by the day, but I missed my mates… and wanted to see this woman too,' and she pinches Wenling's cheek. '*Thanks, lovely, I wonder what you do… You now have a kid, but more sense too: what happen with university?*'

If tolerating her neighbours' kids paid for her depilation, selling pre-cooked meats in the market every Saturday paid for what she liked most in this world. Those saucepans weighed a ton, but the morning flew by! And Mireia could have her computer. 'Yes, love, my uni course was fucked, my profs were really sad I quit…' 'No joking, Mireia, and now what, Computer Engineering?' Christ, she had the marks, she really did. And instead of studying the mathematical bases, programming and structure of computers, Mireia was compelled to learn how to deal with colic, rashes and earache… 'I'm only telling you the worst bits, poor baby… Sometimes when he stares at me for a long time, I feel sad.' And she shows him to us on her mobile. The same blue eyes, the same good-as-gold face, and furrowed forehead. 'Hell, I think I love him… but when I'm feeling down, when I think of the shit in store for me… I'm so angry I was such an idiot, for fuck's… But you'd be amazed at the number of guys who refuse to wear a condom… I've got girlfriends who've fucked without just to look good, so they're left in peace at school, and can put the wretched business behind them. But what happened to me wasn't about a condom, for fuck's sake… Don't look at me like that, Wenling, I can't lie to you. I tell the gang he wasn't wearing a rubber, but that's not it. I didn't fuck. I couldn't get the guy off the top of me, and that's different.'

★

It was in the early hours, the moon was gone and so had the waiters from the beach bar. They were walking up the beach, chatting about this and that. The wind was blowing their long hair over their faces. Mireia liked that taste of salt water and told him to try it. Not to unzip his trousers. At first Mireia wasn't panicked. He must be joking, I don't want to do it with this guy. He was from a village along the coast, a friend from a lifelong group of mates, and she told him to stop, obviously thinking that he would. 'What the fuck are you doing?! I told you I didn't want to! Leave me alone, you bastard.' But he didn't. And he forced her down on the sand with all the might his base instincts could muster. It made no difference if Mireia grabbed him, spat at him, shouted, or kicked and lashed out. He'd got her where he wanted her. He held her down, fumbled in his crotch and didn't mind if he had to wrestle with her a little while more. Until he could round off his attack.

'And as everybody knows everybody in those villages, like an idiot I kept quiet. No going to the cops or anything like that. I don't even remember how I got back on my feet and went home. I only know that I was in a daze, that my body was on fire and my head exploding. I didn't leave my bedroom for a week! I'd never felt so depressed, I was good as dead! And you won't believe this: the guy called my mobile, wanted to see me. The asshole thought we were an item! I couldn't stand the fucking Samsung anymore and ended up telling my mother. I couldn't before that, I couldn't say it aloud. And my mother sobbed and sobbed. But the next morning she said: Not enough piercings, Mireia! You should have had a sharp one down below and that would have punctured his knob and scraped his cock and left him spilling blood and piss night and day! She went after him in his village. She grabbed his T-shirt and dragged him down the street, calling him everything under the sun. And my mum is only five foot tall! She left him in a heap on the ground. He didn't call me again. And do you know what the worst fucking thing was? I didn't dare have an abortion. I couldn't bring myself to do that. And I won't ever be able to forget him.'

*

And she wouldn't. Though they never saw each other or spoke again, that guy never took off, the one who raped Mireia one summer's evening on a beach in a small village on the Costa Daurada. The guy carried on living in that same village and strolling down its streets, as ever. And will become more popular than ever, will be seen as a good man and all that. When it was time to build human towers, celebrate the annual fiestas, the great paella days, he was always in the front row, building his reputation. A guy trusted by parents, friends, partner, workmates and neighbours. A rapist they will respect. Perhaps early on someone will still remember there is something murky in his past, in the relationship he had with that young girl from Barcelona who became a single mother. Because they will call it 'a relationship'. But the rumour gradually fades until not a scrap remains when they see him hard at it organising a solidarity campaign. Such a model citizen, one day he'll end up as the candidate for the party that has always ruled the roost in his village. And will be elected mayor, for we need young blood like you! And that brand-new mayor will give his first speech. And will opt to talk about macho violence. About the programme that must be implemented to rid our society of this canker, and of his personal commitment to fight it. Yes, that guy, the rapist, will make such a pledge. We will establish a twenty-four-hour service to intervene against any form of sexual aggression. And he lays it on thick. I can assure you that we will act implacably against the men who walk our streets unpunished, the sick men who rape and kill women. Yes, he uses that word, 'sick'. That man, that guy, that rapist. As he reads his speech, his script crumples and gets entangled with his fingers. It's the adrenaline, the arrogance of power, the injection of justice. And the humidity. Because that evening, in that other village on the Costa Daurada, gusts of wind laden with salt water will blow. Salt water. The only thing the guy, the rapist, the mayor should have tasted that night.

*

All you can hear is people blowing on their tea, it's as hot as hell. Before we reached the beach part of the story that morning, Wenling saw the storm on its way and ushered us inside. She'd been the first to react, the first to give the order to hands and legs: the order to seek out tender, loving care, shelter and respect. And all that, in a single act, in a Chinese home, means making a cup of tea. Today, refreshing green tea.

The three of us look down, we don't know how to lift ourselves up. If we didn't have to hold our glasses, our arms would hang down too. But Mireia looks up and stares at me aghast. 'Shit, this is horrible!' She grimaces and turns to Wenling. '*Don't be offended, love, but you can't swallow this without sugar.*' And Wenling rises to the bait. '*What you say? You not know! Green tea refresh and calm squabbles!*' 'I don't know how to drink tea,' she says. 'Oh my god. This is worse than the herbal kind my granny gave me for period pains! *You've got it all wrong, Wenling, this is swill.*' They both put their cups on the table, move their chairs back and face up to each other. They're also pissing themselves laughing. They act as if they are shoving and slapping each other; they are playing. Until they get to what they were after. Until they hug.

I slip out of the kitchen: that scene is for them. I look into the hairdresser's and hunt for a chair. I blow on my tea that's still burning hot, then treat it with the respect it deserves.

27

'*You read a lot!*' An imp appears behind Joyce Carol Oates's stories and whisks it from my hands. It's not every day you see Wenling light of foot, cheerful, and not gripping the reins to steer the day. I hope it lasts. To that end, I won't ask her about her father today. 'Do you like to read?' She whispers close to my ear: '*I death books…*' and blushes as red as the reddest apple.

I try to figure out what she means, I can't spin it around mentally anymore. I say out loud what she confided so quietly and, for good measure, repeat it twice. *Death books? Death books?* Fortunately we can now rely on the Holy Spirit of the Screen. Wenling rushes to show me on her mobile: Noir Novels, and now I can come back to earth. 'Ah! Noir! I get you!'

I also get why she is so embarrassed. There's always a reason to feel inadequate. They've created so many that one or the other always comes your way, making you feel uncomfortable, keen to rub in your face whatever it was they hadn't imagined for you. When it's not because you like cars, it's because you couldn't care less about children. When it's not because you prefer angling to patchwork, it's because romantic nonsense makes you want to puke and you only go to the cinema if they're chopping up office workers. And there's always the sly dig, the little question, suspicion and justifications. Please get lost, and leave our hobbies in peace!

'So what are you reading, Wenling?' '*I can't!*' Ever since she's been living here, she hasn't opened a book, not a single one, she confesses. There are reasons enough that combine to snare and corral her. Work from nine to nine Monday to Saturday, two children, a husband, a house, never a measly two minutes to herself, few books in Mandarin available... No need to say any more. And she shrugs her shoulders: '*You lucky, with books head always thinking new things, always learning, I only work.*' And she gives me my book back.

Before she starts my manicure, I should go to the bathroom. 'Just a minute, Wenling,' and I stand up. '*You drink lot water...*' She's right. One day we should tackle the issue of drinking water. Work out the pros and deal with the cons, like, for example, the time you waste getting rid of it. Maybe we'd find the arguments justifying the general lunacy and principle that has us swilling down water when we're not thirsty quite flimsy.

I go into the back of the shop where I find the boy. His Chinese homework is open on his desk but he'd rather rack his brains over Rubik's cube. 'Look,' he says, feeling pleased with himself. 'That's right, Haitao, every colour in its place.' I tell him I'm hopeless and never manage to complete it, and he doesn't believe me. He doesn't think I can be so clumsy, which is comforting. And blinding too, because I don't see the pool of water and go in feet first. The cistern's leaking and it's spreading water all over the bathroom floor. I waste no time, I try to stop the water spilling, I use a piece of paper to wipe up and exit so fast I bang into an elderly man who must also have swallowed that nonsense about dehydrating. 'Watch out, the floor's wet!' 'Thanks for warning me, dear!'

Wenling sculpts my nails and I'm in awe of her skilful hands. I don't know why I'm surprised. She can find no other outlet for her pent-up talent, so must let her intelligence flow through her fingers.

'*Want them shorter?*' Yes, after a couple of days they start growing, don't hold back, file away. She lets the file dance and in the background I hear a voice coming from the cash desk.

'Water, water!' shouts the nightwatchman. It's the old man from the bathroom. After broadcasting his news, he gives Wenling's husband all kinds of explanations. Because it turns out he's left the little room without pulling the chain. So as not to make things worse and create a bigger mess, he keeps saying. And the poor fellow is really embarrassed. 'I'm sorry, lad, nothing worse than leaving yellow stuff in the lavatory... *I said I'm sorry I left yellow stuff in the lavatory!*' he repeats in Spanish with the decibels of a rock concert. Wenling's husband looks as if he's seen hieroglyphics. I have to say that cracking the meaning of 'the yellow stuff in the lavatory' is advanced-level language, and even took me a while. But as usual he doesn't panic, gives him his change and escorts him out, patting him on the back, '*No worry, no worry,*' and then comes back in to fathom what that riddle is all about.

28

'Uh-huh, of course.' More time has gone under the bridge than I reckoned and I make the most of my visit to Wenling to thin out a mop that's threatening to run away. 'Uh-huh, precisely.' Yang is trimming the hairline on my neck, a delicate operation, I can't look round. 'Uh-huh, OK.' I can't catch a glimpse of the individual articulating those painful telephonic agreements. 'Uh-huh, fine.' Even if it were someone choosing their own coffin they wouldn't sound like that. 'Yes, I have everything.' And now it smells as if it's smouldering. 'Yes, indeed, I speak English. I speak English perfectly,' the voice emphasises solemnly. Did it say 'English'? Maybe it's me, mistaking robins for sparrows, but I'd bet my bottom dollar that this isn't about a commission to translate Shakespeare, however canonical and poetic his work may be. And now they're using the dryer, the voice loses all notion of danger and the volume control is skewed. My suspicions are confirmed and my ears trapped. Because there will be no margin for error or an escape. She wasn't choosing a coffin, although they are measuring her up.

'Curves? Yes, typical Spanish. Breast? Yes, that too, obviously.' The scoundrel on the other end of the line can't get enough, he must want every inch of her skin, and the voice has to stop him dead in his tracks. 'No, no, I'm not prepared to mislead anyone, either about physique or anything else.' Yang is so delighted by his quest for scissorial excellence, my desperate play at conversation falls on deaf ears. 'What you see in the photo is what there is,' the voice says with leaden seriousness. I would certainly like to disappear. Or for the children to charge in, or for him to slice my carotid with the scissors, or for Senyora Gripi to create another biblical, Taoist, Talmudic, Buddhist or Koranic deluge, anything to stop that conversation. But nobody listens to my pleas. And what I felt was coming comes. 'Yes, yes, I can adapt to all tastes. Total discretion, of course. In an executive outfit, right. Complete availability during the Congress, completely available, naturally,' she repeats, 'completely available. Uh-huh, ciao.'

And she hangs up, thank God. But her mobile slips from her hand and she has to come to collect it from by my feet, and that's also a slice of bad luck. She looks up and now I can put a face to the voice. We both do. She realises she's not only surrounded by people who were born in China, or by old grannies in need of hearing aids, and her fright is cosmic. The only thing I can think of to lighten the moment is mouthing a yawn, closing my eyes to persuade her that I'm dozing off again. Hey, I bellow to myself, I was on another planet the whole time! Hey, I didn't hear a word! Hey, these knots twisting my gut have got nothing to do with you!

Too much bawling for a head feigning sleep. No, I don't come out of this at all well. Through my half-closed eyes I see her jump up, collect her bag and blouson in one hand and with the other juggle her purse. She scorns her change, gestures to Wenling to pocket it and slips out of the door with a '*Gracias por todo*' that sounds terminal.

'*Girl always serious, always hurry, one day man pushes hard in street and she comes in here, has a bad time…*' Wenling must have put two and two together some time ago, as I just did, and she doesn't know how it will play out either. It was devastating to hear her trying to defend her dignity. And how her defences wavered, after every response.

★

We did the manicure in silence. We were weighed down by our good fortune in not having to mount that kind of defence. '*Now wait a bit, love, I more work.*' Wenling pinches the soft part of my arm, goes into the back and I imagine I'm supposed to stay relaxed, quiet, waiting for my nails to dry? Our guts remember too. When she turns tail, I take my mobile out of my backpack, and tap away, trying not to damage the varnish. I almost let slip an 'uh-huh' as well.

Because, uh-huh, we are three days away from the favours granted us by divine, technological, wireless, global providence. Three days away from the massive whitewashing of fair-goers who will insist on measurements, languages, discretion, executive suits and complete availability. Three days away from making us believe that smartphones are the only item they'll be fingering. And to be clear, it's not only one sector's lunacy; those inside hanging banners for real estate, medical and construction businesses, or tourist, food, automobile or polystyrene ventures, are all likely to be as predatory as the men from the mobile world. Just click on Barcelona Fair and the list is complete. And naturally, those in my guild as well. A trawl of film festivals would soon give us a list on a planetary scale.

Whoremongers and Harvey Weinsteins for every role, every category and every prize. Cinema: the predators' mecca.

★

I see that Wenling's pending work wasn't a customer. She's checking colour stocks. She notes down what is left and what she must reorder. A collection of numbers filling two pages. I don't want to disturb her, I'll go over and see if she'll have a moment later to chat. 'Hey, Wenling, what are you up to?' '*Manicure no dry?*' she wonders, surprised. 'Not yet,' I pretend as if she didn't know the precise minutes it takes me to dry. No matter, I've sat down beside her and blow on my nails, as if that gesture gives me the slightest credibility. I spot the letters of an address on the Thuya glitter varnish stand: Sant Gervasi de Cassoles, 68.

I bet you too would never have imagined that varnishes originating in the same neighbourhood as Mercè Rodoreda preferred not to be associated with a snobby area like Sant Gervasi. And I wonder: what harm would it do to call themselves Toia, so potential buyers could deduce their Catalan origins? Could it be that silly excuse big Catalan firms always make when you put that question to them: globalisation? It must be to keep happy the gods that rule them, the gods who are anglophone when they're not francophone.

And the unexpected links that might be established between Rodoreda's first garden and manicures don't stop there. Sant Gervasi de Cassoles is also the street where my doctor lives, and she was the one who told me to watch out. You're so fussy about your food, she alerted me, you should realise that your skin and nails also need nurturing, however much fieldwork you have to do. Underneath 'Sant Gervasi de Cassoles, 68', they've printed the slogan 'Made in EU', I replied as if that was a sure-fire guarantee. I pretended that I was clueless when it came to chemical hazards, or that I think I'm protected by the EU. I don't know which is the sillier stance. Some time ago I discovered that there were nontoxic nail polishes and I bought myself loads. I'd been painted with all kinds, high- and low-cost brands. When the composition of the product I used to paint my nails was the most important thing, I looked into it. I would lose sleep over such trifles before Wenling entered my life. Now I willingly let my extremities be intoxicated by formaldehydes, toluene, camphor, phthalates and rosin because I don't dare take my supply of all-natural nail varnish to Wenling's.

I'm afraid I'll look like Miss Know-All who on the eve of Twelfth Night had questioned the shampoos.

*

Wenling is opening big boxes and little boxes. One last puff on my nails and I won't bother her anymore. Yeah, I'll scarper the second I reckon my manicure is drier than salted cod. But I will make one last attempt.

She doesn't look at me when she replies reds and light pink in summer, dark in winter. I don't know what I expected when I asked such a stupid question. We should never trust phrases whose sole purpose is to initiate a conversation, because they leave you looking like an annoying customer. The other person thinks: if you are going through the motions, I'll reply in a similar vein and we'll be quits. That's not really how it is with me. On the pretext of asking which tones were more popular, I'd hoped to spark off a conversation that would lead to something more personal and less professional. A mistake. Every time I make more. I always forget I come here of my own free will and that she earns her living here. That I choose the time and the day. That I go in and out. That I always win. That there can be no 'quits'.

29

I wanted to take a different route today. I'd decided to cut through the neighbourhood and pay a quick visit to the market, it's an evening for baked fish. Though maybe not a day for removing scales. Wenling's husband interrupts my train of thought. He saw me coming out of the metro. He's in the café opposite, on his last sip of cortado. I reckon that, rather than waving hello, his hand is summoning me. I walk towards him. He crosses, I cross, and when I'm next to him, the telegram: *Wenling father dead.* 'Heavens, I'm so sorry.' He nods and fills a cheek with smoke before letting it slip out. 'How is she?' '*She crying...*' He laughs as he says that, which shocks me but I immediately see it's because he's coming to terms: when you are sad, obviously, you cry, end of story. It must be the fake conventions about mourning we learn out of habit. We end up internalising a single glossary of the question–answer kind with a standard mourning face, and when someone reacts naturally, we can't cope.

We stand rooted to the spot, face to face. We'd known for weeks that it would happen, and now it has. Wenling's father has died, but hadn't I agreed to go to the fishmonger's today? My feet don't budge. Wenling is thousands of kilometres away and yet I felt she was next to me during that exchange of words.

That might seem odd, but it isn't. You immediately recognise the pleasant goosebumps that make you feel sisterly. I try to find something to say that justifies my presence, and the first phrase to come to mind is a most original 'do let me know if you need anything'. I too have soaked up the fake conventions. But I hesitate. Because if you analyse it literally, without injecting the host of subtexts we inject when we are cradled in the same culture, I realise that the concept of offering to help, if the other person needs any, is quite hollow in a mourning context. When you say that, you're not thinking of a physical list of jobs to do. Nor is it accepted that keeping someone company is part of the catalogue of basic needs. We have become adept at devising actions that lower a curtain over our emotions, because we are lousy at accompanying the living a dead body has left in its wake.

And trapped between what we say and what we really mean, I don't take my interlocutor into consideration. '*I can't be in street all day!*' he says with a flourish so I get the joke. '*I work!*' And with a broad grin he puts out his fag, throws it in the bin and says: '*You come inside, your hair long now.*'

That's not true, he cut it less than ten days ago. And see how quick it was to find an exit... My 'if you need anything' and his 'let's have a little chat' were the excuse we needed. And he jumps right in. While he ties on my gown, he tells me he's always suffered from stomach aches. I glance at him out of the corner of my eye and think I could hold him up in one hand, he's just a bundle of nerves. Working at the rate he does means he eats at odd hours and has only quick snacks, when he hasn't missed every meal. Most days he can't sit down and have a bite to eat like a normal person until he gets home in the evening. '*I ten or more heads a day, I non-stop. If customer come in and you say wait, customer flies off, and customer can't fly!*' Today when it was less hectic and he could have eaten a proper lunch, '*Wenling call, stomach protests,*' and he shut up shop for the day.

I confess I too know how a belly with the pincers on can irritate. When I was twenty-one, not even purées would go down, I lost ten kilos and had to be examined. One male surgeon threatened me with a 'reduction of the intestines' and a woman doctor decided that the best cure would be anti-anxiety meds, because 'at your age they sort everything out'. He barely gets half of my ironic touches, but reacts in surprise as if he'd caught every innuendo and calls me '*poor little thing*' twice. '*In the end, all fine, I was cured,*' I say to lighten the mood. In fact I was on my knees, at twenty-one I had three jobs at the same time and all day I spun like a top, whizzing from here to there. And my life was a life I didn't want, even when I was twenty-one, but I keep quiet about that. And while I keep that to myself, I think about how I would have told Wenling.

He does what she does and shows me a translation on his mobile: *fishing boats*. Yang was born in Taizhou, on the coast of Zhejiang province, a couple of hours by bus from Wenling's city. Once he'd discounted spending his life doing the same as his male forebears – fishermen – and his female forebears – unloaders, fishwives and net menders – he had to go to Qingtian to learn another trade. '*I work one day out to sea and three on land to get well!*' He was like jelly, it seems, judging by the face he made. He also performs the pain he got from mending and I take that with a pinch of salt, as I know what a great artist he is when he has only a few hairs to deal with. But I let him have his say, and he says it was seasickness that was kind enough to turn him into a hairdresser and for him to meet Wenling. '*I lucky, all good from then on!*' he proclaims with that big smile always blossoming in his eyes. He tells me proudly that everyone at home is still alive, and recites them in order of appearance on this earth. '*Grandfather eighty-eight, grandmother eighty-five, father sixty-three, mother sixty-one. All very strong, all talk at the same time, lots of noise my house!*' He waves his arms like a windmill to imitate the shindig. I imagined he would finish my trim, but for a while half my head is cut and the other isn't. Maybe today I'll receive the fatal cut, but no worries. I willingly assume the risk.

I recognise that madhouse and tell him that his family was akin to mine, that my folk natter on even when they're underwater. And I don't know if his fisherfolk come into his head shooting the breeze in the sea fully clothed, but he splits his sides when he hears my picturesque expression. '*The same, the same, my family always talking!*' 'So I don't know where you come from…' I say to tease him, 'because you're queasy out to sea and aren't keen on nattering.' '*Hahaha, I found in rubbish too! Like her!*'

Haijun has just peered around the door. Without following through with her body, she says something to her father, hello to me and then goes back in. '*I say come to the hairdresser's when you finish piano, then I see you.*' It was a brief eyeful, but I'd say she's had a spurt. 'She's grown, is taller,' I conclude, seeing she is shooting up above her dad. It's the first time I've seen a hint of bad temper. '*Haijun not eat, so she lovely!*' 'What!? But she's only ten!' '*I know, I know!*' he says, looking worried. '*I say eat now to grow, but she looks older girls on mobile, and she too wants be lovely!*'

WENLING'S

Lovely means thin. And it's not just these two who see it like that. Our civilisation is about to make women's body diversity disappear and we're all going along with it.

I leave cropped like a raw conscript and quite happy about that. I also leave with the taste of fish in my mouth: fishing boats dancing in my innards, fingers crossed it's not too late to find some.

You're on your way to the market, but you could be in a street in any city, you don't have to look far to register the constant assault on our bodily freedom, the attack that's rebounded on Haijun too. The hoardings perpetrating it continue to be the unrestricted lords and masters of public space, as if they didn't damage lives just like tobacco and liquor. And it makes no odds if the individuals who are presented as model women are famous or part of the crowd. Renown has been no help to Kate Moss: twenty years after the first advertisement she still has to agree to being photographed skinny and showing all her ribs that look as if they've been scraped to the bone.

Four metres on and it's the big French house Chanel that wants to sell lipstick at the cost of caking the face of a girl who's not yet thirteen. If you take a close look, you won't find her anywhere, the advertisers' paedophile brains have looked for that delectable mouth in hundreds of photo books. You simply see a girl who's already trodden in shit. Because she is one of those girls who will have to 'watch out', 'watch out' being the go-to verb of the moment. There is no end to the girls thrown out between one fashion parade and the next... watching out. They're watching out for carrot-coloured juice, and I say 'coloured' because you couldn't swear any residue of that vegetable is left, because they also keep a count of the calories in vegetables. They watch out or drink or eat the meal of the day, or however you want to phrase it. No variety allowed in their appearance: between skin and bone. If the fashion world wasn't so cunning, didn't handle so much cash and wasn't so dazzling, I'd take Haijun and be her anti-guide at the 080 Barcelona Fashion Week.

A truce now I've reached the market! I jostle everywhere between women from A to Z. Dames with their own noses, lively lips and free-flowing flesh – a guaranteed stock of proper individuals. Starting with Prudi, my fishmonger, who is exuberant from her hair down to the blade she's flourishing.

There's always a frightful queue. Today's my lucky day, there are only two customers in front of me. An elderly lady who's already leaving, a 'priority' client. I saw Prudi wink at her and hand over gratis the 'little something for the kittie' – or the four weekly sprats she'd never eat if Prudi weren't a woman with principles. The other, a young woman dragging a three-year-old kid, with another on the way. She's a foreigner, and can't decide what to choose.

The truth is that here the label 'fresh fish' isn't a marketing ploy, and anyone looking for the usual range is fucked. Here, all privileges have been stripped from the representatives of the piscatorial hetero-patriarchy, namely, cod, monkfish, sole and salmon. The drawback is that there's no way you can translate into English *espet*, *bròtola*, *llampuga* and *tallahams*. The poor girl can make no headway on her iPhone. Prudi works up a sweat telling her not to worry, this is blue fish, that one's white and the other over there tastes shrimpy and kids adore it. But she can't convince her. She wants to see back and front of an array of fish that would be invisible on most stalls. And so I take a close look too. And I size up the situation. If I'd been fed on fruit from another sea, I'd also find *espet* to be a longish specimen and tasteless to boot, *llampuga* to be a monstrous big head, and *bròtola* deformed, as if half-finished. And not vouch for any. But the young foreign woman now has to shelve her doubts, the kid outside is pulling on her skirt and the one inside is exercising an arm. She must yield to the unknown. She randomly points a finger and indicates her lucky one. 'A good *tallahams!*' a relieved Prudi declares, although she has to fillet the bones, leave it as clean as a whistle, in two symmetrical steaks worthy of a prize.

★

I'm not going to let the girl with the *tallahams* go yet, I'll give her a couple more whirls. I change her foreign accent to one we'd judge to be immigrant. I'll stick on a label in line with the colour of her skin. I'll deprogramme her European cultural background. I'll withdraw her Kingdom of Denmark passport. I'll snaffle all her credit cards and pocket her iPhone. I'll leave her belly as it is. That way I can see Wenling a little less hazily on that 15th of May 2006. The day she set foot in Barcelona. The day she will remember when she dies.

30

El Prat airport. The old Terminal 1 that welcomed everyone to Barcelona with the colours of Joan Miró. We'll watch the woman over there, in the calf-length cream coat, just off the flight from Frankfurt, who hasn't simply come from Frankfurt. If we unpick her journey we'll find Shanghai, and further back by train, Qingtian, Zhejiang province, south-east People's Republic of China. Total time in airspace: more than an entire day.

We don't lose sight of her. She is by herself and very alert. She doesn't look as if she's travelled half the globe. Her left hand trundles along a medium-size, Bordeaux-coloured case. Her right scans a piece of paper. Those who've already been there would guess she was precisely six and a half months. She shows the bit of paper to at least three people before confronting the first name, RENFE, which is also the first trap. She's crossed the first bridge, is now in the station, and has to buy her ticket.

The young woman in calf-length cream holds up one finger, opens her purse and gives it to the man at the window. It's not a bad ploy, and she takes a breath. Pity that the guy is such an idiot. The idiot clicks his tongue, and looks this way searching for witnesses to agree that giving twenty euros for a ticket is equivalent, at the very least, to losing one kidney and part of the other. He can't find a ready audience and is forced to reduce his fuck to a murmur. But maybe he can make a big deal of returning a load of change. '*See if we can remember to carry change! Today we'll let it go… Chinky.*'

The day trippers on the platform who've been scraping out the Beatles on a pre-war guitar help her to hump her suitcase. They also mime that they'll tell her when she's about to reach the second name: SANTS. And now the girl in calf-length cream is in the carriage. She's still tense, clenching her right fist, but an elderly gent gives her his seat and she can go down a few watts.

They mustn't have 'Don't Let Me Down' in their repertoire: the day trippers have vanished. If she could leave her suitcase and go out and chase down the carriages looking for them, the girl in calf-length cream would find she'd only be pursuing a battered guitar. Ever since she stepped foot in the Far West, everyone looks the same. They're all copies of each other, big-nosed and greedy.

Sants skips by unnoticed. However, she's not upset, no way. Our language says nothing to her at all, spoken or written. She has only one word clear in her head and the loudspeakers stopped saying Barcelona a long time ago.

The train reaches Passeig de Gràcia and there's a general stampede to get off. The girl in calf-length cream takes that to be an unambiguous sign of a terminus and decides to follow the trend. Now shoulders, backpacks, pushchairs, arms, bags and feet start to dribble. It's impossible to stop, first of all one must escape that underworld. Escape it, taking her case and her belly, because her head is starting to spin. The stink of fumes, armpits, metal and soggy chicken is about to sink her when she spots the escalator. She gets on, and each step towards fresh air brings the colour back to her cheeks. She doesn't know where she is or where it stops, or how she'll get to where she has to go, but first things first. She takes a small flask from her coat and dabs her forehead, her wrists and under her nose. She breathes in that perfume of herbal essences and seeks a soul to guide her to her third name. Maybe that lady with the elegant hair. And she stops her and waves the bit of paper in her face.

'Oh, it's half-erased…' The lady investigates close up. RENFE, SANTS, SAGRADA FAMÍLIA. 'Oh, you're not on the…' The girl in calf-length cream realises she hasn't picked the best passer-by. 'Oh, I'm in a hurry, ask someone else, my dear.' She turns her back on her, and everyone hears her chunter, 'All the Japs want the Sagrada Família, lucky old Gaudí, as if there was nothing else in the world!'

A young man has noticed that scene, puts away his iPod and goes over. 'Got any cash? Because it's better if you take a taxi to the Sagrada Família with all that luggage, if I were you, that's… Cash, dough, money?' However hard she listens, the girl in calf-length cream doesn't know what he means. The lad takes a note out of his pocket. She takes that as all help coming with a price and responds by showing him her purse. 'No, not cash for me, for the taxi!' She persists, he does too, without success. Disappointed, the young man departs, she wants to stop him, she jerks her neck round, the only outcome is to send her head back into a spin. She puts her butt on her case; she doesn't know what to do. And her eyes decree a pause.

Now for the first time, she will look at Barcelona.

'Barcelona,' she says softly, 'Barcelona…' A name that should say it all. But she's not swayed one way or the other by streets with so much concrete and a few forlorn trees. She's not seen the sea anywhere. The sky isn't so bright, nor so blue. And the sun doesn't shine like gold. People aren't so welcoming. Or so refined, especially when they stoop to scoop their dog's poo…

The previous young man interrupts her list of disappointments. '*Hey, here, over here!*' she hears him shout from across the road. Unable to gather why, the girl in calf-length cream drags her case in that direction. Now she's in so deep, she really couldn't care less and dares jump into the taxi the young man hailed for her. Because one imagines the driver will be able to read the last signpost, and will take her to the address where they are expecting her, where she will grasp the lifeline they agreed to throw her. Fortunately, she's not got the energy left to feel afraid. And Barcelona will fly by the window as blurry, lethargic and clapped-out as she feels right then.

*

I've rewritten it differently twenty times; twenty times I've crossed it out. It didn't work if I contrived to get her mugged, or pushed to the ground, or have her lose her way in the night. Whatever the ups and downs I brought to the script. There is terror that's hard to explain because it's not thought of as terror. There is terror that's been stripped of grandeur or epic heights by comics. There is terror you can't describe if you're short on inventiveness. This is what happened; there must be a reason why I dismissed the J.A. Bayona option. I have never been able to imagine her tsunami that day; I've never been able to recreate in words what Wenling communicated to me without any.

After she said '15th of May 2006,' I asked her what happened, what she'd done for it to be etched on her mind like that. She closed her eyes and covered her ears. '*Now you.*' She touched my eyelids with a finger, she made me hush and, with a hand on either side, left me only the sound an empty seashell makes. She counted one, two, three, four seconds and then uncovered my ears. '*You alone in Barcelona like that. Nothing happen, everything happen!*'

31

'This is the switch, this the generator, this the wire and, look: electricity!' The boy can see I'm impressed by his invention. 'Wow, you've created a really classy circuit, Haitao. When you show your mother, she'll go nuts.' 'She's already seen it...' He picks up his masterpiece and goes proudly off in search of more fame. Wenling already... Yang doesn't let me even finish writing down that thought, his first greeting is: '*Wenling back, comes fifteen minutes.*' He saw the expression on my face change. Just as well he can't see inside my head.

Names, adjectives, articles, adverbs and interjections compete violently to line up in a winning combination. So my condolences don't sound wooden. But for now I can't get it right, no set of words can move beyond hollow convention. To get over my nerves I pull out all the grey hairs I can and keep checking the door in the mirror, in case Wenling comes in. As I can't think what to do to hide my anxiety, I opt for a change of scene. And I walk inside to the bathroom, which isn't leaking anymore. The cistern lid is in its rightful place and there's no trace of the flood. And today when it's not acting crazy, today I find that yellow stuff in the bowl. And I accidentally slam the door. Take it any further and I spoil everything.

They have their backs to me. Mother and daughter in the

little room before you get to the kitchen. If she was here...
Wenling is undoing her plait and untangling her hair using her
fingers as a comb. Once, twice and a third time... It's a miracle
they don't snag. Haijun's head loving her caresses. Wenling's
body lovingly repeating the movement. Their giving nature.
Night and day that fortress she is always defending. The sound-
less melody she generates... I'd rather not leave. But I tiptoe
away. It would be a crime to disturb that pas de deux.

I also find it unfair they can't prolong it until their hearts say
enough. The alarm will ring, the fifteen minutes Yang said will
soon be up. I won't be the cause.

I pull my jacket off the hook and am about to put my backpack around my neck and disappear, when a hand tugs at me.
'*Wenling come now!*' says Yang, adopting the tone of people who
get angry in advance in case you've got angry first. And I do
what he does: 'No worries, no worries, I don't want to bother
her, I'll come another day.' But I don't calm him one bit and he
persists. '*No, Wenling come out now, you no jacket, you sit,*' he orders
me with the highlights brush. And I sit down.

In a while I'll find material to note down, grist to my mill,
but my head's not fit for anything now. My heart leaps, even
though I've still not decided what I'll say, and now here she
is: Wenling walks across the hairdresser's. She's hidden by the
mountain of clean towels she's carrying to put away, but even
so I can see how she's changed.

It's shocking what a workday apron hides, however much
hers looks like the tabard worn by a Jedi Knight. This is the first
time I look at her without sensing the classism manufactured
by an intermediary, and it's truly striking. The whitest of tops,

the marine-blue jeans I like so much, the camel calf-high boots, the earrings embellished with a small pearl. The more I look, the more reason I think there is to abolish uniforms that aren't technically necessary for the job. Isn't there a world of difference between presenting yourself one way or the other? And of course, doctors' white coats don't play in the same league, there are uniforms and uniforms. Doctors' white coats have prestige so woven into the material that it's really hard decrying them on days they don't deserve it. 'Wenling, lovely!' I rush to welcome her, she's seen me and is coming towards me.

Such play-acting, and I only had to stand up. A single movement. Her arms opened immediately, and Wenling immediately hugged me with a *gracias*. And that's that. Breathing on the other's back is how we managed all the 'I am so sorry' and 'It's a real shame'. Which weren't needed if you think about it. We assume our brains must decide these questions and maybe we'd do better to let our bodies take control.

'*He and I better now*,' she told me, caressing my cheek as we came apart. '*He not eat, drink, he not now… Heart painful, but better for all when doctor say he not live more. His wife many days in hospital…*' And we also move as one to sit close to each other, for what Wenling wants to tell me is said more through touch than sound.

It's strange how she doesn't appear to be exhausted by so many hours on the plane, a kind of electric current seems to keep her going. So many things bubbling in her head that her body can't stop her either. She'd like to have a day to herself to think it all through, to fix it in her head. Not even a whole day. Luckily her friend-sister Xiaolu accompanied her night and day.

On this trip to China she'd experienced more family upsets than expected, things she can't tell me about now. She's longing to have a day when she can have a decent amount of time: Gripi and her twin sister have just come in asking for pedicures, 'We're here, Wendy!' And we must leave our conversations mid-air.

I make the most of the hurricane they unleash and hit the road. Yang is rinsing the hair of a lad with lots of highlights, he doesn't see me. She doesn't miss a thing, ever. '*I owe manicure,*' she points to my fingers that are so discoloured, and winks. I promise to come back this week and blow her a kiss.

And whoa, those two truths. She left them to the last moment, while she does up the tabard that will erase her again. She said the first with a hint of shame: '*My father good so-so.*' The second, with the force of a universal law: '*But I sad because now I have nobody.*'

Good or bad, the face Wenling just buried had to do the work of two. Because it was the only one. The only one that could question, find something missing and fear. Good or bad, it was also the one that told the world she'd not emerged from beneath a cabbage leaf. And that she must keep her father's face somewhere safe. Because it will also be the only one to surprise her when she sees it repeatedly in the mirror, and the only one that someday she will glimpse in her children when they both make that expression of his.

The same with his voice. She could only rely on her father's to nourish the noise made by her nostalgia for her roots. '*When I think China, I always call my father, always. Now can't.*'

From today on, Wenling lacks even nostalgia.

32

'*You come in, snack.*' Yang wants to make me an accomplice on how to slice a melon. A sign that it's time for the kids to come. He distributes the chunks on small plates and pushes one towards me. '*You pick, it's Bollo, siempre bueno!*' I'm stunned. Yippee! A standing ovation for the person who had the outlandish idea to create a melon-selling slogan. As flat as a pancake, no hint of sophistication, that '*Melons Bollo, aquests són els bons!*' and the way it won over customers who didn't know they existed.

Yippee, yip-pee. While I look at Yang clipping me in the mirror, I wind down my applause for that melonary feat. Why… why am I amazed he likes the same kind of melon my father always eats? Don't tell me I'm one of those who believed that nonsense about 'the Chinese always buy from their own'. Don't tell me that despite all my going in and out of the hairdresser's, all my observations and fieldwork, I couldn't see the big difference it makes not to have lived isolated in a ghetto. Don't say I didn't get the basics: that to discover what the hosts in your new city eat, you must first make the acquaintance of one of them. You must know the mood they are in, exchange good mornings when you pull up the blinds, accept the parcel they've brought after hours, the cortado after lunch, the 'it's cold', 'it's hot' when you shut up shop, or – now we're back where we started – you need a Pep the fruiterer at hand whom you can ask which melon you should buy so he can tell you about the unrivalled properties of a Bollo. The ABC of good neighbouring, as always, and it seems so obvious when those who live next door aren't a carbon copy of ourselves.

I was looking forward to seeing the children but they don't turn up. And Wenling is busy stock-taking hair dyes. I must suppress my desire to ask her about the mourning period, it's time for me to scarper. 'What do I owe you, Yang?' But Yang has a perm on his hands. Wenling abandons the tubes of Wella, Schwarzkopf and L'Oréal and stands behind me. When it comes to the finances, they are that sort too, the non-trusting sort.

I bet you're thinking of a grocery store with a line of half a dozen sales assistants where only the boss has a key to the till. Rain, snow, Xmas or Xmiss, or a crowded shop, she is the only one who handles the money. Well, it's the same at Wenling's. Only the family takes your cash. When the children are around, they man the till.

'I've got the right money, do you want it, Wenling?' '*Yes, lovely, me can't count now!*' She gasps as if she's in a photo finish. 'I bet! Tonight you'll dream of numbers, and more numbers, so much work!' '*Today I very busy, come a day we quiet together, OK?*' 'It's a deal!' and we high-five.

When I'm about to zip up my purse, and lock away this small step in friendship – big for me, for humanity who can say? – a customer breaks the spell. '*Pedicure?*' he grunts angrily. Very angrily. '*Yes, just a moment, wait a little, please,*' answers Wenling, offering him the bench. The customer is an elderly guy, tall as

St Paul, who doesn't reply and doesn't budge an inch from the doorway. My instinct discreetly tells me to look away. And I stick my head in my backpack. I rummage enthusiastically, as if I am looking for something in particular, as if I can't leave without it. Just in case. And the guy proves to be a total basket case.

★

'*Who'll do me?*' shouts the elderly guy. '*A pedicure!*' he bawls even louder. '*Who will do me?!*' Wenling is deathly pale. She always does pedicures. Almost in a tremble, she points to Fen, who is standing petrified in the back. 'She better not *cut my toes!*' I tense like a bow and hesitate. Perhaps he's just a harmless rude git? Perhaps he thinks he's being amusing? Better turn a blind eye? I give him leeway for just one more outburst.

'*Like my wife! She did it so poorly we had to go to the hospital! And it was all her fault! We should make an official complaint!*' I'd let him have his little say and Wenling's panicky expression makes me wonder what else is coming. I decide to intervene.

'Halt! Right there!' He's so het up he thinks he's alone in this world. 'Listen! Over *here!*' Now he looks round and sees me. 'Hello, I'm sorry, but I'm an interested party, that young woman also does my feet: what were you saying?'

The impact is devastating. The transformation, total. His arrogance and contempt retreat to the corner of each of his eyebrows, his ears to the level of his shoulders, and he looks a good foot shorter. He's toned his voice down too. No trace of that barking, or of that first language.

'Ohhhh, I was just saying... My wife had an ingrown nail on her big toe. She came here and two days later she had a whitlow and the hospital said it was infected!' He's trying to justify himself but he's not the same man who stormed into the salon. I look at Wenling out of the corner of my eye: all her senses riveted on the performance.

'You're saying your wife already had a whitlow when that young woman, the pedicurist, did her feet?'

'I should say so! Her big toe had been playing up for some time!'

'Well, with all due respect, you walked in here making a very serious complaint and it turns out it wasn't quite like that.'

'What about the pain she was in?' The fellow is still up for it, he won't back down. 'My wife won't let me even mention this place!'

'And how is it you've come back, if you reckon they do such a botched job?'

'Dear, never heard how expensive chiropodists are?'

'But this isn't a chiropodist's, my dear sir! People come here with nails in a fit state! It's the job of these young women to cut, file, remove a few tufts of hair and paint, it's a beauty parlour. If you and your wife need treatment, you'll have to dig deeper in your pockets and not come here bawling so rudely...'

'Are you saying that I'm impolite and looking for a cheap fix? You've got some cheek! You're the one with no manners!'

'Look, I'm very sorry, but that is precisely what I'm saying. Got that? Do you know how accusations like yours can damage a business like theirs?' His tongue, hands and legs seek out the luminous exit sign.

'I didn't want to do you down, dear... I expect I went too far, I expect I did... *Well... I'll sit here and wait for my turn.*' The elderly man turns again to Wenling, who stands there like a statue. '*You know, duck, I'm sorry about what I said… It was a… misunderstanding!* Now that's in the past… *water under the bridge!*' He sits on the bench, grabs a magazine and tries to do a disappearing act.

Wenling is glassy-eyed and thanks me silently, repeatedly. She understood every word. No translation was needed, abuses of power are unmistakable. And that was one, however much the despotic pensioner then tried to win us over. But let's go back to that first scene, before he slipped on the meek lamb's coat. Let's go back to when he thought he'd rule the roost like the bossman, that he'd strut around and not find anyone to stand up to him, nobody he'd recognise as an equal, nobody to whom he should show respect. So we have an elderly white man, a customer and a native, bellyaching and badmouthing a young woman from another continent doing female work, and thus judged to be the lowest of the low. A −10 in terms of humanity, at the bottom of the scale. That wouldn't do justice, not even with all the points from the 'I'm not classist but' test and you'd have to add the ones from the 'I'm not a male chauvinist but' and from the 'I'm not racist but' tests. Rock bottom across the board.

How many days and nights do you need to get over a rash of impotence like that? The one looking at me now and saying goodbye is a Wenling just back from the front. I feel like making a face to ridicule that retired despot to bring a smile to Wenling's face. I wrinkle my nose like somebody disgusted by everything, who always seems to be smelling a fart. It usually works. She manages a so-so laugh, as she'd say, at my performance.

And that guy must be watching us. Because he takes his mug out of the magazine and looks up. '*Keep well, love,*' he pipes up. 'I'm so sorry…' So what do you answer back now? 'Well, see you soon, hope your wife recovers,' and on your way.

33

'Hey, know what? You should read Tolstoy!' One lad to another, in the middle of the street. He blurts that out, digs his finger out of his shoulder and runs off. Bookshops would be cock-a-hoop if every invitation to piss off went like that. And while wondering whether the subtext of that ultimatum inclined more to *War and Peace* or *Anna Karenina*, I hear that girl's footsteps.

I know them well. Learned in a jazz class, perfected at home, tried out in the street. She danced all day long, so did I. Her headset was linked to her mobile, mine to my Walkman. There wasn't really much in it. She must be eleven or twelve, what they now categorise as pre-adolescent and what my grandma would call a little ducky. One too long in the laboratory, the other too long in the farmyard, perhaps we should find a halfway house. In the meantime, I call them kids, ones in the same groove as us: faded jeans, tennis pumps, tracksuits with two white stripes, and a breakdance jacket. She's lucky that padded shoulders didn't survive natural selection, we celebrate the fact that Haijun doesn't have to wear them. Because she was the girl trying to rehearse a routine. I've not seen her for ages… I catch her up.

'Hey, Haijun! I didn't recognise you from the back.'

'New trousers!'

'Very nice too. Do you know that when I was your age I dressed exactly like you?'

'Exactly?'

'Well, not really. You don't wear shoulder pads.'

'Like an American footballer?'

I was going to say it wasn't a man-thing, but the fact is those stupid accessories that make our lives so uncomfortable are always designed by guys who are never going to wear them. When I was a young girl, we'd put lumps of foam up there held in place by our bra straps and we'd forever be feeling them, like this, terrified they might slip down our sleeves. The absurdity of shoulder pads!'

'How awful! And why?'

'You know, Haijun, for no real reason, for the sake of fashion, so our shoulders looked broader, you tell me. Just another piece of nonsense I'm glad to say is past history now.'

'Look, isn't that great?' And Haijun is spellbound again. Three young women are singing and dancing in sync looking at the camera in an endless set, the same video clip formula as Beyoncé's 'Single Ladies'. 'They're from China, like me,' the same formula and every bit as empowering as it was to so many Afro-adolescent girls. Because I don't see Haijun as ever being a pop star. And mirrors must cost her a packet as well.

'Do you like it? They're like me, they are yellow.'

'Yellow? What on earth do you mean?' I keep looking shocked, because the next thing I say doesn't know where it's heading. 'You know, Haijun, what colour would you say I am? Because I'm not what you'd call white…' I pull up my sleeve and put it alongside hers.

'Hey, we're the same!' she shouts.

'Awesome, we're the identical tone. You see, what colour you are is very relative.'

'Well, they call me "yellow".'

'Who do? Your classmates?'

'Yes, some do.'

'Right, you find objectionable folk everywhere. You know, you're a healthy, clever girl and a good person, and that's what counts, it makes no difference whether you're pink or brown or... or have cauliflower ears or lilac eyes, it makes no difference!'

She wasn't convinced, and shrugged her shoulders with a resigned 'Sure'. I wasn't either, I didn't know what else to say, I don't know enough. I don't know enough because I've never had to worry a little or a lot about researching in the library 'the ideology of racism, biological supremacy, scientific racism, social Darwinism...' Before that yellow punch in the belly, forty years on this planet and never a worry. I flounder badly, and then decide there still might be something I could appeal to. At the very least accompany her for a while, in that misery when you're at school and dreading an adjective purpose-built for you.

'Can I tell you something, Haijun?' We are sitting on the bench at the front of the hairdresser's. 'There was a time at school when they called me "handicapped". Do you know what the word means?'

'Yes,' she responds, very impressed, looking me up and down for an explanation.

'No, it's alright now, but when I was a kid I had to wear a metal device from my chin to my hips, a real faff... So one kid started calling me that, and a few others joined in and it was "handicapped" here, there and everywhere, like a scratched record. At first, I was really fed up and miserable and didn't know what to do, but one day I got up feeling determined, went over to the kid who'd invented the tag and gave him a slap that knocked off his glasses.'

'You did? That's awesome!'

'Awesome?' And now I'm the one who's surprised, what an example to set... 'Maybe... hitting someone isn't the best way to fix things, everyone told me off, my mother being the first, and it turns out the kid was the headmaster's son... there was a real to-do... I only told you about it...' because you know that one day or another you'll put those people behind you, I think but can't say, because my case isn't hers, a new idiot might always go after her... 'so you'd have a laugh, Haijun.' And I ruffle her hair.

'When they call me "yellow", I laugh. That way they stop.' And my blindfold falls off. You can't take that route.

'Know what, Haijun? Maybe you can slap the fool who calls you names next time. With your hand open, like this, whack! But first you must tell your teacher. If she doesn't know, she can't tell him off. Promise me you'll tell her straight away, agreed?'

'Yes, but I'm fine, I'm happy... School is what I most like about living here. In China some children...' And she finishes the sentence by slicing her neck with a finger.

'What? You mean...?' I can't bring myself to say the word either.

'Yes, they jump.'

'From the window? From the balcony in their house?'

'Yes, they can't stand any more.'

'Young kids?'

'Like me. In China no games, no school trips, only more and more homework. You never sleep, always scared… I never studied so little and here get super top marks and we've already been to Port Aventura, Montseny, the snow, La Pedrera, the theatre…' And when she finishes the fingers of one hand, she looks up and says: 'And I love everything, every little bit!'

They will never stop her. However many putrid people and words there are out there, they'll never ever stop her.

34

It was after lunch and there were four heads and a few feet at Wenling's. That doesn't necessarily add up to five customers. You can only laugh at Miss Know-All, it's not so easy to maintain a silence with such bad vibes, you have to work at it. The positive side is that I'll probably not meet them again. They were fly-by-nights, the lot of them. Wenling's regulars like every step in the ritual. When they're trimming and spicing you up, it's so delicious, it would be an effort not to savour it. These five are as insipid as they come. None passed the humanity test. Each love-other-foot-inside, love-turn-your head-a-bit, love-go-to-wash was like stirring a half-hibernating brown bear. They couldn't manage a stingy monosyllable in response. It was a spectacle to make you lick your lips. I put the latest Alice Munro translation to one side and switched on my mobile.

Maybe they were even waiting for me. After I clicked on 'Notes', one broke the silence like this: '*Are the children Spanish? Were they born here? Or are they Chinese?*'

Wenling stops the pedicure and looks alarmed as if someone has just rung a bell. The one bringing the fine you weren't expecting, never the parcel you're dying to open. '*Are they Spanish or aren't they?*' The woman who's been silent to that point loses her patience.

'*Yes… both… born here.*'

'Oh!' The customer throws off her gown and drapes it over the arty hairdresser who specialises in retired women, reluctantly looks at herself in the mirror, and goes to the register. '*Is somebody coming to collect or not?*'

Yang is struggling with some very curly hair, the dryer is on full volume and he doesn't hear her. Wenling can't go, she's handling those feet again. She shouts to Haitao and Haijun to come out.

It's down to him. Munching half a banana, he drags his feet through the salon, reduces his irritation with each step and stops by the register. The customer hands him a note and when Haitao grips it: '*Children don't work! That's not allowed here!*' She pulls the note away. Haitao looks at her in a state of shock, but it's obviously a joke and she gives it back to him. 'Is the pay good, boy?'

'No,' he replies knowingly.

'*Well, we are doing well.*' And she extracts a two-euro coin from her pocket and slams it down on the counter. '*For you!*'

I check her out before she beats it. A good eighty, indigenous, rough hands from touching lots of bleached water, a housecoat instead of a dress, espadrilles instead of shoes… It wouldn't be too much of a stretch to imagine she was toiling away before she was fourteen. In the neighbourhood dairy, in her uncle's bacon store, in the cake shop on Sundays. Or sewing flamenco dolls piecework in the neighbour's flat on the mezzanine. Or maybe much nastier things. And you reckon that that's not what has dulled her memory or fostered her contempt… I've still to finish the profile when the lifeless feet Wenling was attending mutate into another bad-tempered customer.

'*The Chinese are like ants!*' I try to glean titbits of meaning in case I might have missed something. I haven't. They don't have souls, they're only good for work, we can see they're all the same and squash them without feeling remorse, after all, there are so many of them. Ants have never been randomly chosen subjects of an animal kingdom, I reflect to myself. And the second who joins in after hearing the first attack is nothing random either: insults need the trampoline of complicity to dare take a running jump.

I look at Wenling, Yang, Haijun, Haitao and Fen and the artist hairdresser for retired women. All transfixed by the same question, all belittled by the hurt it brings. I have yet to say or do anything.

'The Chinese are like blacks!'

Do I need to wait for another attack, after such a xenophobically crafted sentence? I look at them again, I must now!

Must I? She's only a bit younger than my grandmother. We'll be here till kingdom come trying to get her to understand. The despotic pensioner was a specific case, the injustice was demonstrable, the defence legitimate, I found that easy enough. To respond to these two insults would require me to theorise in depth, and repair the whole of their thought, upbringing and culture… And I'd still find more excuses, many more. And they all come from the same source: from our everyday racism. From what the Lord gives us today, from what he gave us yesterday and what he'll give us tomorrow if God wishes and we don't attempt a cure.

I've munched on it too, while eating my St Stephen's Day cannelloni. And the brownies at the fortieth of my mate the sound mixer. And at the drinks party given by the producers. And at the paella cooked by my cousins. And the gin and tonics with my girlfriends. And everywhere I've downed it heartily, hungrily. Racism is almost like garlic: it's antisocial, hard to digest and you notice it only if you don't eat it too often. If you don't have it for breakfast, for lunch, for tea and for dinner and haven't had enough until it comes to be a second supper, and you don't register that it's passed into your bloodstream. And as everything gets mixed up inside, you don't detect it, and you reckon you're not racist, that racists don't exist, dead and buried, kaput. Until one fine day you realise they do. And that you're one too. Because now the taunts, jibes, insults and names we use to brand the skin of others begin to jar. You detest that. You don't want to belong to the tribe of aggressors. But you're still unable to attack one. You don't smash their face in as you would have anybody else's, because first you'd have to smash your own. Because, you know, I too must have laughed, joined in like everyone else, on that day, at that party. Or said something even fouler. Or kept my mouth shut.

★

'*You say nothing today...*' 'I'm sorry, Wenling, I can't get today's stinking customers out of my head. They said things... I'm very sorry.' '*Not many like that here, and gone now...*' And we stare at the three old bags still there, who may still perform. They're spraying two with lacquer, and the other is tying her scarf around her neck, they're all about to beat it. '*Lovely, I think: why fix hair, why fix feet but no fix heart?*'

★

She who follows the advice of Xiaolu, her friend-sister, grabs her bag, sets off, goes to Europe, to Barcelona, has a little girl – alone – and spends four years working as a beautician for the owner of a salon near the Sagrada Família who throws her the first lifeline, her first contract. He arrives a year later and spends three in a barbershop near the Arc de Triomf. In between they have a baby boy. They toil four and three years, twelve hours a day, six days a week, in order to save and find premises on a lease. They search the whole of Barcelona in order to have their own hairdresser's, not depend on the whims of others, continue labouring away twelve hours a day, six days a week, with their minds on their main goal in life, the one that gets them out of bed every morning with no memories of the previous day's excruciating efforts: a decent enough apartment for them to bring the children from China. They negotiate the 'regrouping', which is the label they give that right in administrative terms. What in human terms would be translated into being a family again. Or to be one for the first time, because Haijun and Haitao weren't able to be brother and sister under the same roof until they arrived in Barcelona. Slaving away every God-given hour meant leaving months-old babies with the grandparents, one in Qingtian, the other in Taizhou. Now it looked like all they had to do was work, the four of them were together, they had everything they needed, then those worm-eaten, dried-up, dead spirits had to come along.

Who would want to stay forever in a land with such bad feelings? Nothing to do with their grandparents' chop suey or pickled whatever, they know very well that they'll have to beat the path back to China to die there as their compatriots have always done. No joking matter, ending your days as the target of so many insults. More than likely they'll go once the kids can manage by themselves.

Yang tells me that loud and clear and woefully. '*I no speak good Spanish, I no learn Catalan, I speak all day with dryer and scissors, but I know boys who born here and speak Catalan and Spanish perfect like you, and people no treat like you, people treat like those customers today. Why? Because face is Chinese, face can't change. Here we never equal to you.*'

35

In Vic, in Banyoles, in Santa Coloma de Gramanet, in Cambrils, in Manresa… All around Catalonia, scenes like this one that Haijun and Haitao will have to be tough-skinned to handle:

'You speak really good Catalan? Where are you from?'

'From here.'

'I mean, where were you born?'

'In Sant Pau Hospital.'

'I mean, where do you actually come from?'

'From Gràcia.'

'Where do you originate from, for fuck's sake?'

'I just told you.'

'What country are you really from, dickhead?!'

36

They're giving Senyora Gripi a pedicure, her twin sister is under the dryer, Senyora Mundeta is letting her perm set, Senyora Eulàlia her colour, and Senyora Catalina is simply waiting. She's the one who swung her mop and launched the topic discussed in *Semana*'s 'Consultant's Corner'.

The wick is lit by a small column, barely a quarter of a page. As easily as forests in a summer drought. No need for a pathetic arsonist to grab a rabbit and light its tail for the woods to go up in flame. The red-hot poker is this headline: '*Orgasms in retirement, the good sex women never enjoyed.*' Wait for it, today we are going to garner knowledge vital to our lives.

The first glimmer of a reaction comes from Senyora Gripi, 'Agh!' accompanied by an exclamation the force of which might lead us to describe her as a non-believer: '*That's a load of cobblers!*' But her twin knows that when she lashes out, there's meat on the bone. We all know that, especially Wenling and Haijun. Ever since that day she unleashed her assault on national Catholicism, the day she declared, '*The Sisters are bastards.*' Senyora Gripi's twin lifts the visor on the dryer and retorts:

'*Speak for yourself, dearie... You've only had it with your first, so I'd shush if...*'

'*Well, really! I never needed to, and I'm proud of that!*' she huffed, not sounding genuinely aggrieved.

'Hey, my lovelies, don't take it the wrong way, I read it aloud for all of you, because I thought it was funny, apart from thinking it's dead right…'

And after Senyora Catalina slings her second hook, Senyora Eulàlia grips the arms of her chair and with a strong push from her feet steers into the centre of the salon.

'As we are on our own today…' Swish! She opens her fan. 'Today I'll tell you one thing for sure: what Senyora Catalina read out is as true as my name is Eulàlia. Yes, my love, I mean it! Maybe the bit about orgasms isn't so widespread, but I quite believe the other stuff about the sex they've never had. Or didn't we all go into marriage like animals who've sensed their time has come? I mean, we didn't know what we had between our legs or what it was for! And had never seen a man's knob! And didn't lots of us even fall sick! They told you it was the emotion of marriage. Nonsense! It was fear and terror of the first night!'

'*Stop fanning, Eulàlia, you'll choke, love! Let it be, and carry on, dear.*'

'As I was saying, that wondrous first night. Well, after we married, we went on a trip around Andalusia. My husband earned a good wage and we could afford to stay there for ten days. Well, by the second I had a temperature of thirty-two, we were in Granada. And you know my husband, who has never thought about anybody but himself, saw me looking so bad and said: "I swear I won't touch a hair on your body until we get home, Eulàlia, now let's enjoy the sights." The next morning

I woke up as fresh as a rose and we went to the Alhambra and I thought it was the best palace ever erected on this earth. But nothing lasts for long and at home I still felt poorly, and the roughness of it all, not to mention the disappointment. Such a song and dance for *that*, my dears? To learn what to do when, to keep still and let him get on with it until he's skinned his goose? Know what? I spent every minute it lasted making my shopping list, for I was always in a rush when the kids were little: maybe buy two quarters of chicken, and half a kilo of mince for Saturday's macaroni, two hundred grams of ham, two hundred of fuet, and when I saw him still grinding away, I thought, Come on, lad, get it over with, or it will go clean out of my head before I've jotted it down!'

'*No, no, I'm going to split my sides, Eulàlia, though I'm doing my best not to, I can imagine you and…*'

'It's funny now, but don't tell me it's not a sad state of affairs to see yourself reduced to a piece of meat where someone else unloads. Then I learned from acquaintances that we women weren't here just to be sinks. After finding out on the quiet, some women with grown-up kids felt brave enough to tell their hubbies to go down to their nether parts to see if they could find their cherries and make them happy. Now, it was only a handful, because you had to take care or else you risked being seen as a woman… on the game, if you showed any sign of being desperate for it. It was only quite recently that I dared ask him to seek out my cherry, but he's past it now, and for the one time he finds it, there are ten he doesn't. So, my lovelies, what the magazine said was really true, wasn't it?'

She had an answer in under two seconds.

'Too true!' Senyora Mundeta's memories come flooding back and tears well in her eyes. However, she grips her walking stick tight and says: 'I think you paint too rosy a picture, what about the women who faced a man drunk out of his mind? It cost me dear to say no to him... When he stank of wine, I couldn't, I really couldn't... And then he hit me and climbed on top of me all the same. And while it lasted, no lists, just streams of tears. And I felt that helped a bit, because when it was over, I went off to the wash house to wash clothes and I'd think, Come on, Mundeta, you've had a good cry, now blank it out, for if you put it out of your mind, he's not won. But you can only blank out half... he died thirty-five years ago and I've still not forgiven him.' Senyora Mundeta looks at her leg that went gammy after one of those beatings, takes off her glasses and wipes her eyes. 'I've never missed Sunday mass and never will as long as this stick props me up, but I shall never forgive him, however much the priest preaches that you should. What does he know about the torture we women suffer... About the torture meted out by the man of the house, that nobody can save you from.'

'*Priests know shit all, Señora Mundeta, and now you're making me weep. And as we're... I mean, as soon as he'd deflowered me and given me two kids, he cleared off! I didn't have to put up with a pig like your husband, for sure, but all the same you have to harden your face, because I was the affectionate sort when I was a young girl... Shush, you idiot, I can see you out of the corner of my eye. Ignore the faces my twin sister's making. I've had to live with everything I've suffered. Because I said never another man, never another man, but it always turns you sour to think you don't have anyone to love and hug you. Fondly, of course, not like my husband, who felt a sudden need to do it and stuck it in with one thrust without so much as a by your leave. And, as for enjoying it… I never did. And I'll go to the grave having never enjoyed it.'*

'Come now, Senyora Gripi, you can never say that…' Senyora Catalina knows that after everything that's been said, it's now time to dream. 'My dears, of course they sold us short, but our cherry never dies! There's time to pleasure there until the very last day!'

It makes no odds whether they ever activate their cherries. It was worth their while airing all those inner scars. And the light sparkling in their eyes isn't the morbid kind. The sparks generated by the most ancient of abuses come from quite different depths.

After all, the tragedy yet to be written doesn't end here. Or with them. The tragedy yet to be written would expose rape scenes legitimised behind the walls in every house, every family, every village, every world, every epoch. And would be infinite. And whether you write Zhejiang or Moianès, examples and variations on the living death in women's lives abound in every centimetre of what we have the nerve to call 'humanity'.

37

'Third daughter, do this! Third daughter, bring that!' They've ordered her around like this from birth. Why bless her with individuality if shouted orders will do? Now she's ten or eleven – her mother, the only one who could say for sure, isn't there – she belongs to another voice. And this voice will slice through the air with a different cry: 'You!'

If she knew what to expect after today... She'd hide inside that cave only she knows. Or walk over the hills until her legs give up. But ten kilos of sweet potato and half a sack of rice don't seem to augur ill. They always bring joy to a pantry as bare as hers. A ruddy-cheeked youngster unloads them and he won't charge her father because he'll take her as payment. And that will teach her.

A three-day walk from her home leads her to a hamlet called Kuishi, four stone walls, a mother-in-law, a stove, half a cane with a bucket at both ends for carrying water, land to rake, small animals to watch over and torture she didn't know existed. She can slough off the skin of third daughter; they've just kicked her out.

Her father didn't wait until she was fourteen to marry her off. Her father decided to save himself the years remaining – three or four? – for him to keep her, and the dowry and banquet he'd have to pay for a normal wedding. So he got rid of her in the most profitable way for himself and the most catastrophic for her: as a child-bride in an inferior marriage. Slavery pure and simple that the dust of tradition and so much poverty prevented them from seeing through these eyes. And everyone resumed normal life the next morning after watching the child-bride depart towards the abyss.

Three days have passed. Crags, stones, prickly hedges, shards of stone… all the hazards on the path have left their mark on the soles of her feet. Not a week will go by before many parts of her body are blackened by those same marks required by the work that follows that 'You!'

The one summoning her like that is not the ruddy-cheeked ragamuffin who will be her husband when she is of age. It's her mother-in-law. Finally she had one. She didn't go to sleep a single day until she'd requested a young girl, please, a young girl. She must now take advantage. Bringing children into the world has weakened her lungs, she won't soften because the young girl he's brought her is a young girl who still has soft cartilage rather than bones. The mother-in-law also bore the dust of tradition and so much poverty stuck to the nape of her neck under a bun that keeps her hair in check.

The first weeks go by without her even being able to see their colour. Her eyes have only just closed when morning dawns. There's no lull, no conversation, no warmth, no explanations. Nor any rest apart from what she needs to gulp down her two daily bowls. That's always standing by the fire, when she's served them at the table and they're already belching.

It's when she's almost fourteen that night won't pass her by like daytime. When she's almost fourteen, the ruddy-cheeked

GEMMA RUIZ PALÀ

ragamuffin will begin his assaults on her. He's lived his life to the full and knows his age. It's been three years since he made his purchase. That calculation was also an insurance policy. Many had learned that if they didn't cool their expectations and raped the girls when they arrived, they would cross to the other side after the first birth. The machinery of birth wasn't ready, it was all a mess of blood and flesh and whoops! One more child-bride to bury. Often the child too. No point throwing the baby out with the bathwater.

But having the most calculating of all possible husbands didn't mean she was spared the Night. The first time, she'd have sworn the hands of Death were tearing her apart. But those hands couldn't have belonged to Death, because they left empty-handed. Because she was still alive when the ruddy-cheeked ragamuffin rolled off her and went to his bed.

First she concentrated on one hand to see whether she could feel it. And gradually she brought it level with her face. She cupped it and checked that air was coming out of her nose. Then she inspected her legs. She felt them. Still attached to the same torso. The other hand, both arms, her feet... Everything seemed to be there, intact!

And she thought of an arrangement. If Night agreed to destroy only her innards, to burn only her skin, to bruise only her body, but protected her from the hands of Death whenever he attacked, she would do everything he asked.

Night came from the first cloud of dust, like the Sun, though the latter was bestowed with the title of king. All it had to do was shine. It wasn't by chance that Night was dark. With closed eyes, what mortal would ever know who really did the work?

Night couldn't cope. It was charged with watching over all the wonders of the world. And it was exhausting. Maybe it was time for reinforcements... Despair also creates hope: she might like to do it, ruminated Night. And Night agreed to offer help in exchange for life.

First of all, I'll take your sleep, you won't close your eyes again. Because you must come with me, and help me to guard the earth's treasures. And I warn you that's a never-ending task, you'll be worn out. If you agree, the hands of Death will never come near you again. Agreed, she replied, where do we start? Night ordained that first up would be the treasures of Zhejiang, and they agreed that after every sunset it would take her straight there. Flying.

And now to fly, she told herself. She turned into cotton wool, departed her bruised body and left it lying on the bamboo bed. It was as if she were there when the ruddy-cheeked ragamuffin came to tear her apart. She was already adept at running to take off. But she always lingered a few seconds too long. Because she would look down from on high. Feverish temples, tangled hair, fists like rocks. They were hers. It was her. Then, Night had to retreat. Shush. Deals are deals, it told her, drying her eyes with a puff. Up and away, Luli!

And it was by travelling in the wake of Night that she learned so many things. That she had a name, Luli. Meaning 'jasmine spangled with dew'. That sleeplessness might be a fair payoff. That the path isn't only made of potholes, weariness and dirty feet. There are also miracles. The earth where she was born was sown with seeds, which couldn't be bought even if you had all the stars in the sky in your pocket.

Wonders of water, woods or stone? When they brushed against the clouds, Night always asked her the same question. She inclined her head, tapped her cheek and chose. And now they could begin the day's work: up and away, Luli!

They flew over the Village of New Rivers and checked each bridge with the tips of their feet. They followed the peaks, rocks and waterfalls of the Yandang mountains until they found the Three Perfections intact. They climbed to the moon to see what it looked like in the three mirrors of the Western Lake, in case one had become unhinged. They entered the Big Cave of the Yaolin Fairies to chisel pillars of jade. They sank their heads down and quenched their thirst on the sugary water from the Lake of the Thousand Isles, after counting every single one. They accompanied the Qiantang River in order to curb its powerful swell. They checked the five hundred steps of Yongkang, and from top to bottom the Orchid Pavilion, the Temple of the Soul's Retreat… Each darkening hour, a wonder secured, ready to be contemplated by mortals.

And with the beauty of Night in her eyes she could kick out all that ugliness. Because every day the Sun lit her up with its first yawn, filled her with light and made her mistress of every form. It was impossible not to see ugliness everywhere. In her mother-in-law's scowls, in her husband's red cheeks, in the toil in that house, the sacks she dragged and the rags she wore. But she invoked one word and held out her hand: Luli. And immediately she smelled that fragrant flow of dewdrops and flowers. From the moment she felt that sheen of dew-spangled jasmine on her skin, she felt unsullied by the ugliness. It could hurt her no more. They hadn't got on well at first, she and

Night. But it turned out it had also saved her from the hands of Day.

*

That's one way to tell a life like Wenling's grandmother's. But as she'd require a whole stage to herself, she'd surely have preferred not to start. The moment it was her turn to spill the beans, her voice wouldn't have allowed her; she was so used to being forbidden that space. Though she wouldn't have rejected the opportunity altogether. Those souls had shared abuses very similar to her own; you could say they were sisters. And that's why Wenling's grandmother wouldn't have said a word, but would have looked at them in turn. Deep down. Attentively. Reciprocating. Senyora Gripi, her every breath. Her twin sister, her every revelation. Senyora Eulàlia, her every shudder. Senyora Mundeta, her every scar, and Senyora Catalina, her every feeling of gratitude.

Wenling's grandmother couldn't be with them on that afternoon of sharing wounds. Night had taken her off nine years ago on her eternal round of wonders. But my favourite compatriots at the hairdresser's were already in the street, about to go their separate ways, when there was a sudden breeze. 'That can't be, can it…? Do you smell that scent?' '*Of course it is! What else could it be?*' 'At this time of year, in this street? Surely it can't be…' 'Jasmine?'

38

Wenling has found a discreet way of working out whether I'm in a hurry. When she sees me tidying a few hairs and switching off the dryer, she comes and asks, 'Y*ou working now?*', meaning can I stay on a while. I didn't get that straight away. I relied on a literal take and my ability to communicate, and would say something like: 'No, I only just left!' Or: 'Yes, I'm late, I must be off!' A real disconnect between intention and outcome, there was no way I would see the light. Wenling would say, '*Alright, lovely*' and put away whatever it was she had for me. Now the penny dropped. '*You working now?*' 'Noooo!' I answer, rain or snow. 'I'm free!' I always respond. And no sooner said than done. She goes inside and comes back with an envelope to show me. An envelope from the Caixa.

If ever they land you in it, it will go something like this:

Dear Sirs,

 We take the opportunity in the present to communicate our decision to resolve the contractual relationship that you maintain with this Entity.

 […]

 Nevertheless, in respect of the amounts linked to products with payments pending, we advise that these will be sustained, their

*movement being restricted to the payment of the necessary amount
to cover the payment of the aforesaid.*

   […]
   No other matters pending,
   Yours faithfully,
   The General Deputy Director of Banking Services

I assume that they are happy with them in terms of mortgage repayments. They are blocking standing orders on the kind of account most of us have. A flustered Wenling recites a list: '*School, Haijun piano, Haitao basketball, water, light, hairdresser's… the usual!*' And she gets more and more stressed. '*Owe nothing! I not understand! Always pay!*' She doesn't understand what's behind this, and as soon as she opened the letter, she went to Pep the fruiterer to find a translation. But there's no human–banking or banking–human mobile app yet. And she understands it so perfectly she cannot understand. '*I ask the Caixa why and they no say! I not know what I do wrong! I not know what wrong!*'

I ring the customer helpline and, my friend, this isn't the Sant Pau Hospital. Now I can use my indigenous Catalan accent on full throttle. Sure, we all know that stressing us out is their terror strategy. Amazingly, they have gone one step further. Because now they don't try to soften the torture of the helpline with romantic music. We don't even merit Beethoven's *Für Elise*, that's how grim it's become. When I finally succeed in talking to a live person I've already gone through four routines obeying the orders of an empty tin that

   intoned

   each

word
as
if
it
was
spewing
them
out
of
a
lottery
hopper

And from the response you get, you can barely tell the difference between the empty tin and the live being: '*These consultations will be attended to after the email you should send to the address that appears in the lower left corner of the letter. Do you need any other information?*'

And it also puts my nose out of joint… '*Thanks, my love, no worry, you do nothing else.*' Wenling doesn't want you to go with her to the branch of the bank that has so rudely dispatched these letters. 'Come on, let's do it!' '*No, thank you.*' Nor does she want to send a written complaint to the 'anti-rumours' office I discovered the Town Hall now possesses and which would attend to them. Even though I insist, and insist vehemently, she won't. '*No, thank you.*' They've been able to open an account at the BBVA next to their house straight away and it was no big deal. '*BBVA girl very nice, don't understand why Caixa does this, says we all in order.*' Wenling wants to stay out of sight, make no sound, not arouse the beast, watch her back, and get by.

★

That '*all in order*' doesn't last long enough for payments to be made. It's not even the end of the year and now it's BBVA that's putting the spoke in: it has blocked all accounts belonging to customers with Asiatic names who are in its database. Allegedly because of money-laundering detected in accounts belonging to people of Chinese origin. As if fraud was at all connected to the names of a nation. A quick glance at the Panama Papers will show us that's not the case: the surnames Messi, Bourbon, Almodóvar, Strauss-Kahn, Berlusconi or Al-Assad aren't born from the soil. They're born from the thick skin the rich grow that makes them relatives of thieves, however much they try to hide it. To rub it in, it was her birthday when the BBVA froze all their accounts. '*Do you like my present?*' asked Wenling. She could make a quip like that when we were in the BBVA office, when I'd already expressed my indignation and ranted enough and we were waiting for her adviser to rescue her from a situation that, it has to be said, the wretched young woman found equally unfair and inexplicable. Wenling wasn't joking when she phoned me in a panic because she wasn't able to pay the wages, the electricity, the self-employed quota or the rent on the salon because their accounts were blocked. She hadn't slept for a week when she rang me. Customers were angry because they couldn't use the payment terminal, a bad situation with the estate agents, danger of a fine because of non-payment of self-employed quota, of being cut off, or more direct debits not being honoured… A week of her muscles quivering and shivering at being so defenceless. She looked so shrunken that I barely saw her when we hugged outside the bank entrance.

'Take deep breaths, Wenling, come on, Wenling, it will be all sorted when we leave this place!' I kept my 'I hope' to myself. With her butt ensconced on the BBVA's plastic chair and holding her mobile, she summed up in one word what made me see red: '*Discrimination.*' Ever since her father died, she hasn't been transferring the miserable annual amount to him, or sending a cent to China, because nothing she tries to send leaves Barcelona, it's insulting for them to put her in the same sack as swindlers, she can show all the inspectors whatever numbers they want to see, everything is up to date with her accountant, all the paperwork is in order, all her taxes paid, she can show that she's earned everything through hard work, after her childhood girlfriends gave her money to top up her savings to enable her to take on the lease. From now on, no help from anyone, *ever*! '*From now on, everything with my hands and my head! Everything!*'

How did it all end? They strung Wenling along for a whole week, she rang twice a day to check, and, '*It's under consideration,*' end of story. It only needed a single blast from me. It might have helped that the bank consultant recognised me from my documentaries. And that I requested chapter and verse about the reasons for the account blocking to give to a pack of journalists I had to hand. She was white as a sheet when she said it was all sorted. Staring at her computer, 'Look, they've just sent me a message that allows me to remove the block.' And she said: 'As of now, what a coincidence.'

One can imagine the fallout from any blocking of the accounts of individuals fully fluent in Catalan or Spanish, with powerful social media, guaranteed legal advice, the right to appeal to the courts and right to vote. And if the blocked, humiliated, slandered and damaged had been called García, Molina, Gil or Vila, and not Liu, Xiang, Hung or Chen? I too feel the indignation, the frenzy, the smashed shop windows, the stink from the burnt ATM, the hue and cry, the headlines, the government crisis, the banks' U-turns. And all in less than twenty-four hours.

★

We walked out of the BBVA with the accounts restored, but it was too early to get plastered, so Wenling invited me in for a cup of tea. *'Lovely, I think no want our money because going to throw us out?'* My body couldn't have felt more upset if a beetle had got down my T-shirt. 'Not at all! What a thing to say! No way, Wenling!' *'Sure?'* 'Nothing to do with it!' *'Seguro?'* *'Segur!'* *'We have all papers in order!'* 'That's right!' *'Why do this to us?'* 'Because… because they are bastards! And… thieves! And because banks always end up working against honest folk!'

Rants, harangues, diatribes meant nothing to Wenling. I told her about how they swindled my grandfather over preferential shares, the evictions, the small print, the looting, the rescue… But Wenling knows all that, that the world belongs to the malingerers, a litany of the usual universal woes wasn't enough. She saw another shadow looming, and as I didn't get it she tried to explain it again: *'I no sleep with problem with banks, cannot… Lovely, this very ancient, but I want my children all Catalan… my life here! If Caixa and BBVA always want our money and now not: is it because send us back to China if Catalonia separate?'*

I should point out that we had this conversation after our AD moment: after the referendum on the 1st of October 2017. Wenling, Yang and all the hairdressing staff saw the beatings, also felt frightened. Thank you, dear bankers, for making sure they felt it on two counts. Because the equation solved itself. Ugly times? Well, perhaps we should pack our bags, for if they're throwing our cash back in our faces, nothing round the corner can be good.

The kettle was boiling and I had a few seconds. To find something to say that wasn't a complete lie. Wenling dropped in the dark-green leaves and took two cups from the shelf, we sat down. 'Everything is topsy-turvy, I'm not surprised you feel scared… But nobody is going to throw you out, Wenling. Things like that don't happen here, this is your home now, you're safe here, believe me, you have to believe me…' Wenling sighed and took a sip of tea. I took one too. An 'I promise you' was in the hot tea scalding my throat.

39

A building project like it was unheard of in California. We're in the middle of the nineteenth century, and you could only dream of such a Herculean feat. Too runtish, they'll never cope, and beware... No Chinks! The contractors didn't want them, but with the pittance they pay the labourers who do sign up they don't have enough to make a start, however tall, sturdy, Irish, Catholic and white they may be. And they'd have to eat their own words with the quantity of hands they needed. No option but to take them. And the Chinese in Sacramento are the first.

The Gold Rush attracted lots of brave Chinese twenty years ago, and they didn't perform badly. On the contrary, as sons of rice-growing families, they brought along knowledge about draining land, diverting streams and fishing any precious sliver that gleamed in the sun. The Chinese filled the coffers of the US Treasury Department with their goodwill. They were also more skilled than anyone at tilling unfriendly land and planting it with more resistant, nourishing varieties. And their good efforts filled the bellies of the European colonisers as well. But all their skills went unnoticed. The Waynes, Fondas, Stewarts, Peppards and Pecks belched after lunch and eclipsed any recognition of those who gilded the Conquest of the Wild West as much or more than they did.

They turn up their noses as they hire the first fifty. They give them picks and shovels, tell them to start as the overseers gawp. We might even turn this madness into reality! And they rush to find more peons for their army. More! More! All we can get! They don't have enough with the Chinese already in California and go direct to their country, to Guangdong province. They already have the ships, from when they kidnapped people from Africa and sailed them off to slavery. Now that's forbidden, they may as well make good use of them. And they load thousands of sons of Guangdong into their vessels, thousands who prefer to take a chance on a bitter, unknown fate than continue starving to death or being killed in wars. It's mainly small peasants who embark, but also blacksmiths, carpenters, cooks, doctors… And they'll all look over their shoulders to capture that last view of their village, fight their melancholy and let themselves be swallowed up by the mists out to sea.

They are mostly young men, with two hands like everybody else, though none can imagine working with them in that giant enterprise, because they think we would need eight or ten to remove snow from the mountains, resist the desert heat, bypass salt lakes, dig out mud, fell entire forests, cross craggy peaks, dynamite rock, erect walls, dig, hammer and carry… Searing indigenous lands with a scar that would scream forever.

These scorned 'Chinks' are ninety per cent of the labourers who between 1864 and 1869 build the first transcontinental railways in the United States. Those who, sleeper by sleeper, carry it from the west and make it reach the two sides of the great nation. Those who, with no mechanised aids, mere hands and feet, shape its bends and curves and bestow the new epoch upon it: Hey, America, you can now board the Train of Modernity! You can now power capitalism forward!

Yes, they bestow. The Central Pacific Railroad will pay the sweat and blood of the Chinese toilers less than half what they pay the Irish. A cut-price feat, and they couldn't be happier. What's more, it turns out the Chinese aren't so prone to be sick. The rice and vegetables they cook make them trip along more lightly than those who only gorge on potatoes. The boiled water they drink drowns bacteria so they don't have constant diarrhoea. Nor do they have to recover from nights spent boozing, because they don't touch liquor. So many individuals under suspicion have rarely responded with such efficiency, resistance and reliability. If it is ever built, it will be the work of giants, said General William T. Sherman. Well, we who have built the railway don't expect to be treated like giants, but maybe we could hear a few grateful words, and even a welcome thanks, Chinese labourers hoped.

But on the 10th of May 1869 in Utah, on the top of the hill, that day when tracks were joined and hands applauded the historic moment, they were forced to admit that the day would bring them joy without pleasure. Chinese workers are nowhere to be seen in the famous photograph because the Central Pacific big bosses don't want them at the official ceremony. Their fingers, their sweat, blood, determination and nous don't stretch to joining the two lines with the last nail. It's made of gold and they don't even get to hammer it in. As soon as the governor of California puts on an act, lifts the pick and delivers the triumphal blow they switch the gold nail for an iron one.

And everything else was like that golden nail: that 10th of May 1869 is also the day when the lies begin. Cleansing the

GEMMA RUIZ PALÀ

celebrations of their presence also meant cleansing their contribution from the public record. It transpires that ghosts built the Transcontinental from the Pacific coast. Chinese workers? What Chinese workers? Bah, Chinese... a handful of Chinks! And the terrain was thus prepared for their efforts and the twelve hundred who died building the track to be finally commemorated with a medal. It will come thirteen years late and be enshrined in law.

Once the gold was exhausted and the railway tracks united, recession began to gallop along the West Coast. Jobs are hit; weekly wages too. White workers start to do their sums and organise: you want to continue greasing the industrial revolution and supporting the lifestyle of the middle classes? Well, pay decent wages! And they stand up. The bosses respond by calling on a third party that's always available when the two of them squabble. Chinks are banned from joining the unions, right? Poker! They'll break the strike for us! Without the union's collective strength, Chinese workers who were looking for a way to earn a dime agree to work for the low rate they're offered. 'Stay out of sight, don't make a noise, don't arouse the beast, watch your back and get by.' The bosses restart production of wool, cigarettes and boots, and white workers are a weakened rival. They are quick to point the finger. They first shout 'Blacklegs!' Then it's: 'Thieves! Savages! Enemies!' But the tag white workers prefer is 'Rats!' The bosses can't believe their luck. They've found a scapegoat and have diverted the workers' anger and now they'll come begging for work with their tails between legs that once swaggered. Could anything be more marvellous? An easy way to inflame supremacists and prejudice at a stroke.

And Chinese Americans will discover that 'We the People…' in the preamble to the hallowed Constitution of the US of A, the heading that should empower everyone, doesn't include them. Chinese Americans aren't part of 'We the People' because they're no longer considered to be individuals, they have become a 'question': The Chinese Question, or carte blanche to attack them in any way you fancy. The dailies advertise 'Great Anti-Chinese Mass Meeting'. 'Chinese? No! No! No!' screech the posters on walls. They are caricatured as worse than worms: one tooth, long nails, a spiteful snarl… repulsion in a single squiggle. 'Shall we have Chinese? No!' they shout from the tribunes. 'The Chinese must go,' replies the audience. 'The Chinese are a source of danger to American civilisation,' it is claimed in political debate. And from words to the burning of shops and homes takes no more than a miserable match. And they burn the few belongings they have, pull their hair, stone them, beat them, lynch them… They kill them and nobody is ever punished. 'They call it exclusion but it's not exclusion, it's extermination,' writes Chan Kiu Sing, a Los Angeles police interpreter.

Because the medal they were owed for the railways they built will be minted with these precise words: Chinese Exclusion Act. In 1882 it's nodded through Congress, and signed off by President Chester A. Arthur – 'If Chinese immigration concentrated in cities where it threatened public order, or if it confined itself to localities where it was an injury to the interests of the American people, the Government of the United States would undoubtedly take steps to prevent such accumulations of Chinese' – and earns pride of place in the roll of honour in the Universal History of Shame. The Chinese Exclusion Act denies the status of citizen to those who already live in the United States and decrees that no more Chinese should be allowed in, categorising a whole people as a 'race' for the first time, and banning it. Pioneers to the marrow of their bones, the US of A anticipate Germany's anti-Semitic laws by fifty years. Adolf Hitler will publicly praise institutional American racism, be its protégé, reproduce, extend and inflate it to the... Shoah.

However, if blocking the way to the filthy Chinese muck 'responsible for demoralising our people, bringing degradation and dishonor to our labor and undermining the integrity of the racial composition of America' might have meant losing strategic Chinese businessmen, the most well-disposed diplomats and the most brilliant Chinese students, then it would be a bad move. They shouldn't repudiate 'good Chinamen', those who were worthy of America. And so it was. They approve specific measures so they can have a margin of freedom: problem solved.

From 1882 on, ordinary Chinese will be treated as illegal unless they can prove the contrary: not carrying documents was to be cast into the slough of deportation. There was a world of difference between having exemption papers or exclusion papers in your pocket. With that legislative slamming of the door, 'excluded' Chinese Americans were left with half a heart in America and half outside. They couldn't leave for fear of not being able to return, and they weren't authorised to bring parents, siblings, wives or children from China. And after declaring that marriages between Chinese and Americans were illegal, the Chinese Exclusion Act introduced another sentence, the condemning of affection: bachelorhood. On top of the sadness that always accompanies solitude, they also had to suffer a series of insults. Model American families – father, mother, children – kept away from them as if they had the plague: keep an eye on those little men that nobody wants, it must be with good reason! They didn't want to know the real reason, and clung to their own: rats addicted to opium, dog-eating rats, indecent rats, depraved rats, dangerous rats...

'We are isolated, scattered and segregated. We are trying to do something. Something that only needs water, soap and an iron,' a laundryman will write. 'When we wash and iron our customers' clothes we think of our beloved ones. That hurts, but it keeps us going day after day, month after month. Banned though we are, we have become a curiosity. They study us. They write about us. They take photographs of us. They continue to see us as perpetual foreigners. Are we still not all equal under the sun?'

Those Chinese Americans weren't daft. Like Shakespeare's Shylock, they lamented. But they immediately had to wipe the tears from their eyes and rise to the challenge: a basketful of clothes was waiting.'Eight-Pound Livelihood' was the name they gave to battling with three and a half kilos of iron, standing on your feet, twenty hours a day, six days a week, after sweating hard to wash a load in unventilated dens. They made it their way to earn a living. No American complained they were taking jobs away from them and with the tiniest of loans they had enough to open a small laundry. They stayed unseen, didn't make a fuss, didn't arouse the beast, watched their backs, and got by.

Deprived as they were of citizenship, they had also been deprived of any labour contract. And as there were no Chinese women to fob off with demeaning tasks, that bachelor community saved their bacon by doing 'women's work'. Chinese Americans demonstrated to the most reluctant that cleaning up other people's shit wasn't part and parcel of being born a woman, it was only a matter of degree: the lower they say you deserve to be on life's ladder, the more reason why you belong to those who must soap, rub, rinse, wring and iron.

Chinese Americans also had to confront another truth: racism and classism have selective memories. Because no matter that they found the 'Chinks' disgusting, no matter that they wanted the 'Chinks' far from their doorsteps, Americans forgot that was such a big deal with every gleaming-white, smooth, warm and fragrant bundle of clothes they unwrapped. No inkling that those hands they thought so repugnant and wanted kept out of their sight were the very same that week after week treated so carefully the clothes they would then wear next to their skin.

They earned more by wearing white gloves and serving up dishes to the wealthy, even double. But setting up by oneself, being self-employed, had a virtue: not having a boss. Their self-esteem had been so battered that every day they earned money without being given orders or insulted, they felt it revive a little. Besides, if you worked in an American household, you lost your name. It was invariably changed to Charlie Chinaman. The category of Chinese servant made people identical and blank. It didn't distinguish faces, ages, height, quirks or character: they were all the same Charlie Chinaman. As if their uniforms didn't hide an inner soul. As if they were automata.

Some were talented cooks and preferred to burn their fingers over hobs and not among sheets, handkerchiefs and underpants stiff with dirt. That's how restaurants were the second leg supporting the Chinese of America. In Guangdong province they'd never eaten such trifling, basic, over-fried dishes so bereft of fish and spices. However, the Americans had a coarse taste and licked their fingers, from their pinkies to their thumbs, and spent. They soon had a measure of their tastes and their inventions came: chop suey as king, a dish they could make from everything that was fresh, all shredded but big enough for their suspicious clientele to identify common vegetables and proper meat – neither dog nor rat. They could make chop suey from everything, for those guys crunched the lot. General Tso's chicken also made its mark. If General Tso had ever existed, I'm sure he'd have spat it out with a snarl, it was a cut so soaked in sweet sauce that in no time it became America's national dish.

Americanising an ancient, rich and complex cuisine like that of the Chinese also meant infantilising it, and it upset them no end; it was yet another affront to add to the list. When they went into the shop to make the monthly transfer to their family, the sacrileges they committed daily in their woks flew from their minds. That moment was half their life. Because who says shop says pharmacy-post office-tea salon-social club... everything. What would those bachelors with eyes worn out by so many insults and such grief have done otherwise? Without a friendly spot where they could relax and chat, they'd have thought they'd come into this world only to break their backs. Those little shops gave them proof that they too had been born with individual features, feelings, love and passion that waxed hot and cold in the same winter and the same summer as an

American, and that if you pricked them, they also bled, and if you tickled them, they also laughed.

The old bachelors had to die alone and the young ones had to grow old until the Second World War began. 1943 is the year they can celebrate a common enemy: Japan. The United States and China had to pretend they liked each other enough to become allies and defend each other and President Franklin D. Roosevelt asked Congress to repeal the Chinese Exclusion Act: 'Nations, like individuals, make mistakes. We must be big enough to acknowledge our mistakes of the past and to correct them.' However, the manoeuvre was quite laughable. America will open its doors to a maximum of one hundred and fifty Chinese individuals a year.

It won't be until President Lyndon Johnson feels the wind of change from the civil rights movement that he will sign the Immigration and Nationality Law: 'It has been un-American in the highest sense, because it has been untrue to the faith that brought thousands to these shores even before we were a country.' In that year of 1965, institutional discrimination is abolished: the people who came from China will no longer be proscribed and as many as want can now come in. And that change lights up their faces. And the way they walk. Chinese Americans no longer walk alone as owls, fearful and forever up against the wall. They are now accompanied by a big family that is a joy to see. For the first time their voices are heard, their hands seen to wave, 'Kids, watch out for the tram,' and there'll be the hint of a smile... Hey, they're token gestures. Sure, but gestures made by individuals who are convinced they are real people at every hour of the day and in the pupils of every eye.

But the story that started with a gold dust sieve, a pick and a shovel doesn't get the happy ending that some expect in the cinema. Chinese Americans will no longer be illegal until they can prove the opposite; they can live their lives without so many snares, but they will still be damned. To not finding American compatriots who will rent or sell them an apartment outside their confines, for starters. To huddle in neighbourhoods whose very name indicates they aren't quite America, that where you tread now is Chinatown. It is always the same town planner who designs the ghetto: racism. However much the new generations know the hymn, stand to attention, hand on chest, and sing with each and every star. However much they study, excel, export their talent made in the USA throughout the world. Despite all that, the caricatures that illustrated the 'Chinese? No! No! No!' posters will still be etched on the brains of American Americans. It is those drawings, not the contributions of the Chinese, that figure in the cast for the historical narrative. Radio and television will elevate them into national stereotypes that will become definitive with the advent of television: they will be packaged for popular culture and spread to the ends of the earth, to where the Chinese roam. And primitive, devious Fu Manchus with faces smeared yellow will mutate into mysterious sellers of Gremlins, later into brawny porters, then computer geeks, footloose karatekas and chefs with twenty-four-hour smiles... Roles of extras with the odd sentence to say. And full of 'rrs' to make it seem they still twist everything, which we continue to find a hoot.

Those who are the butt of the gags don't laugh. Even today, in the twenty-first century, throughout the world, they must still endure the slander, the pain and the wailing, and, just like Wenling, seek shelter in the blues of those first brothers who went to America: 'Stay out of sight, make no sound, don't arouse the beast, watch your back and get by.'

40

Chips off the same block, this father and son. Real beanpoles with the same disconcerted faces after landing in this world. The father's in no hurry, he likes Yang to linger over his fringe, they chat and laugh. In contrast the son is never still, he can't find a way to kill his boredom. That's when the first disagreements begin. The kid goes over to Haitao to get an eyeful of the game he's playing, and Haitao moves to another seat and protects his tablet as if he were the United Kingdom denying Egypt the Rosetta Stone. I imagine he needs a degree of privacy to decimate his monsters. And I also imagine how incredibly fed up the poor boy must be, trying to find entertainment in a silly grown-up like me. 'I like your backpack!' 'Oh, thanks, what's your name?' '*I'm*... I'm Han.' 'Hello, Han, pleased to meet you!' and we break the ice with a high five. He tells me he is nine years old, that he adores every kind of animal and that they're going to the Museu Blau tomorrow. His payback for this stint at the hairdresser's. Because his father and Yang chat non-stop and hit it off so well *because they both come... like from the same place in China*. From Taizhou, the city with all those fishermen? And now he has good reason to look disconcerted. 'Yessss! How come you know?' 'Well, because Yang told me.' 'In my class nobody knows what Taizhou is!' 'Why don't you take in some photos and show them? Maybe they'll think it's as great as I do.' 'OK!' And I leave him with that idea and vibes he's never felt before.

More children, more fathers. Mothers. Some mothers see their children as a revealing reflection of themselves, while others feel they're like an extension that flees the nest and sets up all alone. Two world views. I'd say Mireia and Kristin, for example, are one from each category. They've just come in. Not a minute between them.

Wenling is redrawing a young man's eyebrows while she's got me soaking my hands. From where she's standing, she waves a hello that's also an 'I can't see to you right now' and dips the little stick into the fake toffee the wax makes. I get how their cheerfulness goes out of the window as they retreat to the bench in the entrance. '*Fine, I'll wait!*' they both chorus. And although it's common knowledge that the idea that other people's children always shoot up more quickly is much disputed, it seems incredible that Mireia's boy is already walking and that Kristin's girl already talks twenty to the dozen. It came so easily to her, and her battery's always charged… she observes everything and then wants to recite every detail. 'Oh my God, such a gift of the gab… my boy says nothing, laughs and then streaks off doing his own thing. No, Èric, *amore!*' 'Did you put a rein on him?' 'Come here, quick!' 'Like a dog-leash but for a child, I'm thinking of buying one…' 'I didn't need to, Lila has always helped me, I mean she's always behaved so well… Yes, today I'll have a haircut, I really will!'

Kristin gets a storybook for her daughter from her tote bag and stands up. Elegant and refined as ever, and a zombie. 'I'll look after her!' But Kristin's not listening to Mireia anymore. She walks straight to Yang, as if there was nothing more pressing in the Milky Way. He grabs a handful of ends and whispers in her ear: 'Good riddance! *What you say? Your hair short as her?*' 'Her' means me and I act as if I'm half dozing off because the water is so relaxing. But Kristin tries hard to catch my eye so she can give me a wink, and succeeds. She's bolder than I am. 'No, just under my ears, OK, Yang?' '*OK. You different person today… wash first.*' He unfolds a towel for her and stares hard. '*Short, you sure?*' 'Really!' Kristin slumps down in the backwash chair, lets her hair cascade down and closes her eyes.

★

It hadn't been a bad weekend. Quite the reverse, they'd been able to go to Cerdanya after lots of plans fell through at the last minute. It was crisp and cold, the sun shone down and there was not a wisp of mist in the sky. They loaded up their backpacks and climbed as far as the Estany de Malniu. All broad smiles in their photos, a day to remember. After lunch, a good siesta, a strong coffee and a big shop at the Puigcerdà supermarket, and, in the evening, Lila to the neighbours so they could go out for dinner. Carpaccios, smoked delights, reductions and the last word in rosé. A toast. And on the way back, those blank eyes that turn her into the enemy.

Screams and shoves over a passing snowflake, right in the first weeks they were married. Grabbing her by the neck when their little girl made it to six months. Grabbing her by the neck and throttling her when their daughter was about to hit her second birthday. But outright bloodletting that was so hard to staunch, never. Until that morning in the apartment in Cerdanya that was all wood and so cheerful. Floors, walls, carpets, cushions, red and sticky. They were scrubbing hour after hour. Her husband with both hands; Kristin with only the one. The other was holding in place cotton wool soaked in peroxide. Because this time he'd cracked open her skull. On the door.

'Ohhh… ohhh…' Moans that hurt the ear more than any shriek. 'I've got… I had warts, Yang… *the stitches are still there*, sorry, I forgot to tell you.' '*No worries, no worries, I wash more gently.*' We can't know what kind of zip Yang's fingers encountered, but he was taken aback. He frowns, controls the water, tests its warmth with the palm of his hand and rinses hair that now seems made of crystal. He gingerly covers her head and this time his question is no joke: '*Today cut hair really?*'

You'll have your little girl and someone to love, Kristin dreamed. And she had to bolster her self-esteem. She bid farewell to always wearing a helmet, to en-suite double bedrooms, to intimate tables in bar corners and frolicking on beaches under a friendly full moon. She said goodbye, she said thank you, she unhooked herself from his embrace with the expression of someone on a sinking ship, and spent a week writing and erasing the same WhatsApp message. Writing and erasing. Writing and erasing. Writing and erasing.

Lila didn't only learn to speak before time. She was a little imp and could climb up to get the Kleenex. She scratched her legs with the packet and said, Mummy, Mummy, song! She pulled on her skirt when she saw her daydreaming in the middle of the dining room and said, Mummy, Mummy, street! She knocked on the bathroom door when she took too long and said, Mummy, Mummy, game! She'd performed so often for both of them. In the kitchen at home, in the car, in the apartment in Cerdanya. She invented new ones whenever she saw that mouths and words were starting to sag. Lila carried a light from another planet. And a strong beam of light needs space to shine in, not miserable, mean crevices to slip through. Of course it does!

★

The young man's eyebrows are done and Wenling is weighing up the situation. Haijun has just arrived, so can keep an eye on the kids. She pinches my cheek and hands me over to the apprentice manicurist. She'll do Kristin when Yang's finished her hair, and she takes Mireia into the small room. She spots me. 'Hey, hello! I haven't seen you for ages! How are you? Look at me, more piercings, as hairy as ever, but not so dumb: I'm going to uni.' She turns round with a smile and puts her arm around Wenling. 'Only half leg, dear, I'm not going swimming,' and she says that with such clear blue eyes that the blotches on her teeth enamel vanish.

It was the train or the sea, take your pick. She'd often seen the old folks at nine coming back from their early-morning dip, and had a good laugh. Well, Mireia started doing exactly that. She got up at first light every morning. Her mother had no more flesh to pinch, shouting to her to get up: rage is the best alarm clock. She would race along the esplanade, throw off her trainers and run, arms open wide, to be swallowed up by the waves. But Mireia always surfaced panting victory. Then swam and swam and swam until her heart said that's enough and she would let herself float. Who needs palm trees? In the end she thought those apartment blocks that liquefied with each sway and shimmy were a photogenic high point. Grey, white, blue. Grey, white, blue. Grey, white, blue. Mireia needed peace from war. And her opponent was so reasonable, it must be said: the water let her dive in without stunning her. She never again looked at timetables or rail tracks.

And with all those struggles out to sea, Mireia found she became less sharp-tongued. She carried her boy around her neck without being pestered, she called him '*amore*', she planted big kisses on his arms and pulled faces to make him laugh. And all of a sudden she was enrolling for a degree. Deep down she'd never given up on Computer Engineering. The only drawback was coming home by herself, depending on the time, which she hated. And Mireia was always on the lookout not just for anyone but for dreadlocks, mohicans and piercings. Like the police, but in reverse: she looked out for them to be up there with them. It was always the same people at help points and anti-fascist demos; she would sigh in relief if she recognised someone who'd be walking home along the same road as her. She knew how to distinguish rapists in a mayor's clothing.

*

'Wow, Kristin, you look spectacular!' Mireia and Wenling have just come from the depilating session. '*Yes, you very lovely!*' 'You really mean that? Was it a good idea to get it cut?' Kristin has to swallow hard, the effort chokes her and she starts sobbing.

'Do-not let my little girl see me-ee…' And Wenling immediately looks to see if the children are still with Haijun. Yes, and very quiet too, drawing on sheets of paper on the floor. They stand either side of Kristin and listen to what she has to say.

When they stitched up her gash, she left the hospital and went straight to her lawyer's. Now she's got an apartment, a small one. For now she's decided to live near him; she prefers it that way so Lila doesn't have to change school. Who knows what she'll do later, but for now just to get out of that mess. 'Oh my God,' I hear myself exclaiming, and I can't believe it, I've done it, I've taken that step. And the three of them become a huddle of heads, arms and hands.

Until Yang intervenes to defend his handiwork. '*Hey, head not touch! Hair lot of work!*' And he separates them out, wanting them to weep from joy or indignation, whatever. Wenling slaps him with a cloth, '*Get away, loco,*' Mireia lets rip a 'Beat it, you idiot', and Kristin mouths a thank you and holds out her hand. And when Yang leaves, they pick up the thread.

'Apartment, lawsuit, divorce, the lot! Hell, he shouldn't go near her! We can't make life easy for them, sod it! Those hard knocks made me see the light, didn't they, Wenling?' Mireia is full on with her exams. Now they only greet the sea from the sand, when she takes Èric for a little walk every afternoon: the one who gets to the flagpole first can tickle the other's ribs! 'If I tell you what I'd have done to him at the start… And sure it's great we look identical, and not because I think I'm a total cutie, you know what I mean… My degree and a job, so he doesn't get hit with my shit, get me? Well, and my mother too… without her neither I nor my kid would be here now, that's true.'

Kristin can only nod, she faces a tougher climb. But she'll do it, she will, Lila goes over to egg her on. 'Mummy, Mummy, will I get my new bed today? And what about the little stars you can see by night?' They've reduced all the wax crayons to the size of a lentil and Haijun has had to give up. There won't be a brush left intact if Èric is allowed a minute more in the hairdresser's. Mireia puts him around her neck, 'Christ, what a weight!' And walks out blowing kisses in every direction, 'Bye, bye, bye!'

'Yes, I see it, *I see it*, Wenling, *I see it*,' says Kristin, while Wenling spreads a final drop of protective oil on each cuticle half-moon. 'But then, I think…' '*Not think, lovely, you no think anymore, that already late!*'

'*That already late.*' She summed it up precisely with those three words.

41

'*Hola,¡no hablo catalán!*' says a hipster holding his hands in the air. A hipster who's way off beam, who's taken the norm to be the exception. With Yang's good-humoured '*I no speak Catalan either*', he sees it's no crime, that we won't hurt him, that he can take it easy. And he relaxes. '*For a cut and, hey, do you remove… little hairs?*' '*Where?*' Yang asks, and the hipster points to his lughole. '*Ears? You wait a minute, please.*' 'OK, OK,' he replies, sticking his hands in his pockets.

'*Today no cut you.*' 'Hey, I'm so happy to see you too, Yang.' He chuckles. '*You not diez days.*' 'Yes, it's deu, it is,' I protest, 'or a good quinze.' '*No, not quince, I sure.*' 'Yes, yes, quinze, I'm sure.' Our Spanish–Catalan banter could last until tomorrow, we're both so stubborn. '*OK, Wenling busy, you cut with me first.*'

My cut flies by. I may even have dozed off. '*Good?*' 'Very,' I reply, not even needing to look in the mirror, and I go off with the boss.

'*You work now?*' 'No, I'm free, what do you need, Wenling?' '*Sure? No hurry? You can after manicure?*' Yes, but maybe tell me what it's about first?' She laughs and tells Haijun, who is rushing out of the backroom far too fast. 'Great! You and I together opticians.' 'Oh, that, of course, as soon as my nails are dry, I'll go with you.' '*You collect Haijun new glasses, you can, sure?*'

207

'Yes, I can, Wenling. Your mother does go on, Haijun…' And a spoilsport because she stops our banter by landing a slap on the middle of Haijun's back, '*You straight!*' 'Ouch,' Hajun complains; 'Hell, Wenling!' I complain in turn. '*When older, back not move, then I can do nothing.*' No, she's right enough, branches have to straighten when they're still growing, after that, too bloody bad. It's the method, the method is a knockout. 'Hey, let's get going,' I say, shaking the dust off my hands, 'let's move before she blasts both of us.' I stick my tongue out at her and she returns the favour.

'First can we look around here?' Now I understand her ophthalmic euphoria: today is the Saturday street market. We stop at every stall selling pretty little trinkets. 'Hey, look at this. Hey, look at that.' She points at small silver hoop earrings, coloured thread and metal bracelets, with all manner of pendants. 'I love them! Aren't they cute?' She pulls my hand, leads me through the crowd to dally at this stall, now that one, she holds my hand, up and down we go. We'd still be there, if I hadn't made a suggestion.

'Come on, Haijun, choose a bangle, a present from me.' 'Nooo! Mother will kill me!' I could hardly insist. It reminded me of that slap still echoing round my head. I backtracked when I saw Haijun lift her hands to her head as if she'd fished a biscuit in shiny paper out of a box of Birba cookies. 'OK, forget it, some other time, there are more days than *llonganisses* in this life!' I said, pouring oil on the flame, the fear on her face fading immediately. 'Hahaha, did you say *llonganisses*? *Llonganisses* are like long cold sausages, I guess?' 'The same family, and people say that because every home used to have lots of *llonganisses*, and they seemed to last forever. One day we must eat some.' And I put the bag over my shoulder again. 'Should we go to the optician's?'

'Oh dear, it's shut! Now mother will be angry!' Hands on head again. 'No probs, what if we say they shut on Saturday afternoons? Will that fix it?' 'Yes, it will!' We high-fived and endorsed our first white lie together. Because we missed out by so little. They were turning over the sign, and waved us away and it was clear we'd not been a hundred per cent focused on carrying out the mission we'd been charged with.

True enough, the new glasses were really playing hard to get. We turned tail and, as if nothing was amiss, went on rating the awesome stuff on offer that Haijun loved so much. 'If you say, you not forget!' And now I must concentrate and keep my wits about me.

The second we walk in, Wenling starts up her chorus of *thanks-thanks-thanks* and I derail her, 'No thanks needed, we've not got any glasses, we failed, it was shut.' '*Thanks all the same,*' and she pushes us into the backroom. Haijun and I take advantage of her being behind us to exchange victorious winks.

She's prepared a bite to eat and some fine showstoppers before the usual fruit. Some great-smelling meat and mushroom dumplings are steaming on the kitchen table. Tasty! And as it's obvious I say that with my mouth full, Haijun can also say it's lovely and display her half-chewed food without inhibitions. Wenling keeps a firm hold on her hand. '*You and you: shut mouth!*' She can't tolerate such a sight. It goes without saying that the effect she achieves is the opposite of what she wanted, because we respond with an 'Oh!' that's more startling than two choristers from the Orfeó choir. '*So disgusting!*' And she can't help but laugh too. Haijun doesn't miss a trick and gobbles down two more dumplings in quick succession, yum yum, without chewing them. 'They're so nice, I can't stop!' 'Hahaha, but take a breather!' And I now rate everything I'm enjoying in this kitchen, and at the top I put Haijun eating so enthusiastically and ditching that hateful obsession with being skinny.

And Wenling makes me climb three notches at a stroke: '*Next Sunday, no, the next one, no, the one after: you want to come with me and the kids?*' And from the computer screen they ask: 'Do you want the first cherries? Fructus, straight from the branch to your house.'

'Me? Pick cherries? With you? By coach?' Wenling starts to look worried, all the signs indicating the prelude to a short circuit. '*If you work, or something, or don't want, it's alright, lovely.*' 'No, no, I mean, yes, yes!' I titter. I capitalise the event on my mobile's calendar and Haijun says, 'One thing, just one thing! You before ask, now I can say: pianist.' Her mouth is filled with Beethoven, Bach and Mozart with double the enthusiasm she showed for the dumplings we've just scoffed, and that's saying something. I feel so sorry I have to go now, because she's on a roll. She's telling me about how to position your hands, about the keyboard her parents have bought her, about the new piece she's got to study… 'Haijun, have you got a scrap of paper?' 'Yes!' And she comes back with a Post-it. 'Right, let me write it legibly for you… Here you are, look it up on YouTube and tell me if you think it's awesome: it's my all-time favourite.'

42

A mohair jersey after a fifty-degree wash. A city with an architectural heritage in the style of Robert Moses or Núñez y Navarro. A facial expression after plastic surgery. These are things you can't repair. Wenling believes that lost causes are a husband who's mistreated you and a family that's neglected you. They've shot themselves in the foot: *that now late.*

★

It was time to bury him. She'd thrown her handful of earth and was turning round like everyone else when she saw her again. She'd seen her climbing the bottom of the hill that would shelter her father forever. Who could that straight-backed lady be, she whispered to her friend-sister. She didn't ring any bells. Not surprising, after so many years away. But she ought to know her, knowing, as she did, the whole of Qingtian. Perhaps a time comes when your brain eliminates faces to make room for new ones, pondered Wenling, and she scrutinised her again. Something to take her mind off the banging of nails and hammer that were sealing the coffin so tactfully. There was something about her. Maybe it was her profile. Or her majestic neck. She was such a tall, slender old lady. A relative? But everyone in her house was a little runt, no

211

exceptions. Father, grandmother, uncles and aunts, cousins, all shorties.

Obviously, she wasn't counting those on the other side. But you can't count them in a flicker of your eyelids, when you've a hundred families.

★

With a not-yet-one-year-old baby in their arms, the couple who'd brought Wenling into the world decided to go their different ways. And he wanted to hold on to his daughter. Or to put it bluntly: he wouldn't allow the child's mother to keep her. He was vindicated by the chain of obedience, silence and fear that constituted the law of men, that made it easy: he could snaffle her up in one swoop, and no complaints, no reprisals, no judges or deals. That girl bore his blood, end of story, and belonged to him.

What he would do with her wasn't so clear to that young country lad who wanted no more back-breaking agricultural labour. Nor did he want to follow all those men and women from Qingtian who had travelled twelve thousand kilometres from their country. Better be wary of the fame of Xibanya, he'd say: rolling up a bundle of belongings was to risk becoming a leaf blowing in the wind. Inwardly he was thinking: spend your life working more hours than there are on the clock and never a binge on the side? Breaking every bone in your body! Because Wenling's father wasn't one of the bravest men in Qingtian, but one who preferred to live it up. One who believed it was never time to go home. Who wanted to be the life and soul of the party. Who felt a rush of blood, and wasn't satisfied by ruddy cheeks; he wanted his hands to simmer. Only after he'd let rip a good few times would he consider retiring. So Wenling's father opted to stay in town, and be a lazybones during the day and a hellraiser at night. His daughter could be the leaf. The storm came unprompted, with that father of many trades and master of none.

First of all he went to Kuishi, the hamlet to the south of Qingtian where he was born. He tried to do what he'd seen widows do, or those who for whatever reason no longer had a wife and hadn't yet found a replacement: hand the baby over to mother. You can always rely on your mother. However, he was the true son of his father.

Wenling's father saw a spitting image of himself, ruddy-cheeked, vicious-tempered, and was scared. If he didn't take his granddaughter away from there, he'd throw her in the river, Wenling's father's father threatened, get out of here! Right now! Grandfather would keep his reasons to himself until after he'd slammed the door. Did he think he was going to deprive him of his wife? Now he was a geriatric! Her with a runt around her neck all day? Who'd look after him? Who'd feed him? He was a lousy son, a louse!

Wenling's grandmother hadn't moved from behind the stove. She saw that her husband had finished his tirade and was coming over to her, and she dipped the pinkie of her left hand in the embers. Hey, you're not really crying, are you? Her eyes were a fountain, but she showed him scorched flesh. He couldn't beat her.

After that first door slammed in his face, Wenling's father had to knock on others. Literally. Every two months, or three at most, Wenling passed from the hands of a neighbour, relative or acquaintance to the next person who didn't have the heart to refuse a roof to such a live wire. She never blubbed, and was always full of energy and song. That youngster performed so many times. So they weren't shirty and didn't say no, so as not to anger her father. And he trundled his little bundle around the whole of Qingtian, from house to house till she was eight, up to a hundred, easily. Just do your sums.

When she was older, she always found someone to say hello to on any street. She would ask them how they were feeling, and bring a little something and call them 'aunty'. Because it was the wives of those neighbours, relatives or acquaintances who'd said yes who had first cut her hair and nails. Who had taught her to eat with chopsticks, who had held out their arms to help her walk by herself. Who had tied her to a bulrush chair so she couldn't move, who'd let snot trickle down her nose until it hardened, who couldn't squeeze her in because there were already so many bairns in their small den. Wenling had all kinds of aunties scattered around Qingtian, a red dot here, there and everywhere… A map of a hundred families. And she'd have added more if her grandfather hadn't kicked the bucket.

They'd come to be friends because now and then they'd meet up on the sly, as they were so afraid of him. News spreads quickly around villages. Come if you want to see her, your granddaughter is at my place, they got the message to her. And grandmother still remembered how to fly. From Kuishi to Qingtian, as if there were a fire raging. She was breathless when she reached the spot to embark on the tortoise, the flatboat that ferried them across the river. Up and out, Luli! She was the first to jump on land and run off again. Zigzagging down side streets, under wooden porches, between stalls, dodging bikes and carts. Until a pair of eyes peered from behind a door and swallowed her inside. The road from Qingtian to Kuishi always seemed double its actual length. Grief also made her sandals pinch.

Wenling's grandmother had never wished anyone dead but... A stubborn clod like him just had to go where he shouldn't, and bang, he cocked up his toes.

It was the morning of New Year's Day when her father was able to leave her in Kuishi with her grandmother. The moment Wenling set foot in her little house, it seemed to shiver with cold and fill with smoke. Proof that there might be someone who celebrated her life every second rather than complaining that she was a nuisance. She stuck to her and acted like her walking stick for the whole day. It was a real effort to unhook her when it was bedtime! But grandmother's blanket smelled of her: a sprig of freshly cut jasmine. Falling asleep had never been so pleasant.

Wenling grew up in the Nineties without television, radio or telephone. And the wok was never rinsed so as not to waste a drop of oil. A childhood of daily rice, not every day. Filled up on sweet potato. Of soups made from seaweed, cabbage and ginger. A spot of pig's blood to give it strength when cauliflowers grew beautifully in the garden and grandmother could give them as payment to the lad who pushed the kids' cart. A small red-bean bun now and then. And when it was stifling hot, a lolly from the shop of a thousand delights at the side of the main road. Grandmother did everything she could with her hands:

breed hens, cultivate her garden, sell its produce, collect small branches and tie them to canes to make brushes, darn clothes… And all so her granddaughter could answer the question, 'What did you eat today?' without feeling ashamed. That was the only 'Hello, how are we?' in that neck of the woods. All the idlers you met asked: 'What did you eat today?' Whenever people said hello: 'What did you eat today?' And never ill, she was told to emphasise, in case the neighbours became too nosey.

The era of polluting the earth, air and rivers hadn't yet come, but it wasn't far off. In Wenling's grandmother's hamlet nature still acted as a cure for whatever you might catch thereabouts. She had roots and herbs aplenty to remedy all her little illnesses. She also knew how to cure her with one hand, when she thought some germ was taking too firm a hold. She made a pincer with the knuckles of her first and second fingers and began to pinch on either side of her neck. Again and again, however loud she squealed, again and again, however much she begged her to stop. She kept on until the bruising turned blue. Those atavistic squeezes blocked the path of a current that had lost its way and put it back on track. There were treatments that cured dizziness, debility and retching that were taught at home with the same degree of importance as reading and writing at school.

It was also thanks to her grandmother that Wenling crossed the threshold of one of those for the first time when she was eight. It wasn't easy to scorn hands to help her scour her stone-strewn vegetable patch, but she didn't want her to be sold short as she had been. Study is always a first defence, she reflected when she watched her carrying the cloth bag she'd made for her exercise books. She also said: 'Let the girl who has more roads to walk eat!' And she didn't touch her rations for the day.

Whereas her father visited occasionally, but always flat broke. He brought merely black eyes and failure. The good side was that his accordion of wrinkles smoothed a little at the sight of his daughter acting so alertly. Her school work was always spotless, always the best calligraphy. 'That's what I like, you stay top of the class!' And he gently patted the back of her head. Grandmother would fill another bowl, let him chat for a while and he'd soon leave.

Some afternoons, though very few, fewer than the fingers on her hands, her father took her on a little trip around Qingtian. Wenling always hoped that it was time for those strawberries that climb up trees in those parts, because it meant she would see him for most of the day. Her father taught her to choose the ripest and pick them without damaging the branches. He hoisted her on his shoulder so she could reach them and let her pick every one. They ate huge quantities. However much he tried not to be, her father seemed another person amid so much green. A much better one, at that.

*

It was one day when they were coming back from strawberry-picking that she asked him. 'You don't have one. And you'll not have a father either if I hear you asking me that again,' he replied, flaring up like a torch. And she had to appeal to her grandmother.

'Grandmother, where is she? Grandmother, can we go? Grandmother, can you take me?' And that was only the first round of questions. 'Grandmother, who is she? Grandmother, what is she like? Grandmother, do I look like her?' And the third: 'Grandmother, why doesn't she come? Grandmother, why doesn't she want to see me? Grandmother, why did she leave me?' She had to say 'grandmother' to start off every question and chase after her and look her in the face if she didn't want to be left speaking to a wall. It was a cat-and-mouse game, and always a reluctant one. 'Get out of my way.' She acted as if she'd not heard her, never gave her an answer.

That one person could create so much consternation only inflamed her desire to find out. 'Mummy-mummy-mummy-mummy-mummy,' she shouted hoarsely when she was walking across the village. 'Mummy-mummy-mummy-mummy-mummy,' she repeated in bed when she could hear her grandmother snoozing. Just in case, apart from annoying them so, she thought those two syllables she shouted so furiously might serve another purpose. 'Mummy-mummy-mummy-mummy-mummy,' in case she put in a sudden appearance. 'Mummy-mummy-mummy-mummy-mummy,' and clear up all her doubts.

It didn't happen that night. Nor the next, nor the one long after that. She had to wait twenty-seven years and for the last in the queue to pay her condolences. It was that straight-backed, tall, slender old lady who'd made her head spin throughout the funeral. It was her mother's mother and there she was standing opposite her. Wenling disinterred her other grandmother on the day she buried her father. Don't look for coincidences, the conversation began right there, and didn't start well. Now he has left this world, you can be part of our family, she had come to tell her. Wenling still hadn't got her breath back. That lady took advantage of the lull and told her what she thought she most wanted to know: that her mother died when Wenling was eighteen, that she'd gone to the other end of the province, that she'd made her life anew, but never, for a single day, had she stopped thinking about her. Never, she repeated, never.

As if the end of that report was enough to answer all her questions.

Wenling didn't linger long. Her feet were freezing. She beckoned to Xiaolu and they quickly walked off. Her reply was a no.

★

When she was telling me all this, she seemed really convinced. '*Now I have husband, and children, and now a family.*' But she was seething inside, she really was. '*My father acted bad to my mother, but I? I do nothing! And why do I never know mother? Why?*' And let no one tell her that that man was a death threat to her mother, or that the law had her tied, hands and feet. Wenling called for simply one thing: an act of defiance. Daring, mischief, fighting, window-breaking and a gang led by her mother that took her off at midnight with perfectly choreographed feline movements. Simply that. And they'd have confronted her father later, defended their actions, told him you can't just erase people. Later, but first mother and daughter had to be together.

But her mother never came through her window. She would never know the lilt of her voice when she laughed or when she scolded. Or whether she had the same slender fingers. Or the same little nose, or eye colour. Or whether the height that had leaped two generations to give Haijun her bone structure had also been hers.

Wenling's mother was a gossip-ridden ghost. Inevitably when she was older she kept finding out bits, somebody always bursts the balloon and lets slip that the lass was forced to leave town because she'd gone crazy, shouting out her daughter's name and putting her hands on her neck, on the hole she said was spurting black blood that only she could see.

But if she'd believed all the tittle-tattle, she'd have sentenced herself to venerating a burial shroud. Wenling preferred to cherish reproaches that can provoke life. And she wrote the story from the first line. The revelations now coming from her new grandmother dredged up memories of the only flesh and bone she'd known as a parent. It was time to stop making excuses for him. And tear up the page and start another.

And that couldn't be. *That now late.* Wenling tried to turn it over. Time slipped away from her like a stream, she translated for me on the screen of her mobile.

*

I've lost so many other versions of Wenling making their escape between so many reductive words. How many Wenlings does she lose? Few things can undermine your morale as much as to hear a substitute for yourself speaking another language. To know the moment's now come when you have to strip your thoughts bare because you can't make them leave your lips in the clothes they ought to wear. It must be mortifying that shedding complexity, shades of meaning, subtexts and irony must now be your daily fucking bread. Not to mention her first weeks in Barcelona. When she was transformed into an 'illiterate', into the condemned woman Ágota Kristóf wrote she had become in exile in Switzerland. 'When you understand nothing, when the social desert and cultural desert begin for you.'

The day she shared her childhood with me, we exchanged telephone numbers. I don't remember why, it probably seemed a natural step. I looked to see what image she had on her WhatsApp, in case it was anything that might help me to understand her better. I clicked and a bouquet of jasmine blossomed.

43

Cherry Sunday is here already. We jump onto the coach and after a first look around, a question: where are the dads? There's not one, not even a token dad. All mothers with their children, just like Wenling. They look astonished to see me and I'd say they want to ask a different question: what am I doing there? The driver and I are the only white faces. But no nasty glares, only curiosity. And that vanishes the moment they see me sit down with my friends.

We say hello to the neighbours on the aisle and are greeted by a little chap who's immediately glued to his mobile. And his little mouth starts to produce more manure than an industrial farm. He's singing '*Ahora tengo a otras que me lo hacen mejor, si antes era un hijo de puta ahora soy peor*,' by one Bud Bunny. I picture my great-grandmother skinning the rabbit for Saturday stew and reflect that there are many ways to begin the day, with that thirst for blood. I'm grateful that Haijun changes the soundtrack: 'I've listened to the music you wrote down.' She asked her teacher if she knew the cello part, so one day they could play it together. 'It's brill!' And not only because she was deeply moved by the notes and wants to hold them in her hands. 'As I listen, I think of the way home.' And the memory ends on a sigh I know by heart. For her, Arvo Pärt's *Spiegel im Spiegel* drives her far away: 'home' still means her home in Qingtian.

'One headphone you, one headphone me, and play Spotify.' It soothes me. It slips through the crannies of my mind and clears the dust out, where it's been days since I did a spring clean. When the bow skims over the strings, my eyes mist over automatically. No matter how many repeats she does. This score returns me to the womb, I follow the wild horses and begin pushing sand on a beach. Like that, with my face, like a kid would who won't let you tire of playing. I sneeze. 'No worries, Haijun, just an allergy.'

We drive onto the motorway and she wants us to tread together along the streets and lanes of her nostalgia. The *Spiegel im Spiegel* has also resurrected faces, gestures, aromas, food, the landscape… She tells me the only thing she doesn't miss from Qingtian is school. And again she discreetly slits her throat to recall what she told me that day about the lethal pressure they exert on children to study.

And she now makes me focus on the words. Because when you live in another country, there's always language sickness. For Haijun, the cement-solid grandmother, the one who acted as her mother, father and Holy Ghost from three months to eight years old, is there, but it's as if she weren't. When Wenling calls her father's wife, Haijun can only take the phone to say 'Hello'. They no longer understand one another. Her grandchild has lost the variant of the Wu dialect they speak in Qingtian, the only one grandmother ever possessed.

'Hello' and nothing else. She can't even hear her say how she's cooking that dish that was so delicious to eat, or that yesterday she bumped into that classmate of hers who was such a close friend. Or remember with her what she did with her little fingers when she fell asleep, nor what she did that evening when the last loose tooth fell out. 'Now I Mandarin, Spanish, Catalan, English, French…' She stops to check she's not forgotten any, then the crowning paradox: 'Now I can't talk to my grandmother!'

Paradox or disaster, I can't think how to describe losing the first language that welcomed you into this world at the same time as you take on more than ever.

*

'*Haitao sleeping, how are you?*' Wenling peers out. She seems a little weary, but so different. Her face looks soft, as if you could lean back on it and let yourself go. 'Yang say *have a good trip*' and she shows us the text on her mobile. '*He wants quiet, by self, play with his tablet, sleep… I also want for me! I one day travel, you and I travel to my city together, and goodbye!*' and she looks back in front. Haijun doesn't find that amusing and looks terribly upset.

'Your mother works every hour in the day, Haijun.' She was gawping through the window and turns to me, flummoxed. 'I was saying that your mother can never go anywhere to relax, she has the hair salon, she has you, she can't say leave me alone a while so I can recharge, that's why she fantasises about travelling one day, it's nothing to do with you, don't worry.' She ponders for a few seconds, stares at me and says: 'Mother is scary sometimes.' 'I believe you, but perhaps she's most scary when she's exhausted, when she's at the end of her tether?' 'Yes, she's not so angry on Sundays.' I think I've half won her over. But now we've confided in each other in a Catalan that Wenling can't decipher, I'll not be spared her list of grudges.

Her mother's mania with her straight back she doesn't believe needs to be any stiffer, the compulsory daily skipping session because her mother says it helps her grow, the pestering her to do her homework perfectly, when she swears she's already done it... I'm on the verge of interrupting, but don't. I was on the verge of telling her that her mother sees school as the first defence, that poverty didn't just rob her of food, it also filled her with anxiety, and that she's the one who'll have to live with it, never knowing what caused it.

'It's fine, Haijun, I've forgotten what I wanted to say, sorry, go on...' And she carries on all the same. Because her use of her mobile is restricted to a few hours at the weekend. And that's not all, she's forced to have her hair washed at the hair salon when she prefers doing it in the shower... And that's when I stop her mid-flow.

'Haijun, don't you like to loll back in that super-chair, close your eyes and feel your skull being rubbed? I think it's amazing! I'd come every day just to feel that!' And she finds me so over the top, she bursts out laughing. Over the top, but not by a mile, and she is more specific. 'No, I do like that, but at home when I wash and dry my hair myself, I can think my thoughts and I like that even more.' Bullseye! I can't miss that opportunity. 'Know what, Haijun? What you've just said is a description of privacy!' 'Priva-what?' 'Privacy, that time when you have peace and quiet in your bath to plot and plan is private time, which is exactly what your mother never has...' And I'm well into it, when Montserrat appears. 'Hey, look at that, Haijun! See that, Haitao, Wenling? That's the mountain of Montserrat!'

They don't find it anything special. They say nothing, but their faces speak volumes. Reasonably enough. Compared to China's exuberant landscapes, our beloved mountains are small fry. But they are nice people and they pay homage by taking a series of photos worthy of the massifs Gaudí built in Barcelona. The worst of it is that the coach windows' dirty grey filter will make my eagerness to get them to take a look even more incomprehensible.

Time for a brief doze, then they're turfing us out. The grilled-meat banquet Wenling told me we'd enjoy before becoming temporary labour for a day is here: Les Planes industrial estate. '*I not know meal inside factory!*' Wenling is much more annoyed than I am, and I play it down so as not to be a spoilsport.

For those of you who've already guessed, bingo, the lure of these places is the free buffet: the formula that allows you to stuff your face until you can eat no more for the same price as if you only had a small helping on your plate. In rural Catalan, '*un afartapobres*'. The kind of restaurant where we have all stuffed ourselves at some point because we all come from more or less poor stock, give or take two generations.

It's lucky we have children to turn everything into a game because the queues would make you weep. Line up to get a tray, line up to get our cutlery before it all disappears, line up to grab hunks of meat, and line up, naturally, to cook them. And cooking is not grilling, it's more like operating. That spread of metal hobs looks more like a surgical theatre than a kitchen. It's pitiful. So pitiful it makes you want to run off to the cherry orchards with a rumbling stomach.

And after putting on all manner of displays so at least Haijun and Haitao get something out of this fraud that includes cooking your own lunch, we finally park our trays on the table. Phew, that's done, and we can sit down. 'What's wrong, Wenling, don't you feel well?' '*I worried… I worried you not like.*' 'You don't either.' That was straight from the heart and we burst out laughing! Sincerity. We are such idiots, and find it so hard to… Though it always does us good! No need to play that charade anymore, we put behind us the 'I'm so worried about you being OK' and the 'You're so worried about me being OK' and both relax. 'Right, Wenling, it's quite a swindle.' '*I see that now. Another day good restaurant together, alright?*' 'You bet, and don't worry, this is just one of those get-through-it-as-best-you-can meals.'

And I don't have to dwell on what I mean by 'get through', four grimaces do it, and we calm down, and even like our lunch in the end. Wenling eats like a little bird, pecking at the selection the youngsters made. 'Look, more *llonganisses*, they're never-ending,' Haijun reminds me. I should say I'm finding the sub-produce piled on my plate almost delicious. And as if I were starving, I attack the clenbuterol, antibiotics, saturated fats and preservatives we down with each forkful. All down the hatch, no quibbles, as if there could be no better antidote than the glee of those two kids.

They don't stop running around until we get to our meeting point, to the waiting coach. 'Wenling, no need to make them skip today when you get home…' She looks taken aback: '*How you know that?*' She works out why immediately. '*Haijun talk a lot to you, I happy… At school teacher say she always very shy…*'

'Yes, but forget it, it isn't true, you can't stop her, once she feels secure. Like you!' I suddenly erupt. 'Hahaha… look at her, ha…' *'And like I, if you met Wenling in Mandarin.'* Once again I see the gag binding the voices of exiles and my hahahas dry up.

*

Wherever you look, you see cherry trees, how glorious. Wherever! More than you can take in! They welcome us in a shed at Fructus, give each of us a wooden box and then we can go where we want. The young couple who run the store are in sync, eco-friendly and blond. Easy to pigeonhole and stereotype. I'd bet anything they are Scandinavian, liberal professionals, who one day saw the light, grabbed their trappings and headed south to find that authenticity less well-off people still preserve, and rather than go to Greece, they stopped in the Segrià. Perhaps so much yearning for the authentic wore them down with its austerity.

I don't know what nonsense I'm spouting, because four syllables later I'm knocked out by an indication of their first-class migration: it turns out that both are splendid speakers of western Catalan. I move aside Haijun's hair and whisper in her ear: 'Listen carefully to them, we'll discuss it later,' and wink at her. 'Today you've got a couple of wonderful phonetics classes. We must make the most of it.' Wenling wants to know what we're talking about. 'It's all good, fine, our stuff.' And that's the last word I'll say to her. Because Wenling disappears.

I lose sight of her as the cherry-pickers scatter to start their harvesting. I'm about to shout her name in the bustle, to tell the kids to look for her, to ring her mobile. Luckily, I back off in time. I'd have really put my foot in it. 'Let's go, your mother will catch us up, let's start over there!'

Which is what we do. At first a bit distressed by where she might be, then I forget. They make me forget her. Because I didn't anticipate they'd be so inspired by cherry-picking. They get me to dangle them like earrings, thread them into bracelets, classify them according to levels of redness, list them by size… 'Look how many "excellents" I've found!' 'Mine are "very goods"!' 'These small cherries don't merit an "excellent", shall we leave them?' Because I try to give them guidelines: 'No way will we grab cherries at random and then throw them on the ground to waste, we only pick the ones we will eat, not those that are too unripe, or rotten, or yellowish, got that?' As if I'd been doing this all my life. Just as well no expert is around, I spare myself their scorn.

For the last two hours we've been combing rows to find the trees with the most fruit and I'm beginning to feel dead beat. I've been going at their rhythm and their rhythm doesn't ever contemplate resting. So I opt for an activity a bit less aerobic. I wonder if I have it in me, because compared to what they want to do, it's a mental maze. It's about stopping, sitting and remembering ten cherry trees, the most generous ones, the ones that made it easiest for us, and when you're clear on that, giving them a loud thank you. At first they look at me as if I've gone mad. But my efforts can't have been that woeful, because they now argue about who'll do it next. 'Thanks for it being such fun coming to your house!' says Haitao. 'Thanks for not pricking and being easy to pick!' says Haijun. Lots of imagination helps string it out. All quiet for a good while. Now, when they're thanking the trees for giving so much fruit, I sense I can't spin it out anymore and say it's time to leave. 'Come on, let's see if we can spot Wenling…'

'Before you said something like "yellowy".'

'Did I? Heavens, Haijun, I can't think…'

'Before, when you told us which cherries not to pick.'

'Oh, right! You mean "yellowish", don't you?'

'Yes, what does it mean?'

'That's how my family describes fruit that's dried up and inedible.'

'Bad for you?'

'Not really. Rather it's yellowed on the tree, shrivelled by the heat. Have the nasty kids in your class started up again, Haijun? What did your teacher say to you?'

'I never told her. But they've not called me "yellow" again because one day…'

'Let me! I want to tell you! I want to tell you!'

'Go on then, Haitao.'

'My best friend is Pol and he's really cool. And one day Pol went over to the boy who was calling me "*xino*" and asked him: What the hell was that, man? And they had a fight in the playground, but he soon said OK, man, OK, I won't say "*xino*" again. And then I whispered the names of the kids who called my sister "yellow" in Pol's ear and he shut them up too. And as Pol is very cool, the coolest boy in the school and everyone wants to be friends with him, they won't bother us anymore! Whoopee!'

★

To our box of cherries I added the lesson given by a ten-year-old boy who didn't delegate justice to others. And we walk back. '*Cir[e]r[e]s*,' whoops Haijun, 'I'm also saying thanks because today I learn western Catalan!' And she keeps proclaiming '*Cir[e]r[e]s, cir[e]r[e]s!*' Haitao joins in: '*Cir[e]r[e]s, cir[e]r[e]s!*' I just have to add my voice: '*Cir[e]r[e]s!* Long live *l[e]s cir[e]r[e]s!*' When all of a sudden I see her.

She's betrayed by her backpack, which is swinging from a branch. Wenling has made a nest in the top of the stoutest tree, though she needn't have, she weighs so little. Today she has also stuck to the rules for handling cherry trees that her father taught her, when it was time to go and pick the strawberries that climb up trees in China. So they feast on the ripest, and don't damage any branches. Wenling's father could handle things with care, depending who was concerned.

At the shouts of 'mother', she quickly climbs down. She dusts her jeans and holds her hands out to me: '*I so good...!*' Wenling looks up at the sky and takes a deep breath. I recognise the colour in her cheeks that a while under open skies always brings and it makes my day.

Now it's time to go back and I watch them walking in front. Like a cruet, clinging either side to their mother. They keep pace millimetre by millimetre. Words tangle in their mouths, for neither wants to wait their turn to speak. They both want to tell her at the same time everything they've done, every sentence said. And obviously, once we reach the esplanade, after paying for every kilo we picked, saying au revoir to the lovely Fructus couple, and rushing to fatten the coach's belly with our cherries, we crash in our seats. Wenling does too.

★

The cherries were dispatched in a couple of meals, but that day stuck in my head. Up and down a Barcelona without any green, barer than a reed, I felt surrounded by cherry trees. First Sunday together. First excursion. First time Wenling entrusted her children to me. First games and complicity with Haijun and Haitao... Yes, it did really happen. We'd gone beyond the boundaries of a purely 'hair salon' friendship.

44

'Hello, lovely, I've brought you what you wanted.' '*Good, wait a moment.*' An alarm bell rings immediately and it points me towards Fen. To find out what's not right.

She's doing Senyora Catalina's feet with a grimace that doesn't augur well. Even though Senyora Catalina isn't a customer with Parmesan-cheese feet, and has elegant extremities that are hard to find nowadays. No, Fen must be feeling groggy, she's swaying from side to side. I've only run a few steps when Wenling grabs her, before she collapses. Senyora Catalina and I rush to fan her with the first thing we find: she uses *Semana* and I Svetlana Alexievitch. However, Wenling knows that air's not much help and signals to us to move aside. She grips her between her legs trying to keep her upright and starts to revive her by tickling. '*To cure… my grandmother taught me this,*' she says without looking at us, entirely concentrating on her touch.

'That's amazing…' says Senyora Catalina when we see Fen fully resuscitated. '*If you one day feel sick, I help.*' 'You're not kidding, dear, I'd like a miracle too!'

Yang hands Fen a bottle of water to give her strength and has obviously come to stick his oar in. What has just astonished us is perfectly normal in China when your tummy aches or you've fainted; you're taught how at home and it's rated as highly as writing and reading at school. However much it's turned against them and seen as a threat once they arrive in Europe. Their compatriots have to warn them to stop doing it to their children, never again! And not because the healing impact of those pinches changes when practised here. '*Teacher see marks on child's neck and call the police, here you cannot help your children with your hands because think you beating! Everything here cured with pills, here explain but you not understand.*'

We know all about that, it's not hard to imagine the headlines: 'Custody withdrawn from Chinese parents because they physically abuse their children.' 'Scars left by Chinese homespun pseudo-medicine.' 'The Chinese: dangerous quacks when curing their own children…' Headlines to counter the slander are harder to recreate. From lack of experience, in this case. How might they be phrased? 'The marvellous pinches you can learn from individuals of Chinese origin.' 'Knowledge versus prejudice: explaining the marks that endangered some parents' custody.' 'Ignorance was the source of the slander.'

Wenling takes a teeny bottle from her pocket, sprays a few dashes of herbal scent on her temples and sends Fen inside for a bite to eat. She checks all is in order and she can now be with me, '*You show, I wonder.*' I open the prospectus and recite 'standard', 'compact', 'articulated', 'comfort', 'mega-luxurious'… Prices too following an upward curve, logically. '*Which work best?*' When I admit the last one I had was a BH from the Eighties, I'd say she regretted putting her trust in me: Wenling wants to buy a static bicycle, now they've fixed the lift.

For the last fortnight they've been walking up the seven flights and she's missing that exercise, in the end '*like a lot, and breathe better'*. Her children and husband don't share her enthusiasm, for they were fed up to the back teeth of panting breathlessly. And as the neighbours might not understand if they watched her going up and down that unnecessary Everest of steps, she'd thought of the bike, *'for strong legs without eyes looking'*.

'Which would be best for you? You know what, go for a mid-range bike, in case you get bored and stow it away, then you won't have any regrets.' *'Hahaha, you right! Enthusiasm for bike might go like wind. I tonight look and think hard.'* When I go over to give her two goodbye pecks, she looks me up and down and blurts: *'You no want pedicure either?'*

Here we go, I'm licking my lips, now who's got the will to say no? Feet, that puts me in it. I'm always in a quandary over them. I was determined to pass on that and put up with unanointed toes, but the temptation is strong: it's still sandal-wearing weather when Wenling asks me that question.

I succumb. 'OK, Wenling, fine, I'll have a pedicure, I wait till Fen is back.' She stares at me, wondering whether I'm all there and spits out: *'You joking! No need wait, sit down, I do pedicure. And then can tell you something…'*

'I study driving licence!' 'You don't say! You're ace on a scooter, Wenling!' She downloads theory tests every night on her mobile before going to sleep. *'Then dream of numbers and signs!'* And her error rate is on the scale of zero to two, she shows me, without any need for false modesty. I'm taken aback, and dither rudely, as I do, and take an age and a half to respond that makes Wenling suspect the worse. *'You too think like Yang and children? They say that I, bang, accident,'* and she splits her sides. *'I know,*

I think I drive well… I want car for when old, children their own life. Yang with young girl and I, free!' And now she swirls a steering wheel, invites me to join her as co-driver and do a grand tour of Italy. I'm thinking of a convertible, because it's really liberating and all that, but I've always found the whistle of the wind annoying, although nobody ever remarks on that. No, it's decided, we'll go in a powerful, comfortable car: with a roof. '*Yes, Italy, I want Italy, then Paris, you and I and my friend-sister Xiaolu, the three together, and motorways, right? But first…*' and she clicks to do a test while scraping my calluses, which don't exude grated cheese, but hardly let me classify myself as elegantly footed, all things told.

Let's see… I start to read to myself and, ugh, start to get the heebie-jeebies again. Does this surprising move by Wenling mean I must deal with those nonsensical questions? With terrible punctuation and archaic nouns? I try to get shot of that torture and whisper to Wenling: '*Does the compulsory insurance cover damage…*' '*I say A.*' 'Correct! Next: *Traffic accidents generate…*' '*I say B.*' 'Correct as well, Wenling! *When a lane is marked by…*' And I don't know if she will reply A, B or C. I can't get over it, it's so well written, how uplifting, I wonder if the Transport Ministry is the only tentacle of the regime of 1978 that has minimally rinsed out the filth.

After so much badmouthing, who'd have thought this questionnaire could have done me such a favour? Otherwise, I don't know how I'd have survived the pedicure. I mean, that she was the person doing it. That Wenling was the person up close and personal with my feet. And that she was my friend. When we say presumption makes you suffer, we get it all wrong:

'presumption makes someone else suffer' would be the correct way to word it.

She catches me when I'm about to make a pledge. She interprets. '*What's wrong, lovely, you no like?*' 'Quite the opposite! You did it wonderfully, Wenling.' '*But…?*' 'But I'm so sorry we're talking like this, *me on my perch and you with your backside on the floor…*' '*No, I stool, it's my work, no worry, why you say this?*' 'Well, because… Because when you were doing my hands, I could see your face.' '*You work now?*' 'No, I'm free, why?' '*Well, sit, you long time without manicure, and you and I speak face to face: happy?*'

Happy only so-so, I should reply. But I flick her fringe and stand to attention Chaplin-style. At my boss's orders! Whatever, I still have a lump in my throat. A hotchpotch of fists, wrists and knees. Because I've said too much or not argued enough, or not been more thoughtful or not analysed so much… Remorse also has its sharp-pointed anatomical zones, and uses them to clobber you. Or at least mine likes to act that way.

*

Wenling is smoothing my cuticles and the faint tickles remind me of the pleasurable torture when once my nails were ground, chiselled, polished and painted. Alright, maybe I've lost you with that 'once'. Truth is there's something new to tell: I've stopped having manicures. Yes, really. For most people, no big deal; for me, it was quite a feat. For over three years it was a weekly event, the pretext for my fieldwork. I consulted Simone de Beauvoir and, total freedom, each of us can deal with the badges of our femininity as we think fit. Because if we were to dispense with them all, we'd have to remake the planet, and we'll keep doing that as much as we can, but let's not get stuck on whether we paint our nails or not. We'll do our bit, every hand is a step forward.

And life goes on and one morning you pay a visit, one midday you pop in to shoot the breeze, and stay on for lunch. One afternoon you invite her to a pot of tea, and she repays you with dumplings to take away. And even on the evening when you invite her out for some tasty morsels: '*Natural hands also pretty*,' she tells me while we wait for baby octopus with onion. '*That way you get break from varnish.*' Now we've polished them off as an excuse. Now we eat our excuses. But hey, until I dare to cut my own hair and do it at home with a little razor, to have a reason to go to Wenling's, I keep my hair, so Yang can do the monthly clip, that sacred rite. But there's no comparison. Without our hands touching and rubbing I can't think how we would have done so much. So now I've got what I wanted, I can now proclaim: Blessed manicure! Thank you! And why not? Blessed be the dermatologist with sliding specs for squiggling the first doodle of this friendship.

*

It's time for my cheerful partying with polish to end and an arrow whizzes through the salon. Was that Haijun? '*Yes, she looking for mobile, today can, that why the hurry!*' and her expression tells me it's a lost cause, because her daughter is glued to her mobile like the rest of us: trapped. She emerges from the back holding the Holy Grail between her fingers and only manages a polite nod, because she can't afford to miss a like. Wenling pushes her up against the wall. If she has to do that for so long, at least she should keep her arms level with her eyes and her back straight. Haijun scowls silently, but she relents, what else can she do… '*Neck like old folk*,' she bows, reinforcing her stance. 'Wenling, you're so right, we'll all have necks bent by so much mobile!' And I stoop, gesticulate, and we lark around, and nod in accord like two old dears. Right, we do what no youngster would ever do: talk about our mobiles as if it were an issue, an accessory or an extravagance. An option. That's what marks your age and not the number of grey hairs.

She looks at her daughter surfing far away, looks at me and says: '*Mobile is like…*' She puts the little brush in its hole and takes her own telephone from her pocket. '*It like "opium"*,' she reads from the screen. Yes, we're all hooked on this opium… And now Wenling wants to know about me and drugs.

'Marihuana, joints…' I roll an imaginary spliff and smoke it. 'Know what that is?' '*Yes, I do.*' 'I always coughed and it never did anything for me, so one day I made hot chocolate and threw in a few heads of Mary Jane, which is where the real stuff is.' '*And you feel?*' 'Like crazy! I split my sides laughing and the fun went on for three or four hours non-stop.' I act out the jaw ache it gave me and she pisses herself laughing, and more so when I tell her that the girl next to me only felt the darkness she carried within her deepen and spent a night in a corner of the room looking ghastly. '*Effect depend on you.*' 'That's right, Wenling! Have you ever taken drugs?'

If you want to get your kids to tune in, that question is a sublime gambit. Haijun has just raised her eyebrows, put her phone on standby, and – look! – quite disinterestedly become totally interested in us. But I act as if I've not noticed, as if we don't have an audience. Because we don't need to worry about the customers either; the dryers deactivate ears we've not invited to the party.

'Hey, Wenling, what about you?' And she says no great shakes, she wanted to smoke like all her girlfriends, her friend-sister Xiaolu tried to teach her when they were sixteen or seventeen, but rather like me, '*Only cough and no trip.*' And no drugs apart from tobacco, never, in China they know what opium is all about and her grandmother drummed it into her that she shouldn't try even a whiff. '*People here opium?*' 'Bohemians, people from another era.' '*What drugs rich take?*' 'The rich are into cocaine.' '*What is cocaine, also smoke?*' 'No, they stick it up their snifters, Wenling.' She looks at me bemused; I'd better rehearse a good line. My body's had its share of takes. And there's nothing like movies to teach you to get hooked.

'It's a kind of dust… Look, it's like that talc over there.' She gets up and hands it to me: '*Show! Come on!*' I roll up my sleeves, stir inside the tin and spread the dust over the manicure table. The cuticle pusher allows me to spread the powder in two perfect designer strips. 'Shit, I need a tube in order to snort… Haijun, a note from the till!' And with the five-euro note she hurries to get me, I fashion the vehicle that will let me snort the white gold. I've got it ready, look, it's more or less like this… Onomatopoeia for climbing the mountain. Onomatopoeia for mopping up bits left. Onomatopoeia for dopamine that lights you up.

And I leave it there. I don't lick my fingers, or get a euphoric high. It's not as if I want to be that arty. 'Do you want to snort the other one?' '*Hahaha, no I now understand. You very good, I see it once in film.*' You see, you can't find a better teacher.

And sure we've acted all innocent, but I reckon we shouldn't spare Haijun a little nudge, watching a live birth wouldn't have astonished her this much. 'It's all about general culture, Haijun, better to know what it's about.' 'Yes, no worries…' She switches off her dazed look as best she can and connects/disconnects again. 'What's grabbing you?' 'Hmmm, culture, too.' 'Culture means cartoons, a series, a video clip?' I wrote 'connects/disconnects again', she can't hear me now, can't answer me back. Her mother points that out. '*Culture like you think, no.*' This: a video channel with baby pandas tumbling downhill, a competition to see who can swallow the most noodles, a pop-star cock of the roost in a final, a kid skateboarder smashing his face in. The pits, and I'm stunned. Haijun called all that 'culture', we might as well shut up shop and go home. The Audiovisual New Order knocks me out but I've no choice but to take it on the chin. 'Oh, Wenling, look how out of date I am!' '*Not so much, she older and look!*'

It's a chubby lady in her eighties with a rhythm that would be the envy of most. Every day she dances in the street, every day she records herself, uploads it and she's quite an influencer, going by the followers Wenling shows me she has. And the fact is she makes us want to dance. We can't watch her and stay stiff as scarecrows. The sight of her makes us all swing our hips. What a lady, she's sure she was born to be an idol. '*When you and I retire, you and I like her. In my city people dance in street. You know, you already seen that!*'

She's right: every night there is dancing in Wenling's first land. The land where she opened her eyes, the land where she first stood up, the land that taught her to speak, the land that gave her courage, and the land she will always miss. Yes, I've seen Qingtian.

45

I took a few nights to decide. The opportunity for a work trip to Shanghai... Cousin Àlex available to be our guide... Qingtian within a stone's throw... It was an incredible offer, but wasn't I being disloyal? I mean, heading there by myself brought to mind Wenling's '*You and I travel to my city together*'. Or maybe not. Maybe so much guilt-tripping was screwing a genuine interest in getting to know her birthplace, when it was only round the corner. And would make me miss what I'm always telling Wenling I want to do: set foot in, explore and love her city just as she sets foot in, explores and loves mine. And I went for it.

'I've come to say goodbye, I'm going to China tomorrow, Wenling.'

'*For a couple of weeks.*'

'Yes, they'll fly by.'

'*Depends, if you expect a lot, go slowly. First Shanghai with your cousin?*'

'Yes, to the documentary festival.'

'*And then?*'

'Then... Well, then maybe I'd really like to go to... to...' – if I don't dare now, I never will – 'to take a look at your Qingtian.'

'*Oh, that nice!*'

It's not the time to continue this conversation. And not because my blood's turned to ice. It's because it's like someone has stuck a sharp point in Wenling. She grimaces, rushes to get a piece of paper, and starts scribbling. Quicker than telling me. '*Shanghai–Qingtian City with TGV, direct, now very quick, here name in Mandarin. And I write Xiaolu mobile number, eat together, she know you my Catalan friend-sister. What language your cousin? Mandarin like my Spanish? Well, no worry, fine, you get to my city. Also write village of my grandmother, Kuishi, close to Qingtian, all the same. And this name stone-carving village, Shankou, important. And you got hotel? I can look. You got yuan? I can change.*'

Unequipped to respond to that torrent without melting like wax in the middle of the salon, I had to resort to my clichéd defences. 'Come on, Wenling,' I said, clearing the lump from my throat, 'tell me what you want me to bring you, what you most miss from Qingtian, come on, write it down and I'll find it wherever you tell me to go!' '*Thanks, don't bother, lovely, I want nothing.*' She folds the sheet of paper into the size of a visiting card and sticks it in my pocket. '*I only want you happy in my city!*'

46

Here are my jottings from a trip that undid every defining feature. A trip that wasn't 'any visit paid to a community, to a country, et cetera'. Neither was it 'a tour of any kind of space that is significantly distant from one's place of residence, in order to become acquainted with its characteristics, carry out a task or simply have a good time'. Jottings that have to act as a distillation of memories, because everything I recorded on my mobile was destroyed as a result of the disastrous effect of mixing a racing heart, haste and yellow stuff in the loo.

AIR CHINA

In 2001 I filled the first half-hour of my flight with boiled cabbage juice. This time I wet my chops with green tea that reminded me of the warmth of Wenling's. It was served by hostesses Air China rates poorly. Because decorating an A330-200 Airbus has no labour status. Forcing them to over-egg their make-up and stiffen their backs doesn't improve the service on board. Nor does forcing them into straitjacket uniforms guarantee the plane's safety. Who gets their kicks from watching them shuffle along the aisle in such a corseted state?

The screens often switch on of their own accord. And it's always to show us a beautiful array of deer, woods, rivers and waterfalls... Those wonders in water, timber and stone still exist. I'm delighted the capital isn't toxic enough to pollute them all.

HIGH SPEED

Tunnel-landscape-tunnel-landscape-tunnel-landscape-tunnel. We are a sickness that kills. Wherever we go with iron claws, we are the loud belch that erupts. I approach Qingtian by drilling through the belly of nature. At over three hundred kilometres an hour, all that is green evaporates. As if the meekest moss carpeted the mountains. As if there were no pain. Stop in Lishui, the capital of the prefecture, the one that wields the rudder in Qingtian county. You grasp that as soon as you see the mimosa and lavender growing in pretty lines on both sides of its river. Speeding up again requires time. I see there are paddy fields, undulating, sandy terraces on each hillside. Photogenic beauty doesn't make them less onerous to reap, although modern machinery is a big help. A river in between. A river we'd elevate to the category of sea in our little country. More paddy fields. And the orchards of the resistance: guarded by three small cream-coloured cottages with black roofs defended by four corners that rise in the air. Futile, given all those apartment blocks. The warlords are also the lords of brick, concrete and sand. And what's trying to curl up against the skirts of the mountain is no paddy field. A cemetery like the one Wenling had to climb to in order to bury her father. It's pretty, so different from the cells into which we humans shut ourselves to live. It must be pleasant to rest your feet in the grass. And so cool, close to the mists. Paying one's debt to the earth can't be so awful.

ALL ALONE

I dreamed this. No need to speak outside. Pondering all alone, doubting all alone, being overwhelmed all alone. Laughing all alone, if it seemed right. And imagining I was invisible. Walking down Wenling's streets and not feeling obligated. Without bones. A head unravelling, with the last twist of the bandage in the wind becoming infinite. Blind, deaf and mute in her language, I wouldn't have got out of the airport. I'm not like her. I'll always owe you one, Max and Àlex. And leading the way is the least of it. So you don't need to wait for me. And act as if you don't notice I'm always three metres behind. Only a tad lonely.

SHOCK

It took me forty-eight hours to get over it. I can't steel myself against jetlag. It wasn't caused by sleeplessness, exhaustion or disorientation. It was a shock of pure joy. *Live a few days in Qingtian for me*, I read as soon as I connected to the VPN in the hotel. My heart didn't know whether to melt or burn. And I was stuck somewhere in between and it grounded me for two days. Until I could reply to Wenling that they make better coffee than in Barcelona. *Hahaha, yes, buy good machines from Italy.* And with endless green teas and half a dozen espressos I manage to revive. And detect two things: two Barcelona Bars and one Real Madrid bar, grocery stores with Vic fuet and Iberian hams hanging from the ceiling, boxes of wine from the Penedès and Rioja... And they've been selling them from long before the word 'globalisation' was all the rage. I can't deny it wasn't a pleasant surprise to find those gourmet kindred spirits in the People's Republic of China, but I'm bowled over by the young people. All who can stammer a few words of English try to strike up conversation. All have a family member breaking their backs twelve thousand kilometres away. They joke about whether we won't soon be neighbours of theirs, now that Europe's on its knees and China is growing like a pumpkin, soon we'll be swapping places. Now the future isn't a ticket to Spain, many won't be leaving now. Their parents pay for their studies with the money they make over there, and here there's plenty of work. They're not anticipating disillusion any time soon.

HER

I'd caught a glimpse of it when it was in black and white, old-style. That is, in the Nineties, before it was competing with Hong Kong's night-time neon. Before running water, asphalt, the red bridge from bank to bank, the luxury skyscraper blocks, air conditioning, vast shop windows, restaurants and eviscerating trains. Before escalators. Cousin Àlex has everyone in his pocket and that includes the gentleman from the Qingtian Photography Association. We swept by them fast, as if playing a game, bang, bang, bang. And the cops were about to smash the door, bang, bang, bang. But I managed to glimpse the zigzag lanes. The houses' wooden porches, the stalls, bicycles and carts. The river, the embarkation platform, the flatboat Wenling's grandmother jumped on to go and meet her. 'Kuishi,' the retired photographer pointed out in a picture-postcard spot. I had to run and ask Àlex to give my empty stomach, migraine, low blood pressure as an excuse, whichever was the easiest to translate. And that I was already on the mend, I didn't need anything, thank you very much. The poor man can have no idea.

It's not the fuet from Vic or coffee in the Barcelona Bar that makes Qingtian seem so familiar. It has to be the energy, cheerfulness, sense of humour… A hundred families imbued with her attitude must simply have generated that expansive wave. *What you think of my city?* Wenling asked before she went to sleep. As if I'd already been here, I wrote to her, as if it were my home. As if it were you.

CHILDREN

Qingtian is also the city of children. Of children without mothers or fathers. Of children without pushchairs. Their grandmothers carry them around their necks or lead them by the hand. Their carts are piled high with greens. The only sweet potatoes I saw were being roasted by a young lad in the street as we do on All Saints. It's yet another titbit, all these cement-solid grandmothers looking after them can treat their grandchildren without penny-pinching. Just look at them. You can see by the way they coddle them that they know they are looking after little treasures. By the way they dry their tears when they're naughty, by the way they look into their eyes when they speak, by their patience. But those cement-solid grandmothers don't dilly-dally, they have work to do. Looking after the children of their own children now living in Barcelona, Valencia, Paris or Milan isn't all they have on their plate. Many should come and follow a course to find out how to handle their children. For the same price they'd learn how to rule the world. I don't reckon these grannies would charge them half the cash they spend on their Masters and we, the whole family of humanity, would benefit much more.

XIAOLU

She fills me with respect, however much I had expected her to glow. Today she will cease to be an idea. I hope she'll like me. We arrive just as she's lowering the shutters. A simple shake of the hand, not putting a hair out of place. Statuesque and grace-ful. A black ponytail sheer on her sky-blue raincoat. *Wenling's Catalan friend-sister!* And she comes over before I've said a word. Max and Àlex introduced, two kisses all around, and on with the show. '*We'll go to the restaurant next door, a restaurant with a big menu, and you can discover which Chinese dishes you prefer.*' And she takes my fingers. Scrutinises them. '*She's the best… She taught me. Wenling nails, right?*'

Apart from the fact they'd all be women, if they existed, the gods would lap this up. It all tastes like honey. And all is a lot. They brought us well over a dozen special dishes. *'When someone else is cooking, I eat more,'* she says, splitting her sides. And when I congratulate her on her perfect syntax, she tells us why.

Fifteen years in Madrid can make a lot of difference. Two children, a dried-fruit shop in Sol, a small apartment in Casa de Campo, free Spanish classes in the neighbourhood civic centre, a picnic in good weather in the Retiro, movies with the children in the holidays and at San Isidro a trip to Barcelona to see Wenling. A good life, on a roll. Until he was cut down. Pancreatic cancer, he was done for in seven weeks. Without her husband, the business, house and children were all too much. *'Now I think it wasn't, I could have managed, but when you're in a state of shock you don't understand.'* And she preferred to learn the trade in a few months from Wenling and return and settle down in Qingtian. *'My manicure salon just about breaks even, but enough for my children, my mother, and I don't need anyone.'* She puts her arm at a right angle and simulates a ball. *'We women can hold up half the sky!'* She reminded me of Rosie in 'We Can Do It!' mixed in with Mao's saying, which she fires at her mother whenever she harps on about her finding someone. A man? You must be joking, Xiaolu jokes, much better without! And she bursts out laughing again. Laughter you'd like to live with.

I'd also have made her my friend-sister on the spot. I'd also have let her drag me to school, to the make-up counter, to Europe... Wherever... I'd also have asked her to teach me to smoke. And I'd also long to be young again, go out together and hear her laugh... And I think I'll allow her to jump into

our non-convertible. And we'll drive around Italy. The three
of us.

KUISHI

Is that it? From the window we can see a cluster of small stone
houses by the side of the road as if they'd been left there by the
road sweeper. We get off. Three firecrackers blast away. That
was all I needed, I was feeling so down. They weren't in our
honour. We sent Àlex to find out and he figured someone had
just died. The huddle of people in the porch that turned around
to look at us wore mourning clothes. The churchy silence they
imposed was just what I craved. Max and Àlex headed towards
one of the four streets that comprise Kuishi. I couldn't have
caught up even if I'd wanted to. I'd never had to drag my feet so
close to the sea floor outside the water. Until a broken window
pane caught my eye. I slipped my head inside. A yard, a hen
pecking, a basin with a bar of soap and a brush. Two chairs with
bulrush seats and their masters: grandma cutting broccoli and
grandad peeling bamboo. 'Just had to say hello, sorry, do you
know Wenling? Did you know her grandmother? Could you
tell me where they lived?' One of my feet slipped, I bruised my
chin and yelped like a dog. The old couple looked up. Managed
a hello. A wave of the hand. I think they gave me their answer,
with a pleasant smile to boot. A poor woman who has lost her
way. They went back to work, and I didn't see another soul.
I walk up a cobbled path and can survey the whole of Kuishi.
Modest, sheltered and cute. And so solitary. Not a wisp of

smoke. No lines of washing. No puddles. No rubbish. No cats. A hamlet with its cover wrenched off waiting to see how its last leaf will wither and fall, a hamlet that's waiting to join the past.

'*Where did you go today?*' Well, we went to the town with the stone artisans, we climbed up to the park in Shimendong, we got lost in the riverside streets, midday and evening we stuffed ourselves like greedy guts, and I fell in love with some trainers but they didn't have my size... That kind of thing. And we only caught a glimpse of Kuishi, from the coach. I won't send her photos, I won't ask her which of all the cottages that Max and Àlex recorded, I won't wait for her to repeat *I very poor*. I've already forced her to say that too often.

THE LAST ONE

She takes us to her children's favourite restaurant, '*so you can taste proper Peking duck.*' I say she could have brought them, we'd have liked to meet them. '*No! For one night!*' And she acts as if she's pleading for mercy. None of Wenling's bevy of friends have stayed in Qingtian, they're all scattered over the Old Continent. '*I always with my children, or with my mother and aunts and uncles... they're very nice, but family very tiring!*' She gives us one of her smiles and we raise our glasses of beer to toast the gift of friendship. A gentleman brings the lacquered duck cut into small pieces and Xiaolu helps with the first bite. A sliver of meat, the sauce, cucumber, spring onion and down it goes. I start to feel upset halfway through supper, and tell her. If you take a photo of us, and send it to Wenling, that will say it all, and she'll like that. She'll understand why I've not answered any of her WhatsApp texts. Photo? She looks at her watch. Better to call her, this is a good time. She extracts her mobile from her bag and starts the video call. Toot, toot, toot. My throat is bone dry. Toot, toot, toot. My heartbeat races. And there she is, at the manicure table. Our table. We all wave, hurriedly. First the two friends speak, it breaks up, we lose her. The picture comes back and now she must be seeing us clearly, because she too greets us. Xiaolu signals immediately: apparently Wenling is crying. I can't say a single word. If I did, it would bring a pitcher of water with it. The screen goes dark, thanks, dodgy wi-fi, thanks! I can just about deal with voice messages. I first tell Xiaolu to reconnect. 'Hahaha... Wenling says don't drink so much water, or in the bathroom all the time! And asks why you didn't get it out.' Why didn't I stick my hands in my piss to rescue my mobile when it fell in the restaurant loo, the cheeky thing reproaches me. When Xiaolu replies that I did put my arm in up to my shoulder, we hear her still splitting her sides. One more sentence, the last one, because Wenling has got a customer; the messages I couldn't read only told us to have a good time, and she's just seen that we know how. She has seen that I am happy in her city.

Time to leave. A big, big hug and glassy eyes. Inside the taxi I turn around to see if Xiaolu is still there. Rooted to the spot. A candle defying all Qingtian's dispiriting lights. I'm already looking forward to the night out we've promised ourselves in Barcelona.

DANCING

The penultimate evening train to Shanghai. When we cross the square leading to the station we have to evade three or four groups of dancers with sound systems louder than anything at the loudest Barcelona music festival. And each group has its leader, its clientele, its choreography and energy. Could anyone rival such a show on a concrete stage? Utmost admiration for that fantastic spectacle in a public space and utmost admiration for the cement-solid grandmas whose candles never go out. Their energy could electrify the whole of our planet of stressed-out souls.

FIGURINES

At home I take the clasp off the little silk box and remove them from the red bed where they were sleeping. My stone artefacts are a swollen juicy pear and a lion with a snub muzzle and mane bristling on its back from crest to tail. A *pixiu*, a mythological creature. They both fit in my hand, but I would have bought size XXL if I had a big enough dining room. Wenling doesn't revere them for nothing. Without pears, *pixius*, monkeys, elephants, seashells and all forms of forest, sea and fantasy in a suitcase, she would never have forged that path from Qingtian to Europe. And we could never have plaited each other's hair.

47

Yes, I did bring her something from Qingtian. She twists the bag round. No indication on the front, of anywhere or nowhere. She finally finds what she was looking for in the tiny print at the bottom on the reverse side. She touches it and says it out loud! Not to mention the way she swells with pride when she translates it for me: the name of the bookshop, the name of the street and the name of her city! '*I know where, I a big customer, you really see Qingtian!*' She doesn't even glance at the four thrillers that Max, Àlex and I spent two hours choosing, they're piled up, untouched. No complaints. If literature weren't above all evidence of life, would we need it so?

Yang is green with envy and comes to ask if there isn't something for him. 'Heavens, how silly, I could have brought you tobacco, I expect you miss tobacco from over there.' He thinks that's a hoot. '*Hahaha, you bad as Chinese tobacco, Chinese tobacco awful!*' And you know, what choice did he have, when he was living there, because ten years ago only the rich could afford the luxury of imported cigarettes, the real item. But it's OK, they can keep them.

Wenling wants to know if she will really come to Barcelona and not go to Madrid, because she still has a lot of friends there, and sometimes she's visited them. I hesitate. I'd say that she won't, we agreed to meet up here, with Xiaolu… '*China very big, we think Madrid and Barcelona very close.*' 'Hey, if we have to spend a weekend in Madrid, we will!' '*No, better Barcelona, Xiaolu, you and I, nobody else,*' and she winks at me. '*I write, I persuade her. But lovely, I think… I work all week, you and she can go on walks together without me, if you like.*' I explain to her what 'get lost' means, and then set out the programme for when she comes. Saturday night, dinner reservations for the three of us somewhere local, and Sunday, if we want to have more fun, we'll open it up. And go to the Barceloneta with the children, Yang and Max, what do you reckon? '*Yes, that possible!*' And she high-fives me so enthusiastically she almost knocks me over.

They were about to shut up shop and I was on my way out when Haijun walks in. She homes in on what she wants to know. It's been a long time since she's not had to slant her questions for my benefit with *just one thing, just one thing*. 'You've been to China, right? To my city, right? Tell me what you liked most about Qingtian.' I take a deep breath before I fire away and Wenling interjects. '*Can have supper with us now?*'

She tells Haitao to come out; if not, we will leave him there. '*You drink beer in China, I see…*' Yang must get a move on before they shut! And he rushes off to buy a six-pack in the corner shop. I call Max, and while she sees to the day's takings, Haijun rings the number of the restaurant that in their opinion is just like home cooking. '*Half an hour and food as good as Qingtian in my house,*' and she pushes me towards the street.

'You remember everything better with a full belly,' she said when all the orders were shared out and we were arm in arm.

So true. But my problem was emptying my stomach. Freeing it up, so all the tasty morsels in the pipeline could find a space. Maybe you've been there and you ladies will know what I mean. I always choke. I always find it hard to digest so much joy.

48

'Hey, don't be such a doubter, Senyora Mundeta! I agree, Senyora Gripi does too, and Senyora Catalina would if she were here!'

'Such a celeb here? You see so many young women dressed like that, in casual clothes, flashy trainers and baring their navels, I reckon you mistook her for someone with similar looks.'

'*Eulàlia's right, Señora Mundeta, I've found her. And Señora Catalina will find her in Majorca too, if my granddaughters don't delete her from my mobile! Of course it was her!*'

'Well, you can believe what you want, but don't expect me...'

'It was her, love, it really was!'

And with all that banter, 'You're pulling my leg, no we're not,' Haijun walks in from the back. And I walk over as well.

'They seem so hot under the collar today. Who on earth are they talking about?'

'Hey, dear, you'll set us all straight, bring the thingy.' And she raps the bottom of my bag with her fan. 'Go on, get it.'

'Who am I looking for?'

'The one singing in the trailer, who else? She's the singer who's everywhere! She just left, a few minutes before you got here.'

'What?! No way! To get a manicure? You really mean *she* came...'

'Shut up and play the video, go on, then we can all be sure.'

'Is she famous? Who is she? Who is she?'

'It's her, Haijun!' And I press play.

Two and a half minutes later: 'It really was her, love!'

'Not half it was! Wait till I tell my grandchildren! And my sister!'

'Maybe this is the face of the young woman who wanted her messy nails to be repainted, maybe it was her...'

'Fantastic! Is she Catalan?'

'One hundred per cent!'

'As Catalan as you?'

'And you, Haijun!'

'Can you show it again?' And Haijun makes a butterfly with her hands and claps twice.

'*Very nice girl, says her shop shut today and needs a polish.*' Wenling peers in between the two to get a look and can't avoid joining in the back-and-forth. I ask her what colour. She's still got it in the top pocket of her tabard and shows it to me. 'Girls!' I turn around to see my favourite compatriots in the hairdresser's. 'Only an artist could ask for that varnish, I also say it was her.'

I take out the folder and lay out all the paperwork for enrolment. So Wenling can see it's all tied up, so she doesn't have to worry. It was the hardest task she'd ever set me, the trickiest, most important bit of help, but it's in the bag, we've canned it, the children will go to the school we wanted. 'Three cheers, Wenling!' 'Three cheers!' choruses Haijun. 'What mean "three cheers"?' asks Haitao, who's just arrived on his skateboard. 'Wow!' he exclaims when he sees the name. 'It's the same one Pol is going to, hurray, hurray, hurray!' Wenling begins her celebration with a Chinese refrain: *'Who works with brain order around those who work with hands. I want good future for my children, no want work like ours. Strong school is very important for me, thanks so much, lovely!'*

Wenling couldn't look more ecstatic. Nor could I. She's got her eye on the state-of-the-art laboratory they'll have next school year, the reading scheme, the Chinese language option, the certificate in English they'll do as soon as they arrive there… And I have to agree, that won me over too, an educational pro-gramme like that, which is why I suggested it in the first place. But they'd have felt it deep down if they'd not given me the right answer. If they'd hidden their heads under their wings when I asked them how they'd react if they ever heard the words 'yellow' or 'Chink' being used in their school as insults. Now I've laid it on thick, I've had guarantees, a commitment, now I can read them the Riot Act if it happens. Because now they won't be able to leave justice to the kids. Now I'll be the one to go and tell them what's what. And I'll be off there like a flash.

'I like new school but after that piano, right!' Haijun declares, shaking the artist's varnish up and down. 'So when you finish secondary, off to study music at the music school where she went.' 'Really? Great!' Gawping as she watches how Haijun varnishes her pinkie with the gold glitter and how she looks at it against the light, Wenling shows me the change of plans on her mobile: *'Xiaolu say she cannot come this summer.'*

49

We waited a whole year for her. And in this year I saw the kids go to their new school with no fear of any words. I've seen *The Philosopher's Stone* wowing them too; they're on their third Harry Potter. I've done a bake-off competition with Senyora Eulàlia at the hairdresser's and Haitao went to bed with a tummy ache. I helped review the delivery paperwork for the new bio nail polish and I made Wenling lose count every time. I've introduced Wenling, Yang, Haijun and Haitao at home and we've celebrated St Stephen's Day together. I've seen the kids gulp down four cannelloni each and noted how Yang preferred to have a second helping of prawns. I've stopped a couple of racist customers in their tracks and Kristin and Mireia stood up against them too. I've tasted endless Chinese delicacies to celebrate New Year and this time I was the one who got tummy ache. I've received requests from Haijun and Haitao to follow me on Instagram and that meant more than if Rosalía had wanted to follow me. I drove them to the Empordà for a fortnight's Easter holiday camp and saw them rapturously hugging their new friends. I've learned four words of Mandarin and Wenling now says 'come in, wait a mo' and 'so-so' in Catalan. I've watched Yang cutting my grandad's hair and standing proud when he was praised with a 'That's one hell of an artist!' I've tried to make zongzi rice balls and we've celebrated the anniversary of Qu Yuan the poet with oven-ready ones Wenling bought. I've uncorked a bottle of cava to toast Wenling passing her driving theory test and we paired it with the ensaïmadas Senyora Catalina brought us from Palma. I convinced Yang and now he goes to my osteopath once a month for a neck massage. I've palled up with Haijun and her mother now lets her go out with her classmates at the weekend. I've renegotiated Wenling's rental agreement with the Catalan gentleman; they can stay there for another five years. I've applauded Haitao and Pol acting as compères and Haijun for being the star in the end-of-year show. I've witnessed Wenling and Yang shutting the hairdresser's on a Friday afternoon for the first time because it was their children's school performance.

I've seen all this and much more, and now it's July, and the night out we promised ourselves with Xiaolu.

50

Both are wearing dresses. Wenling, black, Xiaolu, olive green. Both low-heeled sandals. Both a touch of mascara and manicure face masks. '*I come and everyone remember they have feet!*' Xiaolu gets off her stool, laughs loudly and hugs me tight. Wenling doesn't laugh, she's suffering. Because of the restaurant, because we'll be late, because she's sorry to keep me waiting... I see only one solution: I must roll up my sleeves. 'Bring me one of your tabards, Wenling.' No way she wants to give me one, and I have to get one from the drawer where I know she keeps them. A bit of a struggle, but finally I'm wearing one. Xiaolu helps me tie it at the back and the two of us manage to stop her moaning. From the other side of the table, Wenling hits the ball back in our court with two pairs of gloves tied together, bang! '*And take care, you have manicure! You mad in head!*' 'Yes, a real lunatic,' I retort. Now I do my own crew cut at home, now I've said goodbye to Yankee gear, gone over to trousers, thrown off discomfort and embellishment, and dispensed with make-up, now I miss a good lather in femininity. Buy us if you get it, right! I slip on the double layer of latex so the blood red of my nails doesn't flake, but most of all to make Wenling happy. Because I'm not going to do anything rash. I'm only good to change the water in the washbowls, dry feet, remove varnish and file a bit, I don't want to tarnish their reputation. But every little helps and in less than an hour all the customers are almost done.

'*I want wash hair, I sweaty, is there time?*' Wenling takes off her face mask and I call the restaurant. 'All done, Wenling, second sitting! They've changed our reservation to eleven, you'd have time to wash three heads if you had them!' And while Yang rubs her head, Xiaolu brings us up to speed. Her niece is now eighteen months old, she leaves her alone with her mother. When they took her, she sobbed her heart out night and day and neither of them could pacify her. Xiaolu's brother lives in Italy, in Prato, and he had to do what she did, what Wenling did: take the newborn babe to Qingtian to find a cement-solid grandmother to look after her. Her sister-in-law's mother was so old she could hardly cope, and Xiaolu and her mother had to look after his treasure. '*So I back to purées and nappies! And I didn't remember… Poor little thing, now she laughs. Now she cries when she hears her mother at the end of the line.*'

'*Watch out! So pretty, lots of boyfriends,*' says Yang, standing in the doorway with the two kids. 'Bye, aunties!' That's Haijun and Haitao. '*Did you know that they call you aunt in China when you're like family? Of course, she Catalan friend-sister, she family,*' Wenling emphasises. I look at them, I feel my eyes misting and hug them in turn: we're going to have a weepy time! 'How long since you drank good red wine, Xiaolu?' '*I could in Qingtian, but very expensive, two bottles today!*'

The trio hadn't walked over the first pedestrian crossing, when suddenly a voice: '*I didn't recognise you, you're so dolled up!*' It's a customer, the owner of the hairdresser's three doors along. 'Have a great time, you beauties!' And we barely have time to collect three chairs in the wine bar before a young woman jumps to her feet: 'Is that you, Wenling?' '*Today out with girlfriends!*' 'So delighted to see you!' And gives her two kisses. 'Wenling is more famous than any actress! Do you see, Xiaolu?' '*You not laugh, it because I many years here, she teacher in Haitao's first year at school, she help a lot.*' The waiter's here. 'What would you like, girls? Mmm... Have you got spritz?' 'Yes, whatever cocktails you'd like, shall I bring you the list? In English for those two?' 'No need, we're all locals and you can bring us a spritz each, please.'

The radioactive orange of Aperol always makes an impression, they're knocked for six. '*Really can drink?*' 'Sure, Wenling, it's delicious.' 'But first some photos,' says Xiaolu. We get out our mobiles and do what everyone does now before taking a sip or bite: we bless the food. Click, a photo, still life of big glasses of spritz and the little plate of olives; click, photo of one by one, photo two by two; click, selfies of all three... But the ice is going to melt even more and dilute our cocktails, because I wasn't expecting filters and their Huaweis have got some great ones. Now we've got feline faces, now we're wearing John Lennon specs, now our cheeks puff out, now we're mice... '*No, not ugly like that, make us pretty,*' Wenling complains. '*Look, like this?*' I have to look at the photo twice, close up. 'A big improvement, Xiaolu, but... On the strange side, don't you reckon?' '*Of course, it's pretend!*' I ought to add that the 'beauty' filter is very subtle, and makes our faces super glam. And quite fake too.

We drain the last drop of spritz and head to the restaurant with the spring in our step that alcohol brings. Xiaolu takes a moment to send voice messages to her children and Wenling goggles at all the wonders she discovers in that stretch of Gràcia. *'I always want like you; leave the hairdresser's, see pretty things, go for a walk... I think that never happen to me and today, I free as you!'*

'Hi there, menu in English?' 'No thanks, we're all locals. They're such a drag...' *'People think Xiaolu and I tourists.'* 'Right, Wenling, people think, or rather, don't think. *Don't think we are friends, because there are still not many like us, when there are more, they'll understand.'* 'That's right!' says Wenling. *'And what to eat here? Because I eat not much...'* 'Well, how about a few tapas, and you must try a couple of sips of red wine.' We order a Montsant and what Xiaolu misses most: *calamares, ensalada rusa, croquetas y tortilla de patatas.*

'Night out, without husband... I very happy! So long since I can't remember!' It's inevitable: good nosh, comfy seating, sophisticated lighting, background music, three girlfriends... In such a favourable scenario, nobody holds back on their hidden stories. 'Wenling, do you remember why you married Yang, or perhaps not?' *'Hahaha... I not so crazy, I do remember.'* And Yang wasn't the one that she preferred. There were some who read and read like her, and she loved chatting to them. *'But Yang, when young, Yang a sweet-talker, always handsome, always affectionate, always everything for you... And finally I marry Yang because... because... How do you say...'* Xiaolu ponders, and clicks her mobile. *'I've got it!'* and she shows us a translation: 'destiny'.

'Want anything else here?' 'Well, why not, you can bring us slices of ciabatta with tomato, please.' *'Yes, please, I too like a lot!'* Xiaolu is still holding her mobile and she introduces us: *'This is my niece.'* *'Very pretty, looks a bit like young Haijun... I cry a lot when Haijun in Qingtian and Haitao in Taizhou.*' Xiaolu is no stranger to that and nods. '*You swallow lots of tears and feel very bad, but to make the business work… And they're better with grandmothers than in nurseries.*' But without a mother it's even harder to bear for Wenling. Having to leave her little girl with her father and her little boy with her mother-in-law gave her months of sleepless nights. '*In China is a song that says*: "*Shi shang zhi you mama hao…*"' Xiaolu joins in and they sing a few stanzas for me, very quietly, heads down. A lullaby sadder than winter that says that without a mother you'll always feel miserable. '*But my father calmer when Haijun born. No longer go out at night, no longer drink, no longer fight… My father look after Haijun better than me, I very happy with him, I am really.*'

'Should we finish this bottle?' 'Yes, you can share it around, thank you.' '*I no more, not used…*' 'This is a one-off, Wenling, and nobody's driving.' 'As if she could, she's still got her driving test to come,' Xiaolu bursts out laughing. Drive-car-trip to Italy: '*When, when? When we're old,*' says Wenling. '*But not retired,*' Xiaolu stipulates, '*long time before that!*' 'Hahaha, let's agree in five years' time?' '*Agreed!*' And we toast our Italian tour in a non-convertible. After that drink, Xiaolu wants to know how we became friends. Wenling insists on answering. '*When she come first, I think: I want her to come back another day, and another day, in she walk!*' 'And the moment I walked out the door, I wanted to be back with you, and back I came.' Xiaolu smiles and quickly lights up that translation on the screen of her mobile. What else but 'destiny'?

ACKNOWLEDGEMENTS

The physical and emotional journeys I made as a result of this book have been very important to me, and I would like to thank the individuals who gave me the opportunity to travel to the Chinese province of Zhejiang and get to know the principal cities of our neighbours of Chinese origins: Qingtian, Taizhou and Wenzhou. The day I spent at the William Koehler Senior Center in Mahopac was unforgettable too; thanks to the trust and friendliness shown by the GlamourGals Foundation: watching that cohort of adolescent volunteers listen to and admire for a moment the residents of an old people's home on the pretext that they were giving them a manicure was a priceless experience. And, last but not least, I would like to give my heartfelt thanks to the MOCA, New York's Museum of Chinese in America, for the warm welcome they always gave me. Without their exemplary concept of a museum and their documentary archives I could never have learned about the history of the Chinese diaspora in such a full, revealing way. I spent many mornings at the MOCA and every single morning I left the museum and walked along the streets of Chinatown feeling deeply moved.